More praise for Lillian M. Roberts and *Riding for a Fall*

"Every animal lover wants a vet like Dr. Andi Pauling with her cool analytical mind and unfailingly warm heart. In *Riding for a Fall*, Andi's soft spot for strays—both animal and human—puts her in the track of a murderer. This is a breathtaking ride into the world of polo horses. Lillian M. Roberts's evocative prose rings with authenticity, and her narrative gallops to a surprising and triumphant finish. A winning read."

—MARTHA C. LAWRENCE
Author of *Murder in Scorpio*

"Lillian M. Roberts's first novel, *Riding for a Fall*, is wonderfully told, opulently detailed, and astonishing in its denouement. Roberts is one new writer who delivers with the expertise of a veteran."

—RODERICK THORP

RIDING FOR A FALL

Lillian M. Roberts

FAWCETT GOLD MEDAL • NEW YORK

A Fawcett Gold Medal Book
Published by Ballantine Books
 Published in the United States by Ballantine Books, a division of Random House, Inc., New York, and simultaneously in Canada by Random House of Canada Limited, Toronto.

http://www.randomhouse.com

Library of Congress Catalog Card Number: 96-96843

ISBN 0-449-14985-4

Manufactured in the United States of America

First Edition: November 1996

10 9 8 7 6 5 4 3 2 1

This book is for my mom,
who encouraged me to try,
and for my dad, who shared his books.
And for every English teacher who never gave up.

Acknowledgments

So many people helped make this book a reality that it feels like a group effort. Special thanks go to my agent, B. J. Robbins, and my editor, Daniel Zitin, for their support and advice throughout the process. Nancy Carlson, D.V.M., and Craig Leary opened up the world of polo to this neophyte. The incredible staff and patrons of the Desert AIDS Project, especially Ed Benbenek, lent insight into the medical and psychological aspects of this unique killer. Frank Ercoli, M.D., and Anita Ciatola, R.N., opened a window into the world of critical care medicine. Officer Don Craiger of the Palm Springs Police Department answered innumerable questions. Joan Baumgarten, attorney at law, made the courtroom process comprehensible. Perhaps most of all, my undying gratitude to the astonishingly clever members of my writers' groups: Janice Steinberg, Martha Lawrence, Janet Kunert, Mary Lou Locke, and Charles Slaughter. Finally, I owe a special debt to Roderick Thorp for his unfailingly accurate editorial comments.

Chapter One

A big weimaraner named Jake was hemorrhaging on my skirt. I tried to apply pressure to the open artery in his left front foot while struggling to hold him still. He'd flown through a plate-glass window and hadn't slowed down yet. Didi, my technician, was preparing the O.R. for an emergency Cesarean on a Maltese. Saturday, one o'clock. The sign outside said we closed at two. My waiting room was full, the noise level stratospheric.

It was my first really busy day in quite a while. Months, actually—since I'd acquired Dr. Doolittle's Pet Care Center upon the death of my partner the previous April. He left me the practice, the building, a mountain of debt, and not many clients.

I envisioned a bank statement with a positive balance, glued a smile on my face, and kept moving. It was late October, not even the beginning of the Season. All through the blistering, miserable summer I'd wished for the day clients would stream through the door, grateful for my services and eager to pay for them. Now they were here, and I was determined to make them welcome.

"Are you going to put that bandage on before he bleeds to death?" demanded Jake's owner, Frannie Worpell. She was a first-time client, an enormous, disapproving woman in black stretch pants, clearly unimpressed with my ability to restrain her pet. She stood in the corner, arms crossed, making no effort to assist.

Someday, I fantasized, I'd hire another veterinarian and a whole slew of technicians, and one would always be free when I needed another pair of hands. Someday I could afford that. But for now I backed Jake into a corner, straddled him, and clamped his head between my neck and shoulder, grasping the offending foot in one hand and a roll of gauze in the other.

I was still bent over like that—bloody skirt riding up my thighs, shoes slipping on the bloody floor, gauze failing to stop the flow of Jake's blood—when a half-forgotten voice spoke from behind me.

"Looking good, Andi. Need a hand?"

Jake started, my grip slipped, and the gauze unraveled itself across the floor.

The owner of the voice stood in the doorway like an apparition. "Ross?" I blinked and he didn't vanish. "Ross *McRoberts*. What are *you* doing here?"

I hadn't seen Ross since vet school. I'd thought about him, wished I'd handled things differently, but never expected to get the chance. Right now I wasn't sure I was glad to see him.

Jake moved to check him out. I lost my hold and the artery erupted again. Bandage trailing, four-inch tail wagging ecstatically, he nearly managed to plant his front feet on Ross's chest. Ross caught them in one hand, gave the big gray head an affectionate pat, and scooped him onto the table. He held him there while I at last secured a bandage around the bloody foot. Ross did this without being bled upon, as usual. The room looked like a low-budget horror movie. My skirt was ruined, though I thought my white smock might be salvageable. Jake still didn't know he was injured.

To Mrs. Worpell I said, "Jake's leg obviously needs surgery. The glass cut to his bone and severed a couple of tendons. He'll be in a splint for several weeks." Maintaining this dog in a splint would not be an easy thing. Was she up to it? Her face gave no clue. "I'll call you when he's ready to go home."

She frowned at my bloody clothes and said, "How much is this going to cost me?"

Anxious now to be alone with Ross, I said, "Sheila will have an estimate for you at the front desk," and ushered her in that direction. She'd probably spend more replacing the window.

Once she was gone I missed the buffer. Ross's presence was so unexpected, I couldn't think what to say. Why hadn't he called? How did he know where to find me?

Glancing at him, I set Jake on the floor and led him to the ward. Ross followed, clearly excited to have surprised me. I caged Jake and turned to face my classmate.

Classmate. How juvenile that sounded, four and a half years later. But it brought warm memories, mostly featuring Ross: late nights studying over coffee and popcorn, dreaming of life after school. Classmates were the only people in the world who knew the pressure and poverty, who got the jokes. Whatever happened now, Ross McRoberts would always be my classmate.

He ignored my bloody clothes and hugged me, laughing. It felt good—I hadn't been hugged in a while. Then he held me at arm's length. "Hope you don't mind my dropping in. I saw Garrett at a conference; he told me you were in Palm Springs." Bill Garrett, another classmate, practiced in L.A. "You look great," Ross said. "I like your hair short."

"Thanks. What are you doing in California? Have you lost weight?" Not that he needed to—he'd always been skinny.

"So have you. Looks good."

I put my hands on my hips and smiled. I'd dropped ten pounds that summer and wanted him to notice. At thirty-two I was a snug size six and thought I looked better than I ever had before. But Ross just looked gaunt. I wondered if he had the sort of stress in his life that had melted my fat away.

But no, I realized, studying him. Ross had a serenity about him, the sense of a man at peace with himself. Which didn't gel with the man I'd known. In vet school

Ross had been intelligent, capable, and kind, but had lacked self-confidence. He'd aspired to wealth and social prominence, at least in part, I assumed, to make up for perceived inadequacies: *I'll show them.* I should know; I recognized much of the same insecurity in myself. I was struggling but believed in myself strongly now. Had Ross realized his dreams, too? Was that what I was seeing?

He'd evaded my other question, though. I said, "I thought you were in Kentucky."

He followed me toward the small O.R. Ross had a wonderful smile. "Took a cab from the airport. I'm playing polo in Indio this season. Tell you about it later. Want me to see a few cases while you're in surgery?"

This was too bizarre. "I was just wishing I had another doctor. Would you mind? Everything out there is pretty routine, but some of them have been waiting a long time."

"No problem. Then I'll buy you dinner, okay? Maybe we can go dancing." He turned away, then stopped. Over his shoulder he said, "Can you put me up for a few days? I hate hotels."

I flashed on a night before a crucial freshman anatomy test, when temperatures had dropped below zero. The wheezing furnace in my tiny mobile home couldn't compete. My cats' water dish froze on the kitchen floor, and the copper pipes greeted me with silence when, wrapped in a quilt, I tried to make coffee. In a panic I called Ross, who smuggled my cats—Hara and Kiri—past his landlord and offered me his couch for the duration. Later he'd crawled under the trailer to solder a cracked hot-water pipe and tacked up insulation so it wouldn't happen again.

"Of course," I said with genuine enthusiasm. "Stay as long as you want."

Three hours later the Maltese and her two puppies had gone home. I locked the door behind Jake and Mrs. Worpell and said, somewhat belatedly, "You *are* licensed in California, aren't you?"

Ross threw his bags behind the seats of my Miata. I'd put the top down to make room, and the October weather was perfect. The day had gone well, and he wore a cocky grin. "Took my boards in June, thinking I might spend some time in the Golden State."

I relaxed.

"Dr. Doolittle's Pet Care Center," he mused. "You've got a nice practice here, Andi. I always knew you'd do well."

Ross's compliment thrilled me more than I wanted to show. "Thanks," I said nonchalantly. "So, polo, huh? I didn't even know you played." I pulled the car onto Palm Canyon.

"Picked it up in Lexington. It grows on you. Coming here now was kind of spontaneous, though. Have you been to Las Palmas? Prince Charles has played there. You've got some of the best polo in the world in your backyard." He breathed deeply, gazing at the mountains that stand watch over the desert. Wind ruffled his curly brown hair and pried open the collar of his shirt. "And I'm gonna be part of it. Listen, Andi, you're not—you *do* live alone?"

I didn't tell him I hadn't had a date in six months. "Yep. All the single men around here are either over seventy or gay. Will Kelsey be coming down?" Fishing. Both of us.

His face clouded and he shook his head. I wasn't surprised. His marriage to the Lexington socialite had been given six months by those who knew them—myself included, but I didn't like to examine my reasons.

"Caught her in bed with a jockey."

"Oh, Ross." That did surprise me. Kelsey had seemed too refined for an affair. But then, I barely knew her.

"Her daddy bought us an Alydar filly as a wedding present," Ross went on. "Half a million bucks. She started hanging out at Keeneland. When it broke its maiden, we took the trainer and his crew out to celebrate. I left early. She didn't come home, and I went looking for her." He grimaced. "Found them at a motel by the track."

"I'm sorry," I lied. I'd often wondered what might have happened if Ross hadn't married her. If I had been less focused on studying, if he hadn't been such a buddy. If.

"Ancient history," he said. "Anyway, I got the last laugh. Took the filly in the settlement. Cute place you've got," he said as I pulled into the driveway.

Cute? I bought it as a repo soon after coming to Palm Springs, since no landlord in his right mind would rent to anyone with my growing menagerie. It's two bed, two bath, tan stucco, no pool. Mount San Jacinto looms in the background between palm trees. The view and a huge yard were its only selling points, but I'm slowly fixing it up. Painting kept me sane over the moribund, sweltering summer.

As usual the cats ignored my arrival, but long-haired Carbon hissed at Ross before vanishing down the hallway. My four dogs acknowledged me with glancing sniffs before proceeding to the newcomer, vying for access to his fascinating shoes.

Ross rubbed the ears of my old coonhound. "Is this Gambit? You've still got him!"

"Can you believe it?" I laughed in painful remembrance of a grueling twelve-hour surgery. The dog came to the teaching hospital with two broken femurs, a dislocated hip, three pelvic fractures, and a face that said, *Oh, boy, I've done it this time.* His owner wanted euthanasia. But the animal's stoic dignity touched a tender place in Ross few ever reached. He pulled strings to get the dog donated as a student surgical case. I agreed to take him, since adoption was a prerequisite and Ross lived in an apartment. I never regretted it. Now eleven years old, Gambit lived on prednisone and rarely moved faster than a slow amble. I'd since brought home many strays, but he was the kindest of the bunch and perhaps the only coonhound in all of Palm Springs.

He seemed to remember Ross, though he'd be glad to see anyone who could spare a pat on the head.

"That was some of our best work," Ross said wistfully.

"He's a wonderful old guy." I patted his arthritic hip, then carried one of Ross's bags into the living room. He followed with the other two. "There's no furniture in the spare room; the couch will have to do. You can see I haven't been bitten by any housekeeping bugs." I scanned the animal hair and chew toys—not to mention pets—that decorated every surface.

"*Streptococcus domesticus* hasn't reared its ugly head, eh? I'll be out of your hair as soon as I find a place near the polo grounds. I really appreciate this. It's a lot better than I had to offer that time your pipes froze."

I studied him, a chunk of my past standing in the foyer of my new life. We'd left a lot unsaid those years ago—was it too late to fix that? "It's good to see you," I said, and put my arms around him. He hugged me back and we stood like that until it grew awkward. I offered him a beer, showed him the spare bathroom, and went to shower and change.

We ate dinner at a pretentious spot with white tablecloths, candlelight, and snooty waiters. It was an ambiance hysterically unsuited to our conversation.

"Remember when you brought that piece of cauliflower to anatomy lab and held it like a cat brain?" I reminisced. "Grimes pointed out the cerebellum and got so frustrated when he couldn't find the pons!" Doctor Grimes, the world's original nerd, made an irresistible target. His expression when Ross bit off a piece of "brain" was worth a semester's tuition.

"And that Angus heifer that fell in the creek?" he said. Trailered in for a "preg-check," it was on to slaughter had the exam proved her barren. Instead, she plowed through the head-catch, trampled me, and took off as fast as her stubby legs could go. With six students and an intern in pursuit, she made for the woods behind the clinic and went headlong over a fifty-foot cliff into the icy water below. "Before you could say 'lawyer,' she went from dog meat to a prize heifer in calf to a champion bull. Think the farmer retired on the check the school wrote him?"

I could laugh now. Ross had been the only one who stopped to make sure I was all right.

Ross wore khaki slacks and a button-down shirt. I'd chosen black jeans and boots. I had a reason for dressing comfortably.

"Is there a good country bar in this town?" Ross asked.

"Got just the place," I said as he paid for dinner with a gold credit card and barely a raised eyebrow. "Let's go."

I drove to the OK Corral, a club on Indian Avenue, with posters from western movies on the walls. Palm Springs being what it is, most were signed by the actors. I locked my purse in the trunk, crammed twenty dollars and my driver's license in a pocket, and we swung onto the dance floor before even ordering drinks. The band was playing an old Hoyt Axton song, perfect for the twists and pretzels I hadn't practiced in years. After a few missteps we fell into the familiar moves we'd once performed to the envy of our classmates.

Then the band segued into "Help Me Make It Through the Night." "They're playing our song," Ross said. I smiled and moved in for the two-step. Ross's wiry arm slid around my waist, and we sang together:

"Lay your head upon your pillow. Hold Bojrab's *Pathophysiology* against your chest. As you lay there sleeping, pray you'll learn by osmosis. Make believe you've studied one more time. Help me make it through this test." When the song ended we were laughing so hard we could hardly stand.

The band took a break. As we returned to our table I asked, "How long will you be in the desert?"

"Not sure yet. Probably till March or so; that's when

the season ends. Then maybe on to Del Mar, I haven't decided."

"What about your practice?"

"It's covered." He smiled. "I'm taking a year off, a little piece of retirement while I can still enjoy it."

I was stunned. "A year? Can you make a living playing polo?"

He laughed out loud. "Not me. I've spent two hundred thousand dollars getting ready for this season."

I took a long sip of my beer.

"I can afford it, Andi."

Ross had always boasted he'd be rich one day. "I'm glad," I said finally. "You must have one hell of a practice."

"Nah, I made some investments, sold a couple of horses."

I'd have to ask about those investments. "That Alydar filly you told me about? You sold her?"

He nodded, a little glum.

"Who else is on your team?" I asked.

"Roger Dietrich—he got me into the game. And each of us hired a professional to play the key positions."

Four players, total. "So some players get paid."

"Damn right. Jaime—that's my pro, Jaime Alegro, he's from Argentina—cost me twenty thousand just for this tournament, and I was lucky to get him. But the expensive part is the horses. Wait till you see them; I've got a great string. All race bred."

The band returned and started a waltz. We headed back to the floor, trying to keep up our conversation. "You've got to come and see me play," Ross shouted into my ear.

His enthusiasm made me smile. "Of course. When's your first game?"

"Our tournament—the Santa Rosa Cup—starts next weekend. But we have a practice game tomorrow, ten o'clock. Come cheer me on."

I leaned back and our eyes met. His arm tightened

around my waist, and I thought he was going to kiss me. I wondered if I'd kiss him back. I'd pushed him away the only time he'd tried, and suddenly all that confusion from the past rushed back. It was too much, too fast—I hadn't thought about it for years.

Then Ross spoke, and the moment evaporated.

"We'll blow those fuckers away," he said.

Chapter Two

We weren't drunk by the time we got back to my house—at least I wasn't. Pleasantly buzzed, though. I helped Ross make up the foldout, wondering again whether we'd be sleeping together soon. I paused in the doorway, on the brink of inviting him into my room. But it was too soon, too unexpected. He smiled awkwardly in my direction, and I flashed a quick smile back, then entered my bedroom, closing the door softly behind me. I slept like a rock.

The Las Palmas Polo Club occupied two hundred acres in Indio, as flat as a tennis court and green as a golf course. The Santa Rosa Mountains jutted skyward to the south and west, and the top of a date palm grove graced the intervening distance.

The club was surrounded by tamarisk trees and bisected by a wide dirt road, with six playing fields to the north, four practice fields and stables for three hundred horses to the south. Between the barns and the east gate lay a series of small pastures and mobile homes converted to tack shops. A dirt exercise track circled the south fields, and horses galloped there as we pulled up at Ross's barn. The atmosphere reeked of rugged but well-padded luxury. Taking it in, I couldn't believe I'd never been here before. It was a forty-five-minute drive but a world away from home.

The pungent aroma of horse manure greeted us through the open windows of the Miata as I killed the engine. A Mexican groom was scooping a pile into a plastic bucket while another brushed a thoroughbred with quick, practiced strokes.

The "barns" consisted of double strings of pipe corrals with corrugated roofs and plywood tackrooms. Ross's was in one corner near the outside fence. A sign hung near the tack room door, white letters over a royal-blue background: BLUEGRASS REVIVAL.

"Are you sponsoring a music festival, too?" I called into the barn.

"Smart-ass. Bluegrass Revival is my polo team," Ross said, stepping into the sunlight. Belatedly I spotted similar signs hanging at other barns.

I pointed to a mobile home between the stables and the southern fence. "Who lives there?"

"The general manager, Bob Talbot. He keeps an eye on things at night, too." As I watched, a pudgy young woman emerged, a brunette wearing a bikini top and miniskirt meant for slimmer hips. Heading toward a group of players at another barn, she cast a speculative glance toward Ross: new blood. Ross was looking at his horses and didn't notice, or pretended not to.

One of the grooms was saddling a bay mare as we approached. "Bunios Dee-yaz," Ross said. I winced at his pronunciation. The Mexican murmured something rapid and incomprehensible.

Ross stroked the bay's neck, then ran a hand down each leg in turn. The mare nuzzled his head. The groom wrapped her fetlocks in blue felt bandages. Similar activities took place around us.

Ross led me to an aristocratic gray mare. A groom followed and began brushing her, more bandages held between his knees. The mare nickered at Ross and pricked her delicate ears. "This is Fandango," he said, stroking her beneath her chin. "My best performer." He pulled a couple of peppermint candies from his pocket, unwrapped them, and held them out. Fandango crunched eagerly, peppermint mingling with the aroma of alfalfa on her breath. "I got her from a high-goal player who owed me money. Gave me the mare in lieu of payment. Look at those legs. Goes back to Seattle Slew on her bottom side. I've already been offered twenty-six grand for her."

I reached out to stroke the velvet softness of Fandango's muzzle. She checked my hand for more peppermints before submitting to the caress. Her broad forehead and wide, dark eyes gave her an air of wisdom and patience.

A royal blue Porsche pulled up next to the Miata and we both turned. A man emerged, tall with astonishing black hair and a cocoalike tan. He wore the remains of a very old T-shirt, and tight jeans.

"That's my car. Check it out," Ross said. But I wasn't looking at the Porsche.

The newcomer glanced from Ross to me and offered his hand. "I'm Jaime Alegro." His thick Spanish accent gave the simple statement an air of seduction.

"Andi Pauling." My hand disappeared in his and stayed there. "You're the professional player Ross told me about."

He smiled, displaying straight, gleaming teeth. "I'm supposed to make him look good. We're definitely looking good today." His eyes moved up my body like I was a horse he might want to buy. Though decidedly not my type, Jaime was the kind of man who knew what women liked to hear. When he turned away, I glanced at Ross. He was looking at his car.

"Nacho, Juan!" Jaime clapped his hands and rattled off instructions in Spanish, and the grooms sprang into action with an enthusiasm I wouldn't have believed moments earlier. Jaime pointed as he spoke, and two more saddles appeared on horses' backs. He walked around to each animal, checking the equipment.

"Who's that?" I asked, pointing over Ross's shoulder.

Ross turned. The man was medium height, fiftyish, Caucasian, and wore a red baseball cap and a button-down shirt tucked into creased jeans. He limped noticeably and leaned on a hickory cane. He leaned forward, shoulders hunched, free hand clenched in a fist: aggressive body language.

"Andi, get in the car. I'll be there in a sec." Ross put a hand on my shoulder and shoved. His face had gone white. I stayed put.

"What's wrong, McRoberts?" The man had a Kentucky drawl. "Didn't think I'd find you here?"

"I've got nothing to say to you, Crawford. Let's go, Andi." He steered me toward the car. Jaime pretended not to see anything, but the grooms stared with unabashed curiosity.

As I started the engine and backed away the man shouted, "It's not all your money, McRoberts. I'll make you wish you'd never met me." At least that's what it sounded like.

"What was that all about?" I asked.

"Nothing." Ross crossed his arms over his chest.

"Who is he?"

"Another sponsor. It's no big deal."

I raised my eyebrows in question. He stared out the window. I dropped it. Ross could be unpleasant when pushed. He'd tell me when he was ready.

He directed me to one of the practice fields. Several horses stood at a hitching post at one end. A single mounted player loped in easy circles, swinging his mallet at a ball on the course but rarely hitting it. A few cars were parked nearby.

Ross got out of the car. He pulled a leather duffle from my trunk, removed a white helmet, and strapped it on. It made him look like a cross between *Easy Rider* and *National Velvet*. He selected a battered white ball the size of an orange and one of two mallets wedged behind the seats of the Miata. He swatted the ball around the grass.

I picked up the other mallet and swung it awkwardly. I had to hold it halfway down the cane handle.

Ross laughed. "Don't strike with the end. Use the side, like this." He demonstrated.

The head was cigar-shaped and made of wood. One end was flat on the bottom, and it attached to the handle at an angle. I tried again, moving the flat part parallel to the ground.

"Much better!" He lobbed the ball toward me.

I tapped it back but it stopped short. He ran up and hit it again, and soon we were laughing and batting it back and forth.

Jaime arrived in the Porsche with several mallets and a few more balls. He changed unselfconsciously into a blue polo shirt, his smooth torso almost as dark as his face.

The grooms followed, each riding one horse and leading two more. Other players joined then, and a few spectators pulled in.

Ross introduced me to his partner, Roger Dietrich, a bluff Kentuckian. Dietrich's hired pro was an Australian named Graehm Block. Dundee accent, easy smile, features like Tom Cruise. I was liking this game more and more.

The opposition was composed of nonteammates, together for practice. One of them, another Argentine, rode more aggressively than anyone else, hit the ball harder, and scored often.

A metallic-green BMW backed in at an angle near the Miata. Two women got out and leaned against the trunk, waving at other spectators. One was the chubby brunette I'd seen leaving the general manager's trailer. "Man, Berto's hot this year," she was saying, watching the men on the field.

"What else is new," said the other woman. She was an unlikely companion to the brunette. In her mid-twenties, she was tall and blond, wearing cutoffs and a tank top that showed off broad, tan shoulders and muscular thighs. She oozed a confident sensuality and physical strength lacking in her friend.

"I can't believe Gracie lets him come up here alone. If she don't want him, just let me know." The shorter woman giggled.

Her friend picked up a stray ball and tossed it from hand to hand. "He's okay, but married is married. Argentines don't believe in divorce. And he's crazy about his kid." She hefted a spare mallet and tapped the ball into the air.

"Jealous," teased the brunette. "You just wish you could play like him." From the look she got, her remark hit home.

After the first chukker the players galloped to our end of the field, where grooms met them with fresh mounts. The blond woman approached Jaime.

"Hey, Tish, glad you came." He dropped to the ground, and a groom exchanged his mare for another one. Tish wrapped her arms around Jaime's neck and kissed him as if no one else were there.

Each time someone scored the teams switched goals. I couldn't see the action at the far end of the field. Whenever the ball traveled in that direction everyone ran after it, except Dietrich, who lagged behind to guard the goal. Jaime seemed to hold back, letting Ross take the ball. Ross swung often, rarely connecting. I felt a little embarrassed for him, but no one else seemed to notice.

As they returned after this chukker, Jaime loped over to Ross. "Okay, like I told you. Don't worry about the horse. Think about hitting the ball, man. Then you can pull up with both hands. But you can't do both at the same time."

"Set me up this time," Ross said, breathing hard. He hopped off the mare and inspected the tack on his next mount, the gray mare named Fandango.

Bluegrass Revival was scoring again at the near end. During a heated scramble, Jaime sent the ball flying from the center of the field. Ross was ahead of him, at full gallop. Berto got there first, with a vicious backstroke, slicing the ball into the oncoming players.

Fandango stumbled, went to her knees, tried to recover, but sprawled forward, sending Ross over her head. When he rolled over and sat up, there was blood on his shirt.

The gray mare staggered to her feet, circling wildly to her left. Ross dazedly reached out and snared her reins, speaking softly. She would not be calmed.

I saw where the blood came from. Where the mare's right eye had been was a pulpy mass of blood and bone.

The brunette woman's scream launched me into action. I grabbed Jaime's cast-off T-shirt and dashed onto the field, approaching the mare from her left so she would see me. Once Ross and I were in her reduced field of vision, she calmed down. He gently pressed the wadded shirt against her wound. Fandango tried to rear but found it was less painful to allow treatment.

"Do you know any vets here?" I asked.

"Get anyone. I don't care who."

I sprinted for the car. The blonde, Jaime's girlfriend, jumped in. I didn't ask questions, glad for any help available.

"I'm Tish Hannover," she said. "Jaime always uses Hal Perkins. Head over to the other field." Three mobile vet units were parked near field one, where a tournament game was under way. "The brown-and-white Ford." She pointed.

I pulled up beside the dust-coated pickup with a vet pack filling its bed and introduced myself to the driver.

Hal Perkins reached through the window to shake hands. He had short red hair, and a wad of tobacco deformed his lower lip.

"A mare was hit in the eye with a ball," I said. "Field seven. Will you follow me?"

"Oh, jeez, lead the way." He started his engine and backed up. We left twin rooster tails of dust as he followed me to the practice field.

Perkins assessed the wound and injected Fandango with a sedative. Her head drooped and swayed sleepily as he numbed her face with local anesthetic and cleaned and packed the wound. "Guess you know the eye's past saving," he said, picking a small shard of bone from the mess. "Look's like your mare'll be okay otherwise."

"Oh, fuck, man," Ross muttered. "Fandango, I'm sorry." Ross's hand trembled as he stroked the mare's neck. "She'll be shit for the game. She loves the game."

Perkins glanced at him. "Jeez, too bad. But that's polo."

"I'm down to twelve horses for two players. Another injury and I'm out of the tournament."

Hal nodded. "I think Berto's got one for sale, a good mare."

Hal was cheering me up considerably. Five nine or so and stringy, he wore form-fit Levi's and scuffed cowboy boots with the ubiquitous polo shirt. His aw-shucks manner contrasted sharply with the machismo of the players.

"Berto just ruined my best mare. Look at her." Ross continued stroking the aristocratic neck, but his face had darkened. "You think I want to buy a horse from him?"

"It was an accident, Ross," Jaime said. "Get used to it; he's in our tournament."

"Accident, my—"

"Man, I'm sorry." We all turned. The man they called Berto stood with his helmet in his hand, at the edge of the small crowd that had gathered.

"You fucker! You may as well have killed her!" Ross picked up a mallet and brandished it at the Argentine, who stood his ground. "Just stay away."

"Will you guys knock it off?" This from Tish, who held Fandango's reins. The mare had picked up her head at the commotion. "These things happen. It's part of the game. She's not dead; she'll make a great brood mare."

Berto eyed her warily. Jaime glanced heavenward.

Ross ignored her. Only I saw that he was on the brink of tears. I knew Ross felt the mare's pain as if it were his own. He would know I saw this, and be embarrassed by it. I decided to wait in the barn until he was ready to go, since the game was obviously over.

As I pulled away I saw the man in the baseball cap who'd approached Ross in his barn. He sat behind the wheel of a green Ford pickup near the tie rail. The truck was new and expensive: a luxury car with a three-quarter-ton payload and a fifth wheel in the bed. The driver stared past me for a moment, then drove away. I saw a Kentucky license plate, before the dust obscured it, and a shotgun in a rack in the cab's rear window.

I glanced over my shoulder to where he'd been staring.

He'd been watching Ross.

We left Fandango in her pen. Her head drooped from the sedative, and a large bandage obscured much of her face. Hal introduced himself again and asked where I practiced, before heading back to the game. Ross left with Jaime in the Porsche, planning to look at a couple of horses that might be for sale. I was getting in my car when Tish approached.

"Want to watch the end of the game?" Meaning the real game.

"I think I've had enough polo for one day."

Her face said that wasn't possible. "Could you give me a ride at least? Daddy needed the beamer."

"Sure," I said. She got in and I gentled the Miata toward field one. The car was a few years old but had been my first new one. I hated to drive on anything but smooth pavement.

"Those guys," Tish said. "Man."

The comment didn't seem to invite a reply.

"Horses get hurt all the time. It's sad, but that's polo. They love the game, though. Me, too. You ever play?"

"Me? No. Are there women's teams?"

"Sure. Coed, too. Mostly low-goal, though. Man, I'd do anything to be able to play like Berto, even Jaime."

I pulled in behind the clubhouse, a pseudo-Spanish building with a lot of glass doors and windows.

Well-dressed people moved around inside. I put the car in neutral.

"Sure you're not coming?" she asked, opening the door.

I hesitated. "Not this time. I'll see you next weekend."

Ross got home a few hours later. I was cleaning house. Silently he began scouring the kitchen sink.

"Find any good horses?" I asked.

"It's too early in the season. They've all been sold, or the prices are unrealistic."

As I put the vacuum away I asked, "Where do you want to go for dinner? All I have is canned and frozen stuff."

"I'll cook. I need to burn off some steam." He paused, then grinned weakly. "No pun intended." He left and returned a half hour later with two fillets, corn-on-the-cob, and beer. He also had a small, lopsided pumpkin under one arm, which he placed on the counter. Halloween was coming, he explained. How did I expect to lure trick-or-treaters if I didn't have a jack-o'-lantern? There was a bag of bite-size Hershey's under the corn.

He fired up the grill, scraped grime from the rack, and put the steaks on. The scene reminded me of a hundred nights at school. As he turned the meat I wrapped the corn in foil and laid them along the edge. I chopped salad greens, and he set the picnic table.

The day's heat had given way to a cool, windless evening. Birds chattered, dogs begged. I popped beers for both of us as he slid the meat onto plates. His scowl had been replaced by an expression of contentment. The steaks were perfect.

Halfway into the meal I said, "I'm sorry about your mare."

The frown returned. "He did it on purpose, Andi. I'll never prove it, but I know it's true."

"Is that possible? A shot like that?"

"Did you know that I lost a couple of horses last week? They were poisoned. Castor beans."

He was serious. "You think this polo player followed you from Kentucky so he could pick off your horses one by one?"

His shoulders sagged. "Gutiérrez wasn't in Lexington. Poison's not his style, anyhow."

"Then what? Some kind of conspiracy?"

Seeing that I was humoring him, he shrugged. "I don't know."

We ate in silence for a while. I felt guilty for bringing it up. Then he said, "I've been thinking. You obviously need help at the clinic. I won't be that busy during the week. I could help you out Monday through Thursday, maybe some Saturdays, too."

I hesitated. "Have you ever done small-animal work?"

"Not much. But it can't be that hard."

Wow. Ross really had changed. He'd always considered dogs and cats beneath him.

"You saved my neck yesterday." Yes, I needed help. But.

I jammed the last bite of steak into my mouth, washed it down with beer, and said, "Last spring, when my partner, Philip Harris, died, I had some terrible publicity. He'd milked the clinic dry, including the pension fund and every bit of cash reserve. Business slumps in summer anyway, since this is a winter resort. What I'm trying to say is, I'm still in debt. I can't afford another veterinarian, even part-time." I hated to admit this in light of how well he was doing.

"Don't worry about it. I'd like to keep my hand in. And with two of us working, the gross should pick up fast. If it doesn't, you don't have to pay me." He grinned confidently.

"That's a hard offer to refuse." What was my problem? Clients were shortchanged by my frantic schedule. I'd been wishing for help. People liked Ross, and his rapport with their pets was astonishing. "When can you start?"

Chapter Three

"You're a natural," I told him. Philip's white coat looked a lot better on Ross, and a paisley tie completed the image.

He slipped easily into the rhythm of alternating exam rooms, smiling at clients, introducing himself, and appearing at home treating dogs and cats. Sheila, my young and eager receptionist, flirted unabashedly. Even cynical Didi tacitly endorsed his presence.

While he saw clients I caught up on long-neglected paperwork. Bills. Insurance forms months overdue, taxes late, a nasty letter from the company holding the lease on my X-ray machine. Nothing in school had prepared me for the paper avalanche that went with running a small business. But for a change I had a little money with which to stave off creditors. September had been a decent month, the first in a long time. October was looking even better. Maybe I really could afford another vet.

Midmorning I was conferring with Sheila at the front desk. Ross escorted a fragile, elderly woman out of exam room 2, carrying her overweight cocker spaniel for her and moving slowly to accommodate her pace. The cocker kept shaking its head.

"Come see me in a week, Mrs. Artimas," he was saying, "so I can make sure Buffy's ear is healing the way it should. And be sure you put that medicine in every day."

"Oh, I will, Doctor. Will you be here from now on?" I couldn't miss the hope in her voice.

"For a while anyway." He ushered her out, smiling

patiently. She clutched his hand when he placed Buffy on the floor and handed her the leash.

Sweet, slightly dotty Ruth Artimas was a client who usually mistook me for one of the office girls. I should have been thrilled she liked Ross.

He caught my eye, winked, and gave me a thumbs-up on his way to the next room.

What did I feel? I stared after "my" client. For six months, my life had been devoted to salvaging the clinic. It had been a hard road, but I was finally succeeding. Could I be so insecure as to envy my classmate's easy acceptance? I shook my head and went back to work.

An hour later Didi stomped in, standing in the doorway until I looked up. The technician's round face was screwed up in irritation, her mousy hair falling out of its ponytail.

"What is it?" I asked, irritated by the interruption. I'd moved half the backlog from IN to OUT and had my momentum going.

"Would you do an E and D? Dr. McRoberts can't get to it."

I sighed. Euthanasia and disposal. A daily necessity in my work, but not the most pleasant. "Get the dog out and snag Ross next time he goes by."

"It's a cat. I don't think he likes cats. He wears exam gloves whenever he works on one."

"Whatever, Didi. I'm busy. The cat won't care if he's wearing gloves."

"Please? It's Bartholamew, and he knows you better anyway."

Oh, hell. "Let's get it over with." The job would take less time than arguing. I followed her into Treatment, thinking Ross's reluctance might have nothing to do with the schedule.

My clearest single memory of Ross in vet school involved the euthanasia of an old gelding that had been his case for weeks.

The horse's condition was painful and chronic but not fatal. Ross read everything he could find, searching for a regimen that might help. Nothing worked, and the owner reluctantly decided to put his old friend down.

It was his first euthanasia on an unanesthetized animal. Ross drew up the "blue juice" with shaking hands. As he approached the gelding, who'd grown thin and apathetic from disease, his whole body trembled. He fumbled for the vein and missed. Ross never missed.

"Fucking useless old shit factory," he muttered, jabbing at the animal's neck. "Hold still." The gelding stood patiently, not even twitching its tail.

After four tries I reached for the syringe. Ross glared at me but let go. His eyes glistened; his lower lip quivered. I never knew if he was more ashamed of his inability to perform the deed or for taking his self-reproach out on the horse. As he stalked away I raised a vein and slipped the needle in.

Ross ignored me for two days.

The cat was an ancient tabby I knew well. Barthola-mew was losing a valiant battle he'd fought against kidney failure for two years. A week ago his owners had broached the subject of termination. Today they'd reached their decision. Like many people, they couldn't stand to be there.

Though weak from dehydration and anemia, Barthola-mew wasn't past struggling in protest of a needle. His veins were collapsed from disease and scarred from many punctures. Rather than restrain him while I poked around, Didi held him on his side as I injected the lethal drug directly into his heart. I rubbed his cheek as I did so. He went out purring.

Ross left the clinic early. As I walked in my house I heard him on the phone. "Give me those numbers again?" He scribbled in the margin of a newspaper. "When can we move? Okay, let me know." He hung up and punched in a new number. As he waited for the call to go through he reached under the paper, washed down two capsules with beer. "Vitamins," he said, then, into the phone, "Jaime, it's me."

I opened the slider and the dogs tumbled through.

Ross was saying, "Bullshit, there's always something for sale! I told you I wouldn't . . ." A pause, a deep sigh, then, "Okay, okay. Go ahead and check it out. I'll be there tomorrow to vet it. But see what you can do about the price." He hung up angrily.

"Of all the horses around, you'd think he could find one that doesn't belong to his brother-in-law." He snatched another beer from the fridge. His shoulders slumped and he seemed tired.

"You're going to buy the mare Hal recommended?"

"I need a horse. Hell, I need more than one. Jaime thinks he'll get the price down. His sister's married to the bastard. She lives in Argentina while he screws around up here."

I recalled the conversation between Tish and her friend. "Who is this guy?"

"Umberto Gutiérrez. He's a nine-goaler—that's his rating, on a scale of ten. There are only about a dozen ten-goalers in the world. Any horse Berto's got has to be up to snuff." He drained half his beer. "What's for dinner?"

"I'll order pizza. You still like anchovies?" Ross was the only person I knew besides me who ate fish pizza. "Is that the classifieds?" I pointed to the page he was using for notepaper.

"I was looking for an apartment. Rent's a bitch out here."

Hiding my disappointment, I reached for the phone. I knew the pizza parlor's number by heart.

Later we sat on the patio and carved the pumpkin. Ross roasted the seeds, and we nibbled as we chatted.

When two vets get together, the conversation inevitably turns to odd cases and weird clients. I shared a few of mine—the dog who'd swallowed the baby-bottle nipples, and the twelve-year-old son of the owners who'd picked them out on the X ray before I did; the couple who'd brought me a rotting dog carcass and insisted I try to revive it. Ross was oddly reticent about his life in Kentucky, but I was so glad for someone to talk to, I barely noticed.

When I got up the next morning, Ross had already left to look at his new mare. I had leftover pizza for breakfast and went to work alone. I found myself missing Ross's help already.

Two clients, recheck visits from the previous day, were disappointed when told Dr. McRoberts wasn't available. I was ushering the second of these, a young woman named Hillary Redburn, to the front desk around eleven-twenty when Ross strolled in. Hillary bristled, assuming I'd lied to her.

"I'm sorry, Mrs. Redburn, something came up," Ross said, glancing at me. "I hope Dr. Pauling took care of you?"

The woman batted her eyes at him and coyly canted a hip. "That's *Miss* Redburn, silly. Call me Hillary." She asked if he agreed with what I'd done. Winking at me, Ross scanned the chart and confirmed my diagnosis. Fortunately for him. But I was laughing as I took the next client.

When I finished he had his feet on my desk and the paper open across his legs.

"Find a place?" I asked.

"Are you that anxious to get rid of me?" He sounded hurt.

I ducked the question. "How's your new mare?"

He flashed his trademark smile. "She's amazing, Andi. Wait till you see her. Let's go to lunch, okay? Come on, we'll catch up on the work this afternoon."

We took the Porsche. Nice car.

Over beef with broccoli at a Chinese place on Palm Canyon, he extolled the virtues of the mare. She was, it seemed, nearly everything the gray had been.

"And I got her for two grand less than he wanted. Since Berto felt so bad about what happened to Fandango."

"X rays clean?" I asked, trying to sound like I knew what I was talking about.

"Perkins was tied up. Berto had another buyer waiting, and I need her for Friday's game. I watched Jaime ride her, and she never took a bad step. She's sound." He smiled. "Guaranteed."

"I thought you were never supposed to pass a horse without X rays." It was the one thing I remembered about prepurchase examinations. That, and never guarantee anything. "This is the guy you said ruined your best mare on purpose, and you're buying his horse without X-raying it from head to toe?"

"She'll be fine. You'll love her." He was practically squirming with excitement. Then his expression turned serious. "Listen, Andi, I have to ask you something."

I looked at him, waiting.

"Berto wants his money up front. It's going to take me a few days to get the funds transferred from Kentucky. Um, do you think you could loan me the cash till then?"

It was clearly hard for him to ask, but I still didn't like the sound of it. "How much?"

"Six thousand. Just till Thursday. Friday at the latest."

I dropped my chopsticks. "Are you kidding? I don't have that kind of money lying around!"

"Please, Andi. It's only a few days. I wouldn't ask if there was any other way."

"Damn it, Ross, you don't understand. The money goes out as fast as it comes in. Faster. I have suppliers and staff to pay, utilities, equipment leases. Not to mention mortgage payments. There's not six thousand dollars to be had."

"How about as an advance on my salary?"

"What salary? You've only worked one day, and you already took this morning off!"

He hung his head. "I had to; there wasn't time to wait. From now on I'll be the most reliable person you ever knew. Besides, you have to admit the clients like me." He wiggled his eyebrows in self-parody.

The waiter took our plates and left the bill. Ross got out his credit card as I cracked a cookie and read my fortune: "If you're generous to a fault, no one can fault you."

Loaning money is a good way to ruin a friendship.

Sure it is, but who else can he ask? And I wanted to keep Ross happy. My clients adored him; business was already improving. I hadn't mailed those checks yet. *Look on it as an investment.* "You'll pay me back by Friday?"

"No sweat."

"It's a loan, not an advance. The mare is collateral."

He leaned over and placed a quick kiss on my forehead. "I knew I could count on you."

We fell into a pattern. Ross got up first and made coffee before I was out of bed. He picked up after himself and cooked for both of us. His suitcases were part of the furniture, his clothes hung in the closet in the spare room, familiar yet utterly alien. Occasionally I resented having someone else in my space, but for the most part I enjoyed his company.

Wednesday night he went to check on his horses and wasn't home when I went to bed. I wondered, for no good reason, if he was with a woman. And how did I feel about it if he were? More likely drinking beer with Jaime—I reminded myself that Ross's reason for coming to the desert had nothing to do with me. Then the door opened: Ross trying to be quiet unfolding the sofa. The dogs didn't even bark, though I heard them snuffling, and Ross spoke to them quietly, giving rough pats. I pretended to be asleep.

* * *

Thursday morning I may have imagined a certain tension in the air. Ross owed me no explanation. Everything was fine. Just fine. The appointment book was full.

He worked that morning but took the afternoon off—by prior arrangement—to practice.

Thursday night was Halloween. Even with the grinning pumpkin out front, we didn't get many takers, but Ross had painted his face white, with huge black circles under the eyes. He wore a hooded black sweatshirt and white gloves, and took obvious pleasure in making eerie noises whenever a group of children approached the door. He was generous with the candy, too, but we still ate most of it ourselves.

Friday morning he left early—I barely had time to wish him luck in his first game. I wished I could watch, but someone had to see clients.

Just before lunch Sheila approached me outside an exam room. "I've got to warn you about this lady. She wants you to put her dog down. It has this cut on its face, that's it. I told her you wouldn't kill it, but she said she'd, like, dump it in the desert. I said you'd talk to her."

Sheila has a way of tilting her head down so her frizzy hair falls over her face, then looking up through the bangs like a Lhasa apso that just peed on the rug. I half expected her to roll on her back and stick one leg in the air. She's hard for me to yell at.

On the exam table was a medium-size mutt with a shaggy, speckled coat. His muzzle was caked with some sort of greasy ointment, globbed on over the hair. He greeted me like I was the best thing to happen to him all day. Maybe I was.

"I don't want him to suffer anymore." The owner was sturdily built and wore an assertive combination of navy and gold. She was clearly accustomed to having her demands granted.

The dog licked my hand, tongue barely protruding from his injured muzzle. I couldn't see the skin, and he yelped if I tried to touch it. I rubbed his woolly gray ears and glanced at the chart for a name. "Mrs. Barton, I don't—"

"It's the only way. I can't afford to take care of him."

I stared conspicuously at the huge diamond on her left hand until she covered it with her right. The dog glanced from her to me, his expression anxious. Who knows what animals pick up from our body language? Perhaps it was merely the animosity between us that confused him, or maybe he understood every word.

I consulted the chart again. Bandit was two years old and listed as an Australian shepherd, though he looked crossbred. "The fee for euthanasia will be two hundred dollars," I said. "For one-fifty, I'll sedate him and treat the wound."

"That's exorbitant! I didn't come here to be raked over the coals. You'll do what I want, or I'll leave him in the desert for the coyotes. I'm the customer here, and I've made up my mind."

I picked the dog up. "So have I. I'm confiscating this dog on grounds of cruelty." I marched out the door, not easy with a forty-pound animal in my arms. The outrage on Mrs. Barton's face would have been comical if I wasn't quaking with anger.

"You can't—"

"What difference does it make to you?" I held the door for her to leave. Sheila and Didi stood in the hallway. "No charge," I told Sheila. Why bother, she wouldn't pay it anyway.

The woman, outnumbered, left quickly.

Great, I thought, once my adrenaline had died down. I certainly handled that well. Now what? I already had four dogs, the legal limit. I did *not* want another one.

I set Bandit on the floor, and he promptly glued himself to my leg and cast a solemn, adoring expression up at me. The goop from his face smeared on my pants. When I moved, he came with me.

"First, you get a new name to go with your new life.

Velcro seems to fit. Now let's see what's under that gunk." We shuffled awkwardly into Treatment and I drew up some ketamine.

It took fifteen minutes to clean the ointment off so I could clip Velcro's hair. The wound went 360 degrees around his muzzle. I tried to look inside his mouth, and that's when I found the rubber band.

"Oh, damn, no wonder it wouldn't heal," I said. The elastic had cut through the tender skin all the way around, and through the lips on both sides. On the right the swollen tissue had grown together over the stricture.

Didi said, "Oh, my God! Who would do such a thing?"

"At least they won't do it again." Not to this dog. I snipped the band on each side and carefully extracted it from the laceration. I spent the next forty minutes debriding and suturing, ten more neutering him. Didi vaccinated him before he woke up, and gave him an amoxicillin injection. She bathed him and cut his matted hair short. Now he just needed a home.

Friday night Ross didn't come home. I was irritated at how quickly I'd grown used to his company. He was an adult—he could do as he pleased. Probably out celebrating his victory and didn't feel safe driving home.

So why hadn't he called to tell me about it?

And what about the money he owed me?

Saturday morning I made my own coffee, went to work as usual, and tried not to think about six thousand dollars. When I got home around three, the Porsche was parked in the drive.

He was hanging up the phone as Velcro and I walked in. "Hi," I said, determined to be casual. Then I saw his face. "What's wrong?"

"That fucking Umberto sold me a lame horse!"

"Oh, Ross, no!" I started toward him, hoping to offer—what? Comfort? Clyde, a ginger tabby cat who'd made himself at home in Ross's lap, hissed at Velcro and slunk toward my bedroom. The other cats had made themselves scarce upon my arrival. Gambit, napping nearby, lumbered to his feet and hobbled stiff-legged to inspect the newcomer. Velcro slid down my calf and presented his belly. The other dogs clamored at the patio door.

"Who's this?" Ross asked.

"Name's Velcro." I told him about it.

"Jesus." He offered his hand to the dog. Velcro strained to sniff him, wagging his tail but refusing to leave my side.

Gambit, satisfied the Aussie was no threat, moved to intercept Ross's pat, then lay back down.

"What happened with the horse?" I asked. "I thought she was sound. Guaranteed." Sarcastic. *Cool it, Andi. You want to piss him off before you ask about money?*

"He blocked her or something. She's got laminitis so bad she can barely walk. Rotated six or seven degrees."

"Slow down." Velcro and I went to the refrigerator for a beer. I gave him some food and showed him the water bowl. "Refresh the memory of your small-animal classmate?"

Ross rolled his eyes. "She's foundered. Her feet are sunk. A horse's weight is suspended by the coffin bone. It hangs from the hoof wall by these microscopic structures called laminae." He held up his hands, fingers interlaced.

"I remember that. Laminitis is inflammation of the laminae. But how can it be disguised?" I sat on the other bar stool. Velcro rested his chin on my foot.

"If you inject local anesthetic into the nerves in the pastern, it numbs the whole foot. That's a block. The horse will go sound until it wears off."

"Then why not just block her before the game?"

"Every step does more damage. See, when she walks—running's even worse—she puts a lot of pressure on the toe. He rolled his fist on the counter until the knuckles blanched. "When the laminae try to swell inside the hard wall, they die from the pressure. Laminar necrosis. In bad cases the hoof literally falls off. It's impossible to predict how far this one will go."

I'd taken a test on this stuff once. "Once they die, they can't hold the horse's weight. The coffin bone sinks. That's where the rotation comes in, right?"

"Fucking A. That *bastard.* How could he do that to a horse? How could anyone? Christ, Andi, she's in so much pain. . . ."

I felt bad about the mare, but I had to ask. "What about the six thousand—"

"You'll get your money. It's just gonna take a little longer than I thought. I'll kill the piece of shit, I swear."

"Suing him seems more practical."

"I can't prove a thing."

Should have taken the X rays. "Too bad you were in such a hurry."

"Yeah. I thought there was honor among polo players. And respect for the horses. Should have known better. That fucking Argentine has it in for me, Andi. I just wish I could figure out why."

"Listen, I hate to bug you, but I need that money, Ross. I need it now."

His eyes met mine. "I guess I could call Kelsey. She'd loan it to me."

Damn. Did he know how I felt about his ex-wife? "I thought you already had it and were transferring it down?"

"I need that to buy a new horse. I'm arranging to cash in some bonds, but it'll take awhile." He reached for the phone.

I stopped him, hating myself and resenting him. "Don't call her. It can wait till next week."

I was quickly realizing that polo was a game for people with a lot of money and a lot of time. Exactly what Ross had always wanted to be. He was overreaching—it was obvious to me if not to him. But it pissed me off that I'd let him drag me into it.

Oh, well. I knew I'd get my money eventually. Ross

was an enormously proud person—he'd pay me back if it killed him.

Unless he'd changed more than I realized.

Chapter Four

Ross and I were not lovers, though I'm sure our classmates assumed we were. But I had my life planned out, and it didn't include a man, not at that point. So the night Ross invited me to his bed, I was completely unprepared.

It was after a block party, a bimonthly event celebrating the end of another clinic rotation. Ross was leaving the next day for a four-month externship in Lexington. We'd be graduating two months after his return. The long ordeal was almost over.

I'd ridden with Ross; my car was at his apartment. He asked me in for a glass of champagne—nothing strange about that. But after he poured and we toasted the future Doctors Pauling and McRoberts, he leaned forward and kissed me on the mouth.

I backed up. "What are you doing?"

"What's wrong? Haven't you wanted . . ."

"Ross . . ." How could I not have seen this coming?

I wavered, wanting him, knowing how this would change everything. Too many of my classmates were married, even had children. Nothing about that attracted me. I wanted to live in sunny California, a place I'd never been—the land of golden sun, and mountains, and blue skies, where it snowed only on the ski slopes, and the sun set in the ocean. Now here was Ross, a man I'd studied with for years, talked with into the night—a man I loved deeply.

I shook my head, turned away from the question in his eyes.

I'd made my decision before the question ever came up.

Sunday I awoke to the incredible aroma of ham cooking. I pulled on shorts and a T-shirt and went to investigate.

"Breakfast?" I asked incredulously. I couldn't remember the last time someone had made me breakfast outside of a restaurant. But he was busily whipping up omelets, and I saw plates full of ham, grated cheese, and sautéed mushrooms next to the sink.

"Harry and Kiwi wouldn't leave me alone," he said. Those were his pet names for Hara and Kiri, which he considered undignified titles for cats, no matter how destructive. "I locked them in the spare room."

I considered letting them out, but they'd be okay for a while. I poured myself a cup of coffee and refilled his. "Are you sure you want to move out?" I teased. "I'm getting used to you being here." I slipped a chunk of ham—still warm—into my mouth.

Ross smiled. "What would people think?"

"Who cares?" I slipped my arm around his waist. "Maybe they'd even be right."

When Ross didn't respond, I self-consciously removed my arm. Moments later I held a plate while he slid a perfect omelet onto it. He then cut it in half and transferred half to another plate. We sat down and dug in—somehow he'd made the toast come out just as the omelets were ready, and everything was hot. But my enjoyment of the food was dampened slightly by his rebuff.

Okay, it would be a stupid time to start something. He was working for me, after all, and he owed me money. It wasn't his fault I'd made the gesture, but I had and now I felt embarrassed. Neither of us could bring it up gracefully. But the subject was there, in the middle of the table, like a centerpiece too big to see around.

Game two of the Santa Rosa Cup tournament was

at one o'clock. We went in the Porsche, Ross prattling intermittently about the game. The trip was better than I'd expected, the beginning of a return to our easy peace.

The sun shone intensely. The water trucks had been busy, and the dust level was down. But something else hung in the air, mingling with the heat and the late-summer humidity, as tangible but harder to place. Anticipation.

The clubhouse was a fashion show. Roses and greenery adorned the tables on the veranda. A few faces looked vaguely familiar, the way people do when you've seen them in the paper or on TV. Spectators sipped champagne and nibbled strawberries. I overheard discussions of agents and accountants.

Tish, sleek and a little masculine in cutoffs and tank top, sat with her brunette friend in lawn chairs, fanning herself with a flyer for a weekend polo clinic. The younger woman imitated her. Their feet rested on a railing six feet from the field. A photographer was setting up a tripod nearby.

"Hi, Andi!" Tish motioned me to join them. "This is Babs Talbot. Her father's general manager of the club." Babs and I shook hands. She wore spandex shorts and a green bikini top, a roll of tanned fat protruding between them.

"Is this your first game?" Tish asked. "What do you think?"

"Very glamorous. I'm surprised there aren't more people."

She looked around as if just noticing the sparse turnout. "Not much of a spectator sport. Polo fans are usually connected to a player or sponsor. See how they all know each other?"

Babs said, "How come you're here? Is Ross your boyfriend?"

I shook my head. Her eyes lit up. *Give it your best shot.*

Ross and his teammates mounted. A number of horses,

apparently the competition, stood tethered to a pair of twelve-horse vans at one end of field three. The rest of their mounts stood patiently at the next tie rail down from Ross's group.

"Who are we playing?" I asked.

"Bluegrass Revival is up against Hats Off Farm."

"Berto's with Hats Off," Babs said.

"Strange names for the teams."

"They're named after the *patrón*'s horse farm, or their business, whatever," Tish explained.

Three people came around the clubhouse: two women and a man, all with shaggy, dun-colored hair and shapeless clothes. I noticed them because they didn't fit in. They carried poster board signs and scanned the audience with a speculative air.

"Who are they?" I asked.

Tish turned, then Babs. They wrinkled their noses, an affected gesture that suited Tish better than Babs.

"Humaniacs. They come every year. Call themselves the Animal Freedom Fighters."

"Animal rights activists?" As paranoid as it sounded to me, maybe Ross was right about the mare he'd bought.

The trio marched around the rail and began pacing the strip between the playing field and the spectator area. They raised their signs and with practiced movements held them facing the crowd, swiveling the posts as they about-faced at the end of each cycle. The hand-lettered signs read POLO IS SLAVERY, FREE THE PONIES NOW and THEIR BLOOD IS ON YOUR HANDS.

Tish snorted. "They want the horses to 'run free.' "

"What's this 'blood is on your hands'?"

"They're against mercy killing. No animal should be put down no matter how much it's suffering. As if they cared about suffering. All they care about is drawing attention to themselves. These horses wouldn't last a day in the wild." She flipped her long blond braid over her shoulder.

The deep voice of the announcer came over the loudspeaker, signaling the game's beginning. Hal Perkins wandered over and chatted with Tish, glancing repeatedly at me.

"How's that mare doing?" I asked.

"Fine," he said. "Healing up real well." He spat a dark glob that slowly soaked into the ground. "See you at the party?"

I shrugged, unsure of what he was talking about. Hal's stare made me nervous after awhile.

When he left Babs said, "You gonna date Dr. P.?"

I frowned. It hadn't occurred to me. "No," was all I said.

The game started and reclaimed our attention. The ball moved back and forth the length of the field almost of its own accord as the players chased after it and vied for possession.

Hats Off scored first, Umberto practically knocking the ball out from under Jaime's mallet. Bluegrass had a one-goal handicap lead—the combined total ratings of their players was only twelve, compared to thirteen for Hats Off—so this evened the score. Babs cheered Hats Off. Tish rooted for Bluegrass.

The ball was knocked back onto the field by a mounted umpire. Jaime wheeled his horse and swung savagely. With Umberto practically on top of him, he passed off to Dietrich's pro, Graehm. Another of Hats Off's players slammed the ball down the field and everyone galloped after it.

"This is kind of a silly game," I said halfway through the first chukker.

"It's the sport of kings," Tish said without irony.

"Eight grown men chasing a ball back and forth, looking like they're ready to kill each other over the results?"

This time she didn't bother to answer.

Ross's team was easy to pick out by their blue shirts. Hats Off wore green. All players wore white breeches, leather knee pads, and helmets. They played with intense fury, knowing how much time and money were at stake. The horses seemed as determined to get to the ball as their riders.

"No women on these teams?" I asked.

Babs shook her head. "There's a coed tournament starting in December. Tish gets to play then."

"I'm rated two goals," Tish said. "That may not sound like much, but most women players have negative-number handicaps. The highest female player just got a four. We're not as strong."

"Ross is a minus one." He'd explained the system to me. The combined goal-ratings of the teammates determined the team's rating. Teams were rarely perfectly matched—a higher-rated team ceded the difference in points to their opponent. For instance, Jaime's seven plus Graehm's six minus Ross's one—Dietrich held a zero rating—added up to twelve. Hats Off was rated thirteen. So Bluegrass started out with one point. "So you only play coed?" I asked Tish.

"I play wherever I can. There's an all-women's tournament in the spring. Plus a few low-goal events through the season. And I get to fill in sometimes if a regular player gets hurt. I have my own horses; that makes me look good in a pinch."

"Plus she's screwed most of the *patrones*," Babs snickered. "She'll do anything to play polo."

Tish glared at her. Then both looked back at the game.

"Patrones?" I asked.

"Spanish for 'boss.' Sponsors. You know, like Ross."

I wondered where Tish had been Friday night, when Ross didn't come home. Then I felt ashamed. None of my business, I reminded myself. Ross had made that clear.

The players ran in a tight cluster to the end of the field. Jaime knocked the ball through Hats Off's goal. I let out a yell. The other two grinned: *Told you so.*

The players paired to await the ball's return. Graehm

took early possession, but Umberto blocked him and stole it. The action moved toward the Bluegrass goal.

"How'd you get started?" I asked Tish.

"I grew up around polo. My father played professionally until he hurt his back four years ago. Then he bought the shop—Hannover Feed and Tack." Tish's eyes never left the game. "Someday I'll be able to make a living at it. Polo, not tack. That's practically unheard of for a girl. Want to try it later?"

"Me? I haven't been on a horse since vet school."

"That's okay. A lot of *patrones* can't ride worth shit. See? Watch Dietrich. Catch me during the last game, and we'll hit some balls around."

I wondered if she was sizing me up as a potential sponsor. Wait till she found out how broke I was. Hats Off Farm scored, and I let out a groan that surprised me. I was hooked.

"You girls having a good time?" We turned.

"Hi, Daddy," Babs said. "Andi, this is my dad, Bob Talbot. Daddy, Andi's a vet. One of the *patrones* is, too. Ross McRoberts?"

"Fine, Babs." He patted her shoulder. He was a beefy man in a white polo shirt and khaki pants. He held a glass of bourbon in one hand. "Mind, you don't stay out too late." He drifted away, sipping and watching the game.

The humaniacs, as Tish had dubbed them, continued their quiet protest. We bought sodas from a woman selling refreshments from the back of a golf cart. They sipped from water bottles on their hips. The fans, for the most part, ignored them.

There were six chukkers in a game, six minutes each. During the one-minute break between the second and third, Ross handed a brown mare to a groom in exchange for a bay gelding. He and Jaime consulted briefly over some tack problem, then mounted. They entered the field at a gallop, bunched with the other players, and the umpire lobbed the ball into play. Umberto got to it first, slamming it toward the Bluegrass goal. Bluegrass took out after him.

The bay gelding stumbled and fell. Ross sprawled on his back and lay still.

Chapter Five

I hopped the rail and ran toward him. From the corner of my eye I saw an ambulance and Hal Perkins's truck approaching.

The gelding struggled up to three feet, holding his left front off the ground. Jaime held the reins, restraining his own horse with his other hand. Ross sat up and shook his head, helmet in his lap. A groom took Jaime's horse, and Jaime unwrapped the bay's injured leg, tossing the blue felt bandage behind him.

Ross waved the paramedics away and limped to his injured horse. He bent down next to Jaime, inspecting the leg. Its ankle bulged obscenely. The gelding kept trying to stand on it, as if he couldn't understand why it wouldn't hold his weight.

"Easy, Rowdy." Jaime stood and stroked Rowdy's nose and neck. Speaking softly, he called to Hal, "Give him something, man." Hal readied a sedative and a bandage for the damaged limb.

"Oh, fuck," Ross said, examining the leg. "I can't believe this. How could he bow a tendon? He was sound on Friday."

"Too bad," Hal said. "A gelding, too. Not much good for anything now."

An eerie hum rose behind us. I whirled to see the three Animal Freedom Fighters standing in a circle, holding hands, and keening to the sky, their heads thrown back and their eyes closed. They reminded me of hired funeral mourners.

Perkins and Jaime exchanged glances and shrugged.

"Get out of here," Ross muttered, but without feeling. The demonstrators appeared not to hear him. I watched Ross's face, recognizing the deadly calm that masked seething pain.

A groom tethered Rowdy and brought Ross another horse.

"Roger, can you loan me Witchie for the last chukker?" Ross asked Dietrich, still carefully emotionless.

His cosponsor nodded. He jumped back on his own mount and loped onto the field. The rest of the team followed.

"How bad?" Tish asked when I returned.

"Bowed tendon. They're going to check it after the game."

"Man, poor Rowdy. Maybe he'll be okay." But her attention was already focused on the game.

At halftime Bluegrass trailed five to four.

"Time for the stomping of the divots!" the announcer said. "The players count on you to level their playing field! Just be careful not to step on the divots with steam coming off them!" Spectators dashed onto the field and began kicking in the upturned clumps of turf that marked the horses' passing.

"Come on," Tish said. Babs and I followed her onto the field where we kicked lumps of turf into place. Halftime only lasted ten minutes, and a considerable number of divots remained when the announcer called us off the field.

The game was set to proceed and the players were already mounted when the animal rights activists laid their signs on the ground and marched onto the field, solemnly holding hands as they neared its center.

The announcer's voice cracked, "Please move off the playing field. The game is about to resume. Please leave the field."

The three ignored him, separated, and lay spread-eagled on their backs. The announcer, and the crowd, fell silent. The sudden muteness ended quickly, however, as the onlookers found their voices and began murmuring among themselves.

The announcer's voice recommenced. "Will those on the field please move away. The police have been called. I repeat, the Indio police are on their way. If you don't move away, Las Palmas Polo Club will be forced to press charges."

The players had been conferring at the edge of the field. The umpires joined them. Now they loped onto field two, adjacent to the one occupied by the demonstrators. As if nothing had transpired, they set about finishing their game.

The activists remained until the fifth chukker, then quietly returned to the parking area.

Ross's team lost, 8 to 6. Tish shrugged. "That's polo. Meet me in half an hour, and we'll hit the ball around."

Babs gloated a little over Hats Off's win. "Are you coming to the party tonight?" she asked me.

Hal had mentioned it, too. "What party?"

"Here in the clubhouse. After the last game—everyone will be there. I'm sure Ross is planning to stay."

I wasn't the least bit sure, but I smiled noncommittally and headed for the Porsche, which I'd driven from the barn. It was parked next to a rusty gray VW van. The van's doors were open. Inside, the animal rights group nibbled fruit.

I glanced at them and unlocked the car door. One of the women held out a brochure. "Here, read about the rampant abuse and needless suffering of horses sentenced to polo."

There was no polite way to refuse. It was a folded page, mass copied and stingy on ink. Below the heading ANIMAL FREEDOM FIGHTERS (Tom Gering, founder) and a poorly rendered sketch of a horse in shackles, was a caption: "Striving To Relieve The Tyranny Of Mankind Over Nonhuman Coinhabitants Of The Earth." Inside was a lengthy hand-printed dissertation that I deferred reading.

"Did you know a nonhuman was murdered to give you those shoes?" demanded the other woman.

I glanced down at my leather Reeboks. What to say? They wore cotton jeans and T-shirts, with plastic sandals. Dirty toes abounded.

"Speciesist!" The woman who had handed me the leaflet spat the word. "Only morally corrupt people use our fellow animals that way. Meat and leather are murder; that makes you a killer by association. I can't look at you!"

"Knock it off, Tina." The other woman, who looked remarkably like the first, turned to me. "We're here to educate, not to alienate. I'm Teri Gering and this is my sister. Did you know that more horses are injured in polo than any other sport?"

I had to admit this was news.

"That poor horse that got hurt today? He's gonna be murdered. Just so a few rich people can have some fun."

I couldn't think of anything to say. Feeling like some subterranean invertebrate, I slunk into the car and shut the door quickly before they spotted the leather seats. Glancing back, I felt the full impact of their contempt. I drove away thinking they were making up for a lack of maternal attention when they were small. No pets. That made me feel better.

At the barn, Hal Perkins had removed the wrap from Rowdy's leg. He and Ross crouched near the horse, who stood placidly with his head down, a wisp of hay dangling from his slack lips. The sedative was still in effect, or Hal had topped it off. One of the grooms held Rowdy's lead while Jaime leaned against the pipe corral, chewing on a stalk of alfalfa and watching.

"I never saw one this bad happen so suddenly," Hal said.

"I'm telling you, he was fine. This horse was perfectly

sound the day before yesterday, and he's barely been out of his pen since then." This from Ross.

"Let's scan it and see what we find." Hal went to his truck and removed a white object the size of a toaster oven, and a metal case. Setting both on a bale of hay, he opened the case and pulled out an assortment of cords and gadgets, which he connected to various ports in the white box.

I looked on enviously. The ultrasound machine would generate images of the injured tendon without X rays or surgery. Live, with video. I could use it to evaluate heart cases and liver problems. But they cost from ten to fifty thousand dollars, not on my likely-to-buy list, and required a lot of training and practice to use.

Hal handed his twitch to the groom, who pulled Rowdy's sensitive lower lip through the loop of rope on one end and twisted the two-foot stick of ash wood until it tightened. The resultant pain—it would hurt only if he moved—would keep Rowdy still during the procedure.

I leaned against the pipe corral stroking the muzzle of a bay mare. This must be the one Ross purchased last week with the money I loaned him. She stood with her weight on her hind quarters, forefeet stuck out in front, as if distance minimized her pain.

I figured she was my mare for now, and I stepped into the pen. Remembering my equine anatomy, I bent down to feel for the pounding arteries in her pasterns, a sight of laminitis. *V-A-N,* I recalled. Vein, artery, nerve, from front to back. Sure enough, the arteries throbbed with telltale vigor. Surely no local anesthetic could mask that. Even without pain, the body knew its part was damaged and would ship extra blood for healing. I wanted to ask Ross about it.

He stood at the end of the barn, speaking with the man I'd seen the first day, the Kentuckian with the hickory cane and the red baseball cap. They were obviously arguing.

". . . exactly what her papers said," Ross was almost shouting. "A deal's a deal. Now get out of my barn."

The other man spoke more quietly. He muttered something that sounded like "all your money." As I drew near he said, "You'll make things right, one way or t'other."

"You got exactly what you paid for! Now get out of my face!" Ross turned, noticing me.

"Sorry, did I interrupt something?" I stood motionless, curiosity making me rude. To whom else did Ross owe money?

He seemed irresolute, unsure whether to introduce us.

"I'm Andi Pauling," I said, offering my hand.

"Jackson Crawford." The man muttered, switching his cane to his left hand to shake. Then he glared at Ross for a moment before turning and stalking to his truck parked a few yards away.

"Who's he?" I asked.

"Bought a horse from me," Ross said. "Now he's changed his mind. Everyone wants something for nothing."

Chapter Six

"I was looking at the new mare," I said. "Would a block mask her digital pulses?"

He went to the mare and bent to feel for himself. He frowned and rested his hand on her pastern. "I checked those. What the fuck?" he muttered, mostly to himself. He seemed withdrawn as we went to check on Hal's progress.

Hal had shaved the back of Rowdy's lower leg and applied gel to the ultrasound probe. The machine was running, a six-inch monitor showing a busy pattern of white dots against a black background. He wedged a lump of something resembling clear Jell-O between the probe and the tendon, and we all stared at the screen. Whenever Rowdy moved, the groom—Juan—wiggled the long wooden handle of the twitch, redirecting his attention.

As Hal slid his probe slowly down the tendon's length, he and Ross mumbled and shook their heads. All I could see was a slightly less disorganized dot pattern that danced and flickered as the probe moved.

"Jeez," Hal said. "Look at that. The deep flexor tendon's completely ruptured. The superficial's almost gone, too."

"No way!" Ross said sharply. Rowdy jumped and Juan wiggled the twitch. "That's impossible," Ross said more quietly.

"You can see it right there." With a flick of a button Hal froze the image.

Ross glared at the screen. I couldn't make out anything.

"See here?" Hal pointed to a black area among the white dots. "The tendon should be here, and there's nothing but fluid. Are you sure he was sound Friday?"

"You think I can't tell when my own horse is lame?"

"I just meant . . ."

"Oh, piss off. Just get the fuck out of here."

They stared. What was going on? Hal was trying to help, doing his job. Ross's reaction was far too extreme.

I knew he was lashing out. "Listen," I said, "Ross has had a lot of horses injured lately. This was so unexpected—"

"Andi, I don't need you to speak for me. I can—oh, *fuck it*!" He kicked the bale of hay supporting the ultrasound unit, missing the equipment by inches.

Hal tucked his machine under one arm, gathered the cords in the other hand, and yanked the plug from its socket overhead. He retreated uncertainly until his back hit a pipe corral.

Ross wheeled and stalked to his car, slamming the door as the engine roared to life. The tires threw sand as he left. Horses skittered in their pens.

Jaime, Hal, and I gaped after him. Hal's expression was shocked, Jaime's disgusted. Mine probably showed embarrassment. It didn't help that I'd seen the blowup coming.

"Jeez. What was that all about?" asked Hal.

"He's upset about Rowdy," I said. "And Fandango, and the two that were poisoned, and now the new mare." I glanced at Hal, who'd recommended that one. Had he blocked her? It didn't make sense. "I just hope he comes back; he's my ride home." But already I was making contingency plans, wondering where I could find a cab. I'd tip extravagantly and add the total to what Ross already owed me.

"Where do you live?" Hal asked.

"Palm Springs."

"I could run you home after the party," he said, looking not at me but at the machine he was dismantling. "If you're staying."

"It looks like I am now."

"You guys live together or what?" he asked casually.

"Not like you mean. We went to vet school together. We're good friends." I emphasized the last word.

As Hal returned the equipment to his truck, he was smiling. "Want to watch the last game?"

"Thanks anyway," I said, glancing at my watch. "Tish invited me to try my hand with a mallet. I'm already late."

I hitched a ride with him to the practice field, where Tish loped a tall chestnut gelding in wide circles, swatting a ball across the turf. When she saw us, she cantered over.

"Hi, Dr. P.," she said to Hal. "How's the tendon?"

Hal shook his head and told her about it as I climbed out of the truck. Then he headed back to the game. A bay mare stood at the rail, saddled and waiting. Babs leaned against the BMW in the same position as the first day I'd seen them. "This is Jojo," she said, indicating the bay. "She's real gentle."

Jojo was leggy and angular, with a benign expression and every sign of an easy disposition. I'd ridden some—weekend trail rides on fat quarter horses. This would be my first thoroughbred.

"Those animal rights people approached me on my way to the barn," I mentioned by way of postponement.

Tish scowled. "Let me guess: They want Rowdy enshrined as a martyr, right?"

I laughed nervously. "Something like that, I guess."

"I wonder what Rowdy wants?"

"For now I don't think he cares. Hal left him pretty well doped up, but the leg didn't seem to hurt as much as I'd expect."

"Poor Rowdy, he lives for the game. If he can't play, he deserves a dignified death. Now let's play polo." She spun her mount and loped onto the field.

Wondering how she knew so much about Ross's

horses, I mounted and Babs handed me a mallet. I looped the leather strap around my wrist and rocked it experimentally, getting a feel for its weight and swing.

"Aren't you playing?" I asked Babs.

"Daddy won't let me. Sometimes I groom for Tish." She spoke wistfully.

Jaime galloped up on yet another bay mare.

"You're ganging up on me!" I said. "No fair!"

"We can play two-on-one." He grinned. "Two pretty ladies on me."

Tish looked at me inquiringly and I shrugged. Jaime picked a mallet from the assortment leaning against the BMW.

The ball looked a lot smaller from horseback. I kept hitting Jojo's legs with my mallet. Fortunately she wore thick padded bandages. The cane handle flexed and arched if I put much torque on it, then whipped around with amazing force. I underestimated how long it would take the mallet to reach the ground, and swung too late. Or I misjudged the distance my horse would cover while the mallet made its arc. In other words, I missed every shot.

"Slow down," Tish finally said. "Stand next to the ball and just tap it."

With Jojo holding still I could concentrate on the ball.

"Good. Now walk her over to it and tap it again, just a little ways. Keep walking. Right, see how easy that is? Now hit it to me."

"Damn," I muttered as the ball rolled casually away at an angle. I nudged Jojo toward it, slowed, and tapped the ball gently, then tried to hit it harder. It hopped off the ground and made a series of inelegant bounces before coming to rest in a divot. Jojo went to it with no instruction from me. I swung the mallet around in a wide arc, extra power springing from frustration. Jojo, grown impatient with my amateurism, skittered sideways and dumped me unceremoniously on the ground. The soft turf cushioned my fall, but I bruised my ego.

Tish and Jaime laughed so hard, I wondered how they stayed on their horses.

"Let me try that again." I stood, dusted myself off, and climbed back on. This time the ball soared across the grass like it knew where it was going. "Hey! I did it!"

We played for nearly an hour, not keeping score or even paying much attention to which end of the field was which. Jaime made a show of keeping up with us despite being outnumbered. He'd fly after the ball, blocking Tish but pretending to reach me seconds too late to block a shot. I felt like a little kid being allowed to win against grown-ups, but still enjoyed scoring.

The humidity was brutal by desert standards, and the heat clung to us like fog, even though it was nearly five. I'd managed to ignore it most of the time, but as I dismounted on wobbly legs I realized Jojo and I were both dripping with sweat.

"What did you think?" Tish asked, dropping to the ground.

"I'd like to try again someday. But you won't have to worry about competition anytime soon. My butt's throbbing and my thighs are about to go on strike."

I walked gingerly to the tie rail, looped Jojo's reins around it, and loosened the cinch as I'd seen Tish do. She was already gathering up equipment. Jaime dismounted beside me.

"Have a good time?" he asked, looking me in the eye with that odd Latin directness that implies both distance and intimacy.

I grinned back. "It was great."

He moved to tie his mount next to mine. She stood fast.

"Hey, Bella, come on." He gave the reins another tug. "Oh, shit."

I glanced at the mare. Her eyes were open and staring, her breathing labored, her haircoat bone-dry. She should have been sweaty like the others.

"Did you play her in the game earlier?"

"Yeah, had to. What's the matter, *querida*?" The last was directed at Bella, who's neck was extended and rigid. I half expected to see a trickle of blood from her flared nostrils.

"Has she had water since then?"

"Of course." He shot me an irritated look. "She never did this before. What's going on?"

"We need Hal," I said. Babs took off in the BMW.

Bella's flanks throbbed—rapid, inefficient respiration. I laid two fingers on her mandibular pulse, which beat a duet with the convulsive flank movement.

"Thumps," I said. "Synchronous diaphragmatic flutter. I think that's what she's got."

"I thought you didn't work on horses."

"I don't. But I had to in school." Once Ross had persuaded me to assist in judging an endurance race. A hundred miles in one day with no change of horses. It was a hot, muggy day in September, and horses were disqualified at every stop. One rider persuaded me to let her continue, though her mount had these same signs. The horse died and I blamed myself.

"Jaime, how could you do this!" Tish shouted.

"What'd I do?"

"You know better than to overwork a horse! Look at her! Andi, do something!"

"We need an equine vet. I don't have any equipment." I shrugged helplessly. The truth was, I had no idea what to do.

"Jaime, walk her or something! Look at her! I think she's going down."

The mare's legs were a bit wobbly, but as we watched she staggered and caught herself. Jaime looked at me inquiringly.

"Don't walk her," I said. "Just hold on and wait for Hal."

"Man, it's too hot. She's not used to the climate. I got her in Colorado." He stared at the heaving flanks, his anxiety mounting. "We paid almost twenty thousand for this one. Nothing can happen to her."

"Money! Is that all you care about?" Tish had begun to walk the other two to cool them out, but she stopped now and turned on Jaime. "What about the mare? She trusted you, Jaime, and look what you did to her!"

"I didn't think we'd play so long!" he said defensively. "*Doctora*, she gonna be all right?"

I shrugged, feeling as powerless as he looked. I took the last of Babs's water and poured it over the mare's head in a feeble attempt to cool her.

Hal arrived and assessed the mare briskly. He inserted a thermometer into her rectum, ran a hand over her dry neck, and listened over her rib cage with his stethoscope.

"Looks like heat exhaustion and anhidrosis," he said, studying the thermometer. "Let's get her into the shade and get some fluids into her. The thumps should resolve pretty fast."

Jaime led the reluctant bay across the dirt path under a tamarisk grove, and Hal inserted an intravenous catheter. He pressed me into service, holding the bottles of fluids over my head so their contents ran into the vein. He got a gallon of rubbing alcohol from his truck and splashed her neck, belly, and flanks, then poured the last of it over her back.

"I'll add potassium to the next two bottles of fluids, and a little calcium," he told Jaime. "Then we'll get her over to the hospital and run blood levels."

"The hospital? Why can't you just give her a big shot of potassium and a bucket of water?" Jaime asked.

"Potassium stops the heart if you give it too fast. Don't worry; with a week off she'll be okay. Just take it easier on her in the future. And be sure she gets a couple of these in her water every day. It wouldn't hurt the others, either." He tossed Jaime a pint-size white plastic bottle of tablets.

Jaime studied the bottle's label. "This is potassium?"

"Among other things. Now go get a trailer. I'll let

them know you're coming." He set the doctored case of fluids next to me on the ground.

Jaime left with Hal. Tish had mounted Jojo and was leading the tall bay back and forth on the road, watching me closely. As one bottle ran out I closed off the IV line, popped it out of the empty and into a new one. I was on the last bottle when Jaime arrived with a pickup and a two-horse trailer. Bella's breathing was less frantic, and she pricked her ears when Jaime reappeared.

The truck was a green Ford pickup with Kentucky plates and a shotgun rack in the window. The same truck driven by the man named Jackson Crawford the week before. Umberto Gutiérrez—Berto—was behind the wheel.

Chapter Seven

While Ross was in Lexington on his externship I began dating a surgical resident. Ross's sudden advances before he left had disturbed me, yes, but he'd also awakened sexual stirrings that had lain dormant for years.

Uncharacteristically, Ross didn't call during the entire four months. When he returned, he was aloof and very cool toward me. I asked him what was wrong, and he simply said, "Been busy, Andi. I'm moving to Lexington after graduation."

Which hardly came as a surprise. It was, in fact, exactly what I'd expected when I'd pushed him away the night before he went. I'd flown to Palm Springs and been hired at Dr. Doolittle's. We were both taking huge steps toward seeing our dreams become reality. I wanted to celebrate with my best friend.

Not for the first time, I realized Ross had a shell a tortoise would envy, a secretive complexity walled off from the world. He could be extraordinarily sensitive about my feelings and maddeningly pigheaded about his own. Quick to anger but prone to tears. He boasted of doubtful exploits and made unlikely, elaborate plans for the future but rarely claimed credit for actual accomplishments. I knew how to avoid his sore spots but not why they were sore. But this time I knew my rejection had hurt him, and the fact that I was sleeping with someone else made it so much worse. So I assumed.

One night I knocked on his door, determined to confront him, planning seduction. I brought a bottle of wine and a couple of steaks for the grill. A woman answered, slim and dark-haired and elegant. Blood pounded in my ears as Ross introduced Kelsey.

My fling with the resident ended a month later. Ross invited me to the wedding, but I had already moved to Palm Springs and somehow couldn't face the trip back. We never had that talk.

The crowd inside the clubhouse was small and intimate. I knew hardly anyone and didn't speak the predominant language, which was polo. Tish introduced me to Graehm, the Australian player, then drifted away with Umberto. Graehm soon headed for the men's room. I saw him later, chatting with one of a throng of what I thought of as polo bimbos.

The men came in two basic styles. About half were modeled on Jaime—slender, fit, astonishingly attractive, and disproportionately Argentine. The *patrones*, on the other hand, tended to be older and overweight but with a sleekness that said Money—capital *M*. I'm uncomfortable around people like that unless they're my clients—home-turf advantage, I guess.

Hal had gone to the equine hospital to check on Bella, the bay mare. Ross never returned after his dramatic exit, and I wondered where he'd gone. I bought myself a beer and smiled vaguely at people who caught my eye. A few men smiled back. Not my type, but hey, I could still look.

Where the hell was Ross?

Across the room Umberto fended off Babs, who seemed ready to rip his clothes off. Definitely a polo bimbo, with an air of desperation. Bob Talbot came in and glared from across the room until Babs noticed and slipped out. Then he followed.

Jaime turned up, bought a beer, and zeroed in on Tish, who by then was flirting with Ross's partner, Roger Dietrich. She was almost as tall as Jaime, with strong shoulders and slim hips, but he was bigger. They made a striking pair—slender and poised, her sun-bleached blond fairness contrasting with his dark challenge.

The conversation began tense and hushed, then Jaime shouted, "You'll never play like me." She said, "I might if I had a fair chance," then something I couldn't make out that caused Jaime's face to darken with anger. He leaned forward, lips moving: ". . . *whore.*" She stepped back. *"Stay the fuck out of my life,"* she hissed, and turned away. He jerked her back, slapped her, stalked out the door. She raised her hand to her face, gaping and motionless for a moment, then followed him, shrieking unintelligibly.

After an embarrassed pause, conversations resumed.

I looked around for some sign of Ross. He wasn't in the clubhouse. Hal hadn't returned, either. I hoped there wasn't a problem with Bella. Maybe I should call the equine hospital and check on her. Or maybe Hal had another emergency to attend.

"Buenas noches, señorita," a sensuous male voice spoke into my left ear.

Umberto Gutiérrez stood so close, his breath moved my hair. He smelled of sweat and leather and whiskey. He gazed at me with hypnotic black eyes. Full lips framed startlingly white teeth. The open neck of his polo shirt revealed a trickle of hair and skin the color of coffee beans. Taut muscles in his arms and shoulders—*The better to sweep you away, my dear.* And those dark, tantalizing eyes were fixed on me.

Mentally I shook myself like a dog after a bath. "Hi," I said, not too breathlessly, inserting my right hand between us. "I'm Andi Pauling. You're Berto, aren't you? I saw you play. You're good," I babbled, smiling the same smile I used on my most challenging clients.

"Yes," he said. "I am. *Very* good." He ignored my outstretched palm and reached to touch my hair.

I stood motionless. Berto was the most dangerous of men—seductive and without conscience, if the wedding band on the hand holding his drink was any indication.

But I stared back, rather helplessly entranced, flattered and flustered to be singled out for his attention.

Then he jerked away. I blinked, suddenly diminished, to see Ross yanking Umberto around—Ross, who was four inches shorter, fifty pounds lighter, and obviously drunk.

"You fucker, you switched horses on me!"

So it wasn't jealousy.

Umberto caught Ross's erratic fist in one huge hand. "What are you talking about?" he asked wearily.

"Don't act stupid. It took me hours to find her at your place in Coachella, but I know the mare I vetted isn't the foundered piece of shit in my barn. You're crazy if you think you'll get away with this." Abruptly he saw how ridiculous he looked with his fist high in the air, held fast by Umberto. He pulled back. The Argentine waited a beat, then let go.

"You did something to Rowdy, too," Ross said. "I don't know what yet, but I will."

"McRoberts, why would I hurt your horses?" Umberto feigned boredom. "I can beat you on a Shetland pony. You're making an ass of yourself in front of your girlfriend."

Ross saw he was the center of attention. His mouth opened several times, soundlessly. He wasn't too drunk to imagine what everyone in the room was thinking: *Who is this asshole?* Humiliated, he wheeled and stormed out through the back door. By the time I recovered from my shock, he was out of sight. Umberto stared after him, then left through the same exit.

This seemed to act as a catalyst to break up the party. People began drifting away, mostly in pairs. If all polo parties were as much fun as this one, I thought I'd pass on the next invitation.

Hal Perkins finally showed up. "I've got one more horse to check; then we can go. Want to come with me?"

I was suddenly very tired, as well as deeply embarrassed for Ross. Even if he was right about Umberto switching horses—and that seemed pretty far-fetched—surely there were better ways to handle it. "I can't let Ross drive anywhere in his condition," I said to Hal. "I need to find him and take him home. It looks like you're off the hook, okay?" I smiled weakly.

His disappointment was pathetically obvious.

"Thanks anyway." I headed resolutely through the front door and down the drive, which was lined with cars and pickups. I looked for Ross's Porsche, hoping he'd left his keys in it. I found it at the end of the queue, parked crookedly a little apart from the others. With relief I pulled the keys from the ignition and shoved them into my jeans pocket.

As I shut the door, I saw I wasn't alone. Fifty feet away, parked under a stand of tamarisk trees, was the VW van belonging to the Animal Freedom Fighters. One of the women—Tina, I thought—stood nearby.

"Hi," I said. "Did you see the man who got out of this car?"

She nodded.

"Did he come back this way?"

She shook her head.

"I have his keys, but if you see him and he's got another set, would you please try to keep him from taking off? He's way too drunk to drive."

"Why should I help you?" she asked.

I sighed. "It's not me. I won't be on the road. But someone else could be injured or killed."

"One less slave driver to worry about."

"Look, forget it. I'm sorry I bothered you." I started back toward the clubhouse, then stopped. "Do you really think the polo horses would be better off running loose?"

She studied me intensively, as if trying to decide whether I was capable of understanding. "Nonhumans were intended by God to roam free. We feel it's our calling to bring liberty to the animals, as the abolitionists freed the slaves."

She was serious. "But these are thoroughbreds.

They've been pampered for generations. They would die in the wild."

"Nature is harsh. Perhaps they aren't meant to survive. We have more literature if you'd like to educate yourself."

"Maybe another time."

She glanced back at the van. "If I see your friend, I'll ask him to wait for you." And she turned to go.

I shook my head and went to track down my classmate.

People milled around the front door of the clubhouse, chatting about the earlier confrontation. The general consensus held Umberto innocent of the switch. No one could imagine a man who made his living at polo deliberately abusing a horse. They knew Umberto, and everyone liked him. Ross was a newcomer, an unknown. I wasn't sure what to think.

I approached Roger Dietrich. He was a broad man, on the short side, with receding gray hair and a soft-looking paunch. A cigar dangled from one side of his mouth, and his left hand held a bourbon tumbler. He looked more like a banker than a polo player, despite the white breeches.

I'd barely met him sober, but drunk he was a bore. I interrupted a running monologue on the finer points of penalty shots, directed at a willowy blond woman in a red-knit minidress. She had an empty martini glass and a vacant expression. He may have missed these, since he was speaking to her chest.

"Excuse me," I said. "I'm Andi Pauling. I came with Ross. Ross McRoberts?" His eyes focused on me. The blond woman left as soon as he turned his back to her.

"Yes, ma'am, I noticed you earlier. Lovely taste he's got, that Ross." He squinted at my face, swaying a little and blowing boozy cigar smoke in my face. "Always had a thing for blondes, myself. What can I do you for?"

I stepped back. "Any idea where he went?"

He peered around the room, giving the matter his full, inebriated attention. "Had a disagreement with one of the players, took off that way." He pointed to the back door, where we'd all seen Ross vanish twenty minutes before. No help.

I touched the keys. If all else failed, I could simply wait for Ross in the car. He was bound to turn up eventually.

"Might have gone to the barn." Dietrich slurred his words. "Make one last check on the horses." It came out "hausses." "He's a vet, d'ja know?"

"Thanks, I'll drive down." If Ross came back to find his Porsche missing, it would serve him right.

"Hold on. I'll come with you. I left my car down there." Dietrich took his cigar out of his mouth and followed me.

I wasn't anxious for his company but felt even more reluctant to go alone. The barns weren't well lit, and I didn't know my way around.

On the way to the car Dietrich said, "He's said right along there's something off about all this. He's a vet, you know. If he thinks that Spanish fellow had something to do with his bad luck, don't be too quick to doubt it." The slurring grew worse. But at least Ross had an ally of sorts. I finally got him inside the Porsche.

"Got a bottle in here?" he asked as I started down the dirt road. "I need me a li'l sip of good ole' *Ken*-tucky bourbon." He had the glove compartment open and was rummaging through the old maps and paper napkins.

"No," I said, though I wasn't sure. "How far do you have to drive?" I was worried about letting him get behind the wheel.

"Condo's just down the road," he said. "In'erested?"

"What? No, I meant—oh, forget it!" Flustered, I almost passed the turn to the Bluegrass barn. The light faded as we got farther from the lamps lining the main road. Spotlights scattered among the barns inadequately illuminated the stables.

"Let me give you my number, case you change your mind. Though I'm flying out in a couple hours, so you'll have to be quick." He pulled a business card from a pocket and a pen from somewhere, scribbling in the dim light of the glove box door. What was it with these polo players? They all seemed to think every woman was salivating to jump in the sack with them. Then again, the women didn't do much to challenge that belief.

"Flying out? There aren't any red-eyes out of Palm Springs."

His chuckle was only a little condescending. "Comp'ny jet," he said. "Out of Bermuda Dunes. Leave whenever I want."

Oh. Well.

I didn't see any sign of Ross—or anyone else—in the aisle or any of the pens, but nosed the Porsche around next to a pale Cadillac Eldorado, which Dietrich identified as his. My headlights swept the pens, the horses already agitated, and illuminated the far end of the aisle.

That's where I saw the body.

Chapter Eight

I was out of the car, running before Dietrich opened his door. "Ross," I screamed. "Ross?" But even in the shadow I knew the figure was too large.

He lay facedown, head toward me. Dark hair absorbed the light from the car. As I dropped to my knees and rolled him over, dull, sightless eyes stared past me. Dietrich tramped heavily down the aisle.

"It's Umberto," I shouted. "I think he's dead."

I touched a dry cornea, checking for reflex—nothing. Searched in vain for a carotid pulse, wished for a stethoscope.

"Call nine-one-one," I said, and hopped over the body to try CPR. My knee landed on something thin and hard, and I shoved it away. I tilted Umberto's head back, and my hand touched the unmistakable warm stickiness of half-clotted blood.

Suddenly the coppery smell assaulted me, and I wondered how I'd missed it before. Beneath the blood, I felt the hollowness of a depressed skull fracture. *Kicked by a horse? How did he get back into the aisle?* The injury was to his temple, the weakest spot in the skull. Death would have been instantaneous. CPR was clearly pointless.

Not a horse, I realized, as my knee again brushed the pole on the ground. I touched it, picked it up—cane. A polo mallet. The Argentine had been murdered.

Oh, Ross, what have you done?

Dietrich had gone to call for help. He didn't have to go far—naturally, he had a car phone.

Conscious now of the damage I'd already done to what was suddenly a crime scene, I went back to the Porsche to await the authorities. They weren't long in coming. An ambulance and two squad cars, lights flashing. Horses circled and paced in their pens, already distressed by the smell of blood, now made frantic by the swirling beacons and strange visitors at this hour.

One policeman, carrying his flashlight like a weapon, escorted a paramedic down the aisle to confirm that Umberto was dead. The other cop approached me.

"Officer Bryant, ma'am. Who called this in?"

I gestured toward Dietrich, who was leaning against his car. "He did, but I found the body. His name's Umberto Gutiérrez, and he's—*was* a polo player."

Bryant was a large-framed black man with a gentle demeanor, carrying a clipboard. "What's your name?" he asked.

I told him and he wrote it down. He then asked for my address, and I jotted it on the back of a business card for him.

"Did you see what happened?"

"No, we found him like this."

The other cop approached, and Bryant moved away for a quick conference, then returned. "How well did you know the victim?"

"I only met him tonight."

The paramedics got in their ambulance and left, lights off.

"What were you doing in his barn at this hour?"

"It isn't his barn. It belongs to that man"—I pointed at Dietrich, who was talking to the other cop—"and a friend of mine. I was looking for my friend."

"What's your friend's name, ma'am?"

I took a deep breath, feeling like a traitor. "Ross McRoberts."

Bryant wrote it down. "Okay, we'll need you to wait

here until we can take your statement. It may be awhile. Do you know where this McRoberts is now?"

"I have no idea."

The second officer must have radioed for help. Other vehicles began arriving. A curly haired detective and a coroner's investigator came separately in unmarked cars. A crime lab van and another brown-and-white with two more uniformed officers followed. They set up spotlights, photographed and measured, collected the mallet and other items near the body.

While they worked I had time to reflect. I'd assumed Ross killed Umberto because the body was in Ross's barn, and I'd heard him threaten the Argentine less than an hour before. A week ago he'd brandished a polo mallet at him in front of several witnesses. I knew he believed the other player had sabotaged at least one of his horses and defrauded him of another. But I couldn't believe he'd kill him—not this way.

Eventually they slid Umberto's body into a bag, zipped it up, and carried him to a coroner's ambulance. It left slowly, the need for urgency long past.

The curly haired detective had bushy black eyebrows to match. He offered identification, which I couldn't read in the relative darkness. "Dr. Pauling, I'm Detective Braun." And he proceeded to ask the same questions as Bryant, only in more detail. The whole thing felt unreal.

"Where does your friend live?"

"Ross lives with me. I don't think he killed Umberto."

"And why's that, ma'am?" He raised one of those caterpillar-like eyebrows in query.

How best to answer that? My gut feeling wasn't likely to convince him. "The blow was to the temple, the only place on the skull you could count on it being fatal. Whoever swung that mallet had to have perfect aim. I've watched Ross play—he's not that good."

"I wouldn't know about that. Of course, it could have been an accident. Wild swing, killed him by mistake."

The other eyebrow joined its partner halfway up his forehead.

"I don't understand why Umberto was in Ross's barn to begin with," I said. "He was at the party in the clubhouse and left early. He'd just had an argument with Ross." He'd hear about that anyway, might as well be from me. "Why would he come here?"

Detective Braun walked over to the crime-scene van and spoke to the tech for a moment. He returned with a plastic bag containing a glass injection vial about as long as my thumb. It held clear liquid that appeared to be amber, though I couldn't be sure in the poor light, and the label had been obliterated.

"What is it?"

"We're not sure. It was found in the deceased's pocket, along with this." He held up two more bags. One contained a 3 cc syringe, new, the kind with the needle already attached. The other held a larger, 12 cc syringe filled with clear fluid. "And this was on the ground near his right hand."

I took the bag with the vial, held it to the light, but couldn't make out anything new. "Could be anything."

Irritably he snatched it back, the eyebrows now pointing at the bridge of his nose.

I yawned and glanced at my watch. After one-thirty.

"Right. You can go. I may have more questions, and you could be called to testify."

Officer Bryant and the other cop were stringing yellow crime-scene tape across the aisleway. I wondered how the grooms would feed the horses.

Velcro greeted me ecstatically at the door, leaping in circles and doing his best to become part of my leg. I flipped on the light.

"Velcro, what did you do?"

He squirmed at my tone of voice but didn't move away.

Two of the sofa pillows were in shreds on the floor. The trail led from the living room into the kitchen and on toward my bedroom. He'd added a bag of flour I didn't know I owned, urinated on the remains, then run circles in the cramped center of the room, grinding the mess into the blue carpet I'd so carefully selected when I bought the place. The manufacturer had claimed it was dog-proof. Probably they didn't mean this dog.

"I thought you were housebroken?"

He whined apologetically, sorry for whatever he'd done to offend me. But oh, how glad he was to see me home. How relieved to know he hadn't been abandoned yet again. Whatever punishment he had to endure now was worth it.

Separation anxiety. I should have expected it. "Okay, it's my own fault for leaving you inside."

I put him out and greeted the others, who sniffed my shoes intently. Only Romeo, a Dobie mix I'd saved from the pound two years earlier, paid attention to Velcro. The latter immediately rolled on his back against the house in abject terror, which was why I hadn't left him outside in the first place. He feared the dogs as much as he did desertion. But he'd have to deal with it while I cleaned up and got my anger under control.

I pulled the vacuum out and began, thinking a rake and shovel might be more appropriate. The pillows were past repair, but the rest wasn't as bad as it looked. I'd have to shampoo the carpet, of course, but it was due. Had been due for a while.

Cleaning was therapeutic. By the time I finished I wasn't even mad any more—at Ross or Velcro. I was just worn out.

I let everyone in. Velcro defended my right knee as his territory, pulling his cross-stitched lips back in empty threat. Romeo growled back but I shushed him.

I undressed with some difficulty, tossed my clothes into the washing machine, and crawled into bed. The water-bed mattress surrounded me with welcome warmth.

Velcro jumped in beside me. I put him on the floor.

"We had this discussion last night," I said. "No dogs on the bed."

He jumped back up. I pushed him off. He jumped back up.

In the end, I let him stay. I was too tired to argue.

I awoke suddenly and in great pain. Every centimeter of my body felt like it had been beaten with a chain.

It was bright sunlight out, and for a disconcerting moment I wondered what day it was. I forced myself to sit up until a back spasm pulled me down again. The previous night's activities rushed back.

God, I wished I could stay in bed all day.

There was no sound from the other room, no smell of coffee. Did Ross know the police were looking for him? I had his car; surely he'd turn up soon.

I hugged my knees to stretch sore muscles, rotated my ankles, massaged aching calves and my inside thighs. With one hand I reached for the phone and dialed the clinic, told Sheila I'd be an hour late.

"But there's two people waiting already!" she squeaked.

"Have them leave their pets and pick them up later. I'll call them first chance I get."

"Only one's a client. The other one's from the newspaper. They both want Dr. McRoberts."

"I don't know when he'll be in next. Take a message or something. Get rid of the reporter." I hung up on her protestations, feeling guilty. Sheila was a loyal employee. She and Didi had stuck with me over the long and uncertain summer, waiting patiently when their paychecks were a few days late, when it wasn't clear how I would pay anyone. Of course, they hadn't been working very hard for their money, either.

The shrilling phone intruded on my thoughts.

"Hello?" Expecting Ross.

"Let me talk to Ross." Argentine accent.

"Who is this, please?" Like I didn't know.

"Me, Jaime. He there?"

"No. Listen, I'm sorry about Umberto."

"Thanks. I gotta call my sister in Argentina today. Gracie, she got a two-year-old kid. What's she gonna do, huh? So, where's Ross?"

"I was going to call you today, see if you knew."

"Haven't seen the *pendejo* since last night."

Pen-day-ho? It didn't sound like a compliment. "Can I give him a message if I see him?"

"Tell him I got a better offer. I quit."

The line went dead before I could get his number. "I don't need this," I shouted at the receiver. It responded with a dial tone.

My body screaming in protest, I rolled onto my stomach, climbed out of bed, and hobbled to the shower. None of the dogs moved.

The hot cascade rolling down my spine helped loosen my muscles. A couple of ibuprofens and some mild exercise might help, too. I couldn't believe I was this out of shape. All this pain from playing a little polo?

Sheila handed me a cup of coffee. Her enormous brown eyes peered apprehensively through layers of brunette fluff, and I felt like patting her on the head. Even after nearly four and a half years of working together she still had that effect. Besides, I really wanted that coffee.

"I take it the reporter's still here?"

"Unh-uh. He left a card. But Mrs. Artimas is waiting and she's, like, real upset. That news guy said Dr. McRoberts might be arrested. Is that really true? For murder?"

"I'm afraid so." I scanned the Artimas chart. Today's visit was a recheck on Buffy's ear infection. Piece of cake. "Don't worry," I said, noting Sheila's crumbling expression. "He's innocent, he has to be. Once he talks to the cops it'll be cleared up in no time." I wished I really felt that confident.

I put Velcro in a cage. He immediately started yipping.

I went up front and ushered Mrs. Artimas into an exam room.

"It's not any better," she informed me before I shut the door. "You should have told me the other doctor was a criminal."

"He's not," I assured her weakly. "The police just want to ask him some questions. Now let's have a look at that ear."

I lifted the cocker onto the table. Buffy was not a happy girl. Her ear was a mess. As I lifted her matted, stinking pinna, the normally cheerful dog snapped at my fingers.

"Oh, my, she's never done that before! She certainly didn't try to bite Dr. McRoberts!" Mrs. Artimas stared dubiously across her pet's back. Buffy bared her teeth in warning.

Why did she wait so long to come back? "The medicine she's on isn't doing the trick," I said by way of understatement. "I'll need to sedate her to clean the ear thoroughly."

"Oh, dear!" Her face registered near panic.

"Has Buffy eaten this morning?" I tried to distract her. "I need to know since I'll be giving her an anesthetic."

"No, I feed her at night. Are you sure this is necessary? I've heard it's not safe. She's not used to being away from me."

"Mrs. Artimas, I would never do anything to Buffy I thought was dangerous. There's always some risk with any drug, but we'll do everything we can to make sure she does fine. You can see she's in terrible pain. You do want her ear to heal, don't you?"

"Well, I suppose."

"And I promise to call you the minute she's awake, so you can come and get her."

"Oh, dear. Are you sure it's the only way?"

It was several minutes before I persuaded her to leave Buffy, and by then I had two more clients waiting. I handed the cocker to Didi, who drew a blood sample and put her in a cage. Buffy howled and began digging at the cage door. Velcro provided harmony. I should have stayed in bed.

Once I finished with the other clients—a vaccination and a minor skin problem—I headed for Treatment with Sheila in tow.

"There's a lady on line two who says her dog swallowed a wristwatch. Can she wait? It's a German shepherd."

"No problem. He should pass it easy."

"Yeah, but she wants to know how long it will take. The watch was a present for her husband's birthday tomorrow. Will she be able to get it back in time?"

I glanced at her in momentary disbelief, then snatched up the nearest phone. "Was that a Timex, Lara?"

A low chuckle. "Caught me again. What are you doing for lunch?" Lara Barrett, my friend and attorney. She always calls when I'm least available, frequently presenting herself as a battier-than-usual client. This time I'd expected her.

"God, I'm so far behind. But we do need to talk. I may have a client for you."

"Murder at the polo field. Ross McRoberts, right? Thought you might know something."

"Not much, but I can tell you later. When and where?"

"Little Burro, twelve-thirty?" She meant our favorite Mexican food restaurant, El Burrito, which thrives in a converted house around the corner from the clinic.

"Fine. You're buying."

I hung up and turned to my patient. Sheila held Buffy while I gave her a small dose of ketamine. The drug immobilized her for a few minutes, allowing me to flush the pus and debris out of her ear without pain or protest. Then I clipped the hair away and peered down the canal through an otoscope.

Foxtails. Three of them, nestled against the eardrum. I extracted them with an alligator forceps, muttering under my breath about equine practitioners from back east who didn't know about the dry grass awns that wriggle into ears and cause nasty infections. The longer they're left, the worse things get. Cocker spaniels are designed for ear problems anyway. If Ross had scoped the ear, he would have seen them. If he'd asked, I'd have told him. Buffy could have avoided the anesthetic, and I could have saved some time and aggravation.

Well, I thought, irrigating the canal with chlorhexidine, no real harm done. A good client was upset, but she'd get over it when her dog recovered. I'd make it easier by reducing my fee.

I gave the dog an antibiotic injection and made it to lunch with minutes to spare.

Chapter Nine

"What's with this McRoberts?" Lara asked over a basket of tortillas and guacamole. "You know where he is?"

I shook my head, dragging a chip through the spiced avocado mixture. Lara leaned forward, elbows on the table, waves of dark-red hair cascading over her shoulders and framing her triangular face. "No," I said. "He hasn't turned up and I'm getting worried. The police are looking for him. I have his car. His partner is in Kentucky. Jaime is the only other person he really knows out here. He's the victim's brother-in-law and not likely to hide him. Besides, Jaime called me looking for Ross. He quit the team."

"Needs to turn himself in," Lara said. "Longer he waits, worse it'll be. He shows up today, maybe he just heard about the murder. Nobody saw him after you found the body, right?"

"That's true. If he does turn himself in, what will happen?"

She shrugged. "Depends on the evidence. Know anything?"

I recapped the previous night's adventures for her, adding every detail I could dredge up.

"Huh. That's all they got, I could get him bailed out like that." She snapped her fingers.

A smiling Mexican waitress set our lunch on the table and left. I dug into my chicken tostada.

"What kind of money are you talking about? For the bail. In case I happen to see him."

She regarded me warily over her fork. "What aren't you telling me? Never mind. Minimum, two hundred grand. Could go a half million. His part, ten percent. With collateral."

"How much for your fee?" Lara might be a friend, but that didn't mean Ross got any discounts.

"Twenty-five to start. Could be more, depending."

Forty-five to seventy-five thousand dollars. At least. Plus what he owed me. If I tracked him down, it would be time for some hard discussion about finances.

After lunch I stopped by the house and unlocked Ross's Porsche. He kept his car spotless, which made the search easier. Somewhere in here was that phone number.

I ran my hands along the crease in the seat, hoping Dietrich hadn't taken his card with him last night. I glanced into the backseat: nothing. Glove box: some maps and paper napkins, a packet of fuses, a screwdriver, and a flat key with a number stamped on it. No business card. Damn.

I sat in the passenger seat pretending I was Dietrich. Scribbling my phone number on a business card, leaning on the glove box door. Car stops, see the body. Open door, scramble out, confusion. Could it have fallen on the ground? If the cops found it, they might get to Ross long before I did.

One last possibility: I knelt beside the car and looked under the passenger seat. *There*: nestled in the plush carpet, like a prize in a treasure hunt. Buff background, gold embossed letters. "Roger Dietrich, President." At the top it said "First National Bank of Lexington," with an address on Versailles Road.

I'd guessed right. He *was* a banker.

On the back was a barely legible phone number with an Indio prefix.

Closeted in my office, I dialed and waited. The line was answered by a mechanical whir and "You've reached the weekend home of Roger and Debbie Dietrich. We're not home . . ." A wife. What a prince. I tapped my fingers on the desk. The beep came.

"Ross, if you're there, pick up the phone. It's Andi. I need to talk to you. It's not as bad as you think." I paused a beat, out of ideas, unwilling to give up so easily. "I've got a good attorney. She can get you out on bail if you just turn yourself in. She says the longer you wait, the worse it will be. She says—Ross, *will you pick up the damn phone!*" I was about to hang up in frustration when a change in the quality of silence told me someone was on the line.

"Ross? Is that you?"

"Jesus, Andi, won't you leave me alone?" He sounded weary beyond words.

"I can't do that, Ross. You know I can't." I had six thousand good reasons why not.

"Have you seen the fucking paper? The cops want me for Gutiérrez's murder. All I want is to get out of the state. Maybe the country. Just live out my life in peace."

Live out his *life*? "You're being melodramatic. Did you kill Umberto?" A question with only one answer.

"No. But that won't stop the fuckers from railroading me."

"True. And I admit it looks bad right now. But you can't keep running forever. If you try, you'll only look guiltier."

There was a long pause while, I hoped, he considered the truth of what I'd said. Then, "What about this lawyer?"

"She's a good friend of mine. I had lunch with her today, and she wants to represent you. If you'll turn yourself in."

"Set up a meet. I'll call you back tonight."

I didn't ask him how he'd known about Umberto's death in time to elude the police the night before.

Judge Eleanor Wood banged her gavel, demanding quiet. Clear blue eyes stared down her nose, daring anyone to waste her time.

"People versus Ross McRoberts."

Ross and Lara approached the bench. Ross had lost more weight in the past two days and had enormous black circles under his eyes.

An intense, black assistant D.A. approached as well. At the judge's request he gave his name, Victor Franklin. Lara waived reading of Ross's rights. The judge continued.

"Ross McRoberts, you are charged with violation of Penal Code Section one-eight-nine-A, murder in the first degree. How do you plead?"

"My client pleads not guilty, Your Honor," Lara said.

Ross fidgeted, looked at the table, the walls, anything but the judge.

Wood turned to Franklin. "Recommendation as to bail?"

"The defendant moved to the area less than two weeks ago and is an obvious flight risk. Due to the violent nature of the crime, he's a danger to others. We ask he be held without bail."

Ross tensed. Lara placed a restraining hand on his forearm, speaking quietly, calming him. She had anticipated this. It was her turn to address the judge.

"Your Honor, my client is innocent and was unaware of the warrant until last night, at which time he sought counsel and immediately turned himself in. Contrary to Mr. Franklin's contention, Dr. McRoberts is employed locally." Meaning by me. She emphasized the word *doctor*. "He has no intention of leaving his employment. He has no criminal record, has never even been arrested. Holding him would serve no purpose.

Defense requests bail in the amount of fifty thousand dollars."

"Bail is set at two hundred fifty thousand dollars." I let out a breath I didn't know I'd been holding as the judge held up a hand to ward off the assistant D.A.'s protestation. "If anything changes, I'll entertain a motion to revoke. Preliminary hearing four weeks from today."

Ross's shoulders slumped with relief as he followed Lara through the courtroom door. A husky bailiff followed them. I caught up in the hallway. If bail had been even a few thousand more, Ross couldn't have met it.

I stood next to him at the window. He met my eyes, his reflecting brutal humiliation. I reached for his hand and felt his answering grip. My own trembled at what I was about to do.

The previous night Ross had arrived by taxi at my house, circles like black smudges on the ghost-white canvas of his face. His dead-looking eyes mirrored the effect of the makeup he'd worn on Halloween. I hugged him, relieved to be taking action, shocked again at his thinness.

He held me for a long moment, then handed me a cashier's check for six thousand dollars. "Sorry this is late," he said in a wooden voice. "I wanted to make sure you got it before the shit hits the turbo jets."

Lara was already there. I put the check in my purse and went for Chinese takeout while they talked. Coming home, I pulled in the driveway ahead of a bail bondsman invited by Lara, a faintly greasy man named Chuck. We all discussed Ross's prospects while the food got cold. Nobody ate.

Ross had fifty thousand in cash. As collateral he offered his car and his horses.

Chuck said, "Car's good for maybe forty. The horses I can give you a hundred on."

"That's not going to be enough, is it?" Ross asked.

Lara said, "You'll need another forty thousand collateral. More like a hundred, to be safe. You want to make bail as soon as the judge sets an amount, otherwise you go to jail."

"I can't go to jail!" Beneath the frustration I saw panic.

"What about Dietrich?" I asked. "He's a banker."

"I tried him first. No go. Guess his board of directors frowns on loans to bail out murder suspects." He tried a smile. It came out as a grimace.

"Do you own any real estate? In Kentucky, maybe?"

"No, nothing worth that kind of money."

"Can you call your father?" My gut clenched at the idea of asking my own pop for help, but the situation was extreme.

Ross shook his head, despairing.

"Just try," I said. "You haven't got anything to lose."

I saw what the call cost him in the way his body shook and his voice caught when he mentioned the word *bail*. I heard the click as his father disconnected. He'd paid Ross's way through vet school, but only under duress from his wife. He considered students parasites. When she died in our third year she'd named Ross beneficiary on her life insurance policy. It was enough to pay the last two years' tuition and rent on his apartment and had freed Ross from the quarterly ordeal of asking his father for money. Apparently they hadn't reconciled since.

"Isn't there anyone else?" I swallowed. "Kelsey?"

"She doesn't own anything," he said sourly. "And her parents wouldn't help. Believe me."

Lara, Ross, and Chuck leaned back in their seats, dejected. Lara said Ross would be in a better position to help in his own defense if he were out on bail. Being in jail would make him look guiltier in the eyes of a jury.

I pictured the cashier's check in my wallet. Lara's retainer was twenty-five thousand, half of what Ross had left. If bail was set at more than two-fifty, he wouldn't have his 10 percent. Yet he'd paid me first.

"I own my clinic free and clear," I said quietly. "The building the land, everything."

Chuck's eyes lit up. Ross turned paler than ever. "No way, Andi. You can't do that."

Lara stood and motioned me into the kitchen, frowning intensely. "Have you thought this out?" she asked in a harsh whisper.

"It's not like I'll lose it," I said quietly. But I already knew I'd help him get away if it looked like a conviction.

Lara studied me and I saw comprehension dawn. "Are you in love with him?" *He's not worth it* was implied.

How could I explain it to her? My whole life had been directed toward independence: getting into and through college, then vet school, emerging unencumbered. Everything I had went toward proving I could make it alone, proving I was good enough. Even my pets represented professional triumphs—I'd saved each from death, and got a little rush when I stroked one, beyond the usual pleasure of petting an animal. But proving to whom? I'd lived from goal to goal, but the unattractive realization was dawning on me that I'd left out the reason. All the work I'd put into keeping the clinic—for what? So I could buy more stuff? To impress strangers?

"Ross is innocent, Lara. You probably don't believe that, but I know it's true. By doing this I'll lose him—he can't stand needing someone. But if I let him go to prison without doing everything I possibly can to stop it, my life is nothing."

"Okay," I said. "Let's sign those papers and get out of here."

"Sure you haven't changed your mind?" Ross said. Lara glanced sharply at him.

"Hell, no," I said with false lightness. "I took the

whole morning off to be here. I need you to help me catch up on appointments."

The relief on his face was pathetically obvious. As was his shame.

Papers were shuffled, money changed hands, and Ross was free to go. Now all we had to do was to prove he was innocent.

Chapter Ten

That evening started out awkwardly. Ross sat in front of the television. Methodically he swallowed several capsules and tablets—megavitamins, I surmised—while I fed the animals and microwaved frozen dinners. He was exhausted and humiliated and sick of the furor surrounding Umberto's murder. But there were questions I had to ask, things I hadn't wanted to bring up in Lara's presence.

"How did you know the police were looking for you?"

His eyes reminded me of a puppy being reprimanded for the first time—wounded and confused. "It was all over the news."

I shook my head. "The night of the murder, Ross. You disappeared before the body was found. What made you run?"

"What, you too?" he said. "You don't believe me now? You think I killed him, don't you."

"Don't start, Ross." I swallowed my irritation. It wouldn't do any good to pick a fight. "I'm in this up to my eyeballs. I need to know everything I possibly can, even if only for my own satisfaction."

He ran a hand across his face while I slid one plastic tray onto a plate and put the other in the microwave. "You weren't the first one in the barn," he said.

"Tell me."

He took a deep breath and began. "When I left the clubhouse I knew I'd screwed up. Everyone was laughing at me, and it was my own damn fault. God, I hate that, Andi. More than anything." He paused, staring at and through the television. "Things in my life, before I came here—I wasn't totally honest with you." He flashed a weak smile. It was like seeing in the face of a very old man a glimpse of the boy he'd once been. "I wanted to impress you, I guess. Bet you're really impressed now, huh?"

I refused to subject Ross to a depressing exposé of flaws and past failures. I simply wasn't up to being supportive and understanding in the face of Ross's self-pity. "The night Umberto was killed?" I prompted.

"Right. I went walking. It's so peaceful at night in the barn—snorting and stamping and munching, contented sounds of horses with their simple needs met. I needed to calm down. Berto ruined one of my horses and sold me a ringer with laminitis, maybe lamed another of mine so bad it'll have to be put down. I thought if I could prove it, they'd quit laughing." Ross was a little drunk, his thoughts rambling but the words clear. If he had any more beer before eating, he'd be incoherent. I set the plate in front of him, but he ignored it.

"So you went to his barn?"

"Yeah. It's a couple of rows over from mine, on the way. Figured if anyone saw me, I could tell them I was taking the scenic route. I wanted to look around, see if I could get something on him."

"Did you find anything?"

A sick little giggle escaped his lips "Locked tack room. Not a fucking thing. But then the horses at my place suddenly got agitated, and I looked over and saw them there. Couldn't tell who it was. Tried to sneak up on them. Then Berto shouted, and I recognized him and thought he'd seen me. I ducked down about the time the other one rose up and swung something at him."

"Did you see who it was?" Stupid question. He'd have said by now.

He shook his head. "Just a shape from behind, silhouetted against that spotlight in the corner. Then it bent down over the body."

"Damn. What did you do?" Like I had to ask.

"What else? I yelled and ran over, but whoever it was took off. I saw Berto, and he was already dead. How would it look?" He stared blankly in my direction, probably picturing the scene from the point of view of everyone who'd come later. Maybe wondering whether things would have been different had he pursued the actual killer. "I panicked and ran."

I needn't have worried about my clients' reaction to Ross's notoriety. They swarmed to see him, to get the juicy details firsthand. It was the age of the celebrity villain, and clients who'd deserted me in droves last spring now flocked through the doors. Despite his weariness, Ross didn't disappoint them.

I tried not to be too obvious watching him, pointing out a case of Ehrlichiosis, a blood parasite carried by ticks, common in the desert but rare elsewhere. Explaining the difference between pyoderma and mange. Making sure he scoped infected ears. He learned fast and we worked well together. I enjoyed having him there.

Wednesday night he called Jaime. I heard him say, "I wish you'd reconsider. Finish the tournament with me, at least." Jaime would never know what it cost Ross to ask. But I gathered the Argentine was less than convinced of Ross's innocence. He'd been offered Umberto's position with Hats Off Farm and he'd accepted. The officials understood. End of discussion.

"Will you get your money back?" I asked after he hung up.

"Yeah, he has to repay most of it to break the contract. That'll help, but it'll cost at least that much to get a replacement this late in the season. If anyone will play for me at all."

"What about Tish?"

"A woman? Right, and Jaime's girlfriend to boot. Great idea, Andi."

I made myself pause a beat before answering. "She's not his property, Ross; she's his girlfriend. I think she wants to play enough that it won't matter. After all, Jaime played against his brother-in-law. And Tish and Jaime had a pretty bad fight the other night." I told him about the scene at the party, where he'd slapped her.

He considered it. "We'd be the only coed team in the cup. It would give us a hell of a handicap, but it would keep us alive." He called Dietrich and spoke for almost an hour. When he hung up, his head fell back against the single remaining sofa cushion. His hand rested on Clyde, who slept in his lap. The Ayatollah, a seventeen-pound-but-who's-counting Siamese, was stretched out beside him, and sleek gray Evinrude kneaded her de-clawed feet on his shoulder. Gambit sprawled at his feet. I acknowledged feeling much the same toward Ross as I did the animals—in some ways he was just another stray who'd wandered into my life and refused to leave.

"Well, what did he say?"

"He said hire whoever I want."

"It's getting late. You want me to call Tish for you?" Why did this seem more important to me than to him? Then again, he had more urgent concerns at the moment.

After a moment I repeated the question. He still didn't answer. "Ross?" He'd fallen asleep. Staring at him, I realized he looked worse than tired: He looked ill. His face had a pasty sheen and a drawn, dehydrated look. He'd continued losing weight since the arraignment. The past few days had been devastating.

Tish had given me her number Sunday. I fished it out of my purse and dialed.

"Andi!" she said when I announced myself. "How are you doing? Is Ross okay?" Her voice held sympathy. I was relieved.

"We're both managing, thanks. How about you?" Last time I'd seen her, Jaime had slapped her in front of most of the people she knew. I hoped she had the sense to dump him.

"I'm fine. Me and Jaime made up. I swore I wouldn't go out with other guys, and he promised not to hit me again. You want to get together for some stick-and-ball?"

"Coming from anyone else that would sound like a proposition." I laughed. I didn't comment on Jaime's promise. Or her own, for that matter. "Maybe I will. But I called to ask you a question. Want a job?"

"Doing what?" She sounded puzzled.

"Playing polo, what else? Jaime's job, actually. He quit."

She didn't reply immediately. "With Bluegrass Revival? How come Ross didn't call me himself?"

"He, um, figured I knew you better," I hedged.

"Oh, man, I want to, but I don't know. Jaime . . ."

"Quit. He left Ross hanging."

"I feel really bad about that. But working for Ross right now . . . I'm kind of surprised he'd even keep playing."

"Look, Tish, I suggested you because you said you don't get to play enough. Ross happens to be innocent, though it sounds like you and everyone else at Las Palmas already have him convicted. If you don't want the job, just say so. If you do, I'll get Ross to call you in the morning to discuss the details."

"Man. I'd never get another chance to play thirteen-goal polo." She paused, then, "Okay, but he's gotta pay me good."

"How much?"

"Five hundred a game."

Her breathless silence told me she was afraid it was too much. I did some quick calculations. It amounted to less than a third what Jaime had received, and Tish had her own horses.

"How about six?"

She shrieked with delight. "All *right*!"

* * *

Ross barely woke as I dragged him to his feet and unfolded the sofa bed. He allowed me to remove his shirt and shoes, then stumbled off to the bathroom. It was nine o'clock.

Tired myself, I lay awake, obsessing—the possible trial, all the events that had let up to it. How would my life be different today if I hadn't pushed him away on that night four years ago? Was it too late to change my mind?

Moving silently, I got up and removed the T-shirt I'd worn to bed. I slipped out of my panties and confronted my reflection in the mirrored closet door. Enough light filtered in from outside to silhouette my figure. A little soft here and there but not bad.

Hardly daring to breathe, I stepped silently into the living room. I stood over Ross, watching him sleep, suddenly terrified he'd wake up. What would he do if I crawled in beside him: welcome me, or feel obligated to service me like one of the stallions he'd treated in Lexington?

After all, he was paid for.

In buying Ross's freedom, I had humiliated him. We had no chance at a relationship. A sexual encounter would only make things more uncomfortable.

He mumbled in his sleep and rolled over. The shadows deepened the hollows of his cheeks.

I turned around and went back to bed.

I dragged myself out of bed in time to start coffee. Ross was stirring as I went to shower. When I emerged, he was dressed and had poured us each a cup. He was flipping through an old veterinary journal but not reading it. The morning light accentuated his gauntness and pallor.

"Ross, do you feel okay? If you need to take the day off, I'll understand."

"I can handle it."

I started to protest but saw it would only irritate him.

He was an adult. If he said he was okay, then who was I to argue?

I went on and he showed up half an hour later. I tried to take most of the clients, but Ross drove himself like a robot. Several clients remarked on his appearance. One or two even chastised me for allowing him to work. As the day wore on I felt guiltier and guiltier.

Late morning I found him by the lab printer, where blood test results came over by modem from the big veterinary lab in Los Angeles.

"Did you use the last of the large Di-Trim?" I asked more sharply than I'd intended. "I wish you'd tell me when we're out of an antibiotic. I had to send a rottweiler home on six of the little tablets a day."

"Sorry. Listen, I had this case yesterday," he said casually, scanning a printout and marking abnormals with a yellow highlighter. There was a lot of yellow on the sheet. "Bad kidneys but a lot of other problems, too. Glucose is four twenty-two."

A plea for help disguised an offhand remarks. I studied the list of numbers.

"This is prerenal—she's dehydrated. Her BUN's almost eighty but the creatinine's not even three. She drinking water?"

"Not drinking or eating, for a couple days now."

"Vomiting?"

"With blood. That's why I thought it was her kidneys."

"Most likely she's got pancreatitis. That can shut off insulin production, sending the glucose up. See how the liver enzymes are elevated? That's common. Call the lab and ask them to run amylase and lipase—those are the pancreatic enzymes."

"I know that," he said defensively.

"Anyway, the kidneys will probably be fine once she's rehydrated. Abdominal X rays might distinguish it from primary liver disease. What kind of fluids is she on?"

"I gave her subcutaneous Ringer's."

"This dog isn't in the hospital?"

"Um, I'll get her in." He reached for the phone, thumbing through the file for the number. I glanced at the name on the chart.

"Oh, damn, not Buffy Artimas again?"

His frown deepened, then was replaced by a nearly full smile. "Hello, Mrs. Artimas? Dr. McRoberts. How's Buffy this morning?" A pause, then the smile wilted and his shoulders slumped. "Oh no. I'm sorry. Well, I'm sure it's for the best. They said that? No, ma'am. Really sorry to hear about this. Bye, now."

Ross stared at the sink. "She took Buffy to the emergency clinic last night and they put her to sleep. She thinks the anesthetic you gave her on Monday caused the kidney failure and that's what killed her."

"They repeated the blood work?"

"I don't think so. I told her it was the kidneys." He leaned back against the counter and tilted his head back wearily. "It looked like the cat that came in the other day—weak, depressed, losing weight. So that's what she told them, I guess." He pulled his lower lip between his teeth and raised his eyebrows, staring at me apprehensively. "I'm sorry."

"It didn't occur to you to hospitalize her? Pancreatitis or renal failure, either way she needed fluids."

"The owner wouldn't leave her. I thought I'd wait for the lab results. . . ."

"Ross, listen to me. I don't expect you to know everything about dogs and cats." I could barely keep from screaming. "And I know there's not time to read up on every case. From now on, anytime something confuses you even the tiniest bit, you *will* get the animal out of the exam room, and you *will* consult with me. If I'm not available, you'll do your damnedest to hospitalize the animal until I can look at it."

He held my gaze for a moment, then sank back against the counter. "You're right, Andi. I don't know what I was thinking, coming in here and trying to practice—

God, dogs and cats, I thought I could handle it. Do you want me to leave?"

"Ross, I—" Damn, I could be such an ass. If I was irritable, how must he feel? "No, not unless you've changed your mind about taking a sick day. She probably would have died no matter what you did. This is a serious condition. Let me talk to Trinka at the emergency clinic. But let's be more careful, okay?"

"Yeah. Andi?"

"Hm?"

"I'm supposed to go practice with Tish this afternoon. I don't think I'm up to it. Could you do me a favor and go in my place?"

"Go practice polo? Me?"

"Yeah. Please. You're right: I'm not feeling too hot. I'm okay doing this, as long as there's not any surgery. Tish needs to get the horses out and work them. But I don't think I can ride. And I've got a game tomorrow. . . ."

"I don't know how much use I'll be, but I'll give it my best shot."

Chapter Eleven

Actually, I was thrilled at the unexpected reprieve. I needed to get away and cool off. I bought myself a quiet lunch and met Tish and six horses on the practice field at three.

"Where's Ross?" she asked.

"He's not feeling well. He asked me to come instead. He wants to be in top form tomorrow." Also I thought he wanted to postpone showing his face at Las Palmas as long as possible.

She put her hands on her hips, exasperated. "We've got our first game tomorrow. Dietrich can't be here to practice and Graehm's in Colorado looking at horses. How are we supposed to be a team?"

There wasn't much I could say to that.

"Oh, well. You can at least help me tune these guys up a little." Meaning the horses. "I've let them get lazy, since I didn't expect to play for at least a month."

They didn't feel lazy to me. Instead, the three I got on acted like they'd been confined too long and wanted to make up for it all at once. It was all I could do to keep any one of them in hand, even gentle-natured Jojo, whom I'd gotten along so well with before. They seemed to sense a real game approaching and wanted to do their best—their love for the game showed in their pursuit of the ball. My time was more a riding lesson than a practice game. Babs walked the hot ones as we switched.

I developed an awe of Tish. I admired the way she handled her mounts and the mallet, her strength and agility, her obvious talent at driving the ball. The horses, while clearly not in Fandango's league, seemed to give her everything they had. You didn't get that kind of performance out of any animal without spending long hours working with them day after day.

When we finished I felt both exhausted and exhilarated.

Tish approached me as I unsaddled Jojo. "I guess you wonder why I didn't jump when you—well, when Ross offered me this job." She watched her mares walking with Babs.

"Something to do with Jaime?"

"He won't like it, but he understands about keeping competition away from personal. It's this whole thing about working for Ross."

"I understand you'd have reservations about working for an accused murderer."

"It's not that, exactly." She stared gloomily into the distance, then abruptly focused on me. "If he'd killed some stranger it might even be an asset—intimidate the competition a little. But see, Berto was real popular. Man, he played at Las Palmas since he was eighteen. Everyone considered him a homeboy, even though he was Argentine. He expected to go ten goals eventually."

"Ross didn't kill him."

She shrugged. "It doesn't really matter. People will always think he did, even if he gets off. He's the no-name who came from back east and killed our best and most promising player. Even if . . ." She trailed off.

"And you're afraid of having your name associated with his?"

"When this is over, he'll be gone—either in prison or back east. I'll still be here."

"Then why did you agree to play for him?"

"Maybe to set things right. Anyway, I know Ross wouldn't have hired me without your help. I wanted to say thanks." She stopped and looked up. Babs was approaching, riding one horse and leading three more.

I'd had such a good time today, I felt it was me who

should thank her, and said so. "Want to go for a beer?" I asked her.

"Can't," she said. "I've got to get these guys bathed and rubbed down so they'll be ready to play tomorrow. Maybe Babs would want to go."

I opened my mouth to protest, but Babs's eager expression stopped me. What the hell, she might even be able to tell me something about Umberto that would help Ross's case.

"Let's go to The Tenth Goal," she said. "It's just down the road."

As we headed for the Miata Tish called to me from horseback. I walked over and she sat pensively for a second before saying, "Berto wasn't everything he seemed." Then she left at a brisk jog, the spare horses jostling for position.

As I started the car I wondered what she meant.

"Down the road" turned out to be past a citrus grove, an RV resort, and a couple of small, run-down desert dwellings with rusty pipe corrals in front. Indio felt refreshingly real after the glittery patina of Palm Springs. You could almost smell the sweat of the farm workers and the dust from plowed fields, with a sweet overlay of citrus and fertilizer, hear the revving of tractors and the cheerful curses of date pickers. Many of the billboards were in Spanish.

The Tenth Goal was a honky-tonk dive. Its only real distinction was a neon sign bearing an image of a polo player. The player's mallet arced downward again and again toward a ball that never left the ground. The bar's front door hung open, and only two cars occupied the parking lot.

A couple of Mexican men in dirty jeans and old sneakers sat on bar stools drinking beer from cans. Conway Twitty crooned from the jukebox in one corner. Autographed eight-by-tens of polo players decorated the walls. We sat at a table, but it was clear we'd have to go to the bar for service. Babs asked for a beer, and I got us each one. I figured if I didn't ask her age, she was smart enough not to tell me.

"I sure had a good time this afternoon. I'd like to do something for Tish," I said.

"You already did. Playing with a thirteen-goal team is a really big break for her. She lives for the game."

"She takes good care of her horses, too."

"Better than anyone I know. They're her life."

I took a long draw of my deliciously cold beer and said, "I guess everyone misses Umberto."

Her eyes clouded wistfully. "Yeah, he was pretty special. Too bad he had to die for Tish to get to play."

"I understand he had a wife and son in Argentina."

She shrugged. "So? A lot of polo players fool around."

In her mind that made it okay. It wasn't what I meant, though. "Why did they stay behind? Why not come up with him?"

"He brought Gracie once, before Carlos was born. They were thinking of moving here for good. I guess she didn't like it; she never came back. She wanted him to buy an *estancia* in Argentina and become a *patrón*. With enough money he could form the best team ever. So I think he was trying to save up."

"Had he been with his current team long?"

"Hats Off Farm? Years. He got a great deal. His *patrón* let him buy all the horses, gave him a car to drive, and flew him back to Argentina two or three times a year. As long as he kept winning, he could have anything he wanted."

"How much does a good polo player make in a year?"

"Someone like Berto? A lot. Prob'ly a hundred grand or so. Plus perks." She shook her head. "I wonder what Gracie will do now?"

She spoke with genuine concern. If I hadn't seen her throw herself at Berto the night of his death, I might have thought she was an old family friend. Instead, I thought she was pathetic.

"Did he have any enemies?"

"Unh-uh. How come you're asking these questions? Don't you think Ross killed him?" She sounded ready to fight about it.

Careful, Andi. I changed the subject. "Babs, what you said about the players fooling around—I just hope you're careful."

She smirked, then spoke with the arrogance only a self-centered, insecure adolescent can muster. "You mean AIDS? That's not a problem in polo. Only queers get it. These guys are all man." She hesitated, and I was sure she wanted to tell me something else. Then she downed the last of her beer and stood up.

"I gotta go. If Daddy finds out I was here, he'll kill me."

Friday morning Ross left the house when I did. He planned to meet Lara for a strategy session before heading to Las Palmas for the game.

I managed to clear most of the afternoon by cramming extra appointments into the morning and postponing some till Saturday. I drove to the polo field feeling like a truant. I'd been taking too much time off, and neglecting the practice was a good way to lose clients. But I really wanted to see this game. After all, I now had a vested interest in the team.

The first chukker was under way when I pulled through the back gate. I sat by myself on the green to watch.

They were pretty bad. The opposing team, Red Flag, held a two-goal handicap—second in the tournament only to Bluegrass's new five-goal handicap. But Bluegrass's lack of practice gave a dramatic advantage to the other team. Ross played listlessly, seemingly having given up before the game started.

After Red Flag scored, Graehm caught the throw-in and tried to carry it down the field. When a Red player blocked him, there was no one for him to pass off to. Where Jaime would have been clear, Tish was struggling against a superior player for access. The Red player took possession and hit the ball to a teammate.

Red Flag evened the score. Bluegrass had only their handicap points.

As they reconvened for the throw-in, Graehm upbraided Ross loudly. " . . . *guard the frigging goal! Let your girl do her job and chase the ball!*" The Aussie was team captain by default. Polo is peculiar that way—the hired players get to boss their employers. Ross brushed him off.

An umpire threw the ball in, and Tish pounced on it. I watched proudly as she hit a powerful stroke down the field, and Graehm, having ridden down the field in anticipation, received the pass and steered the ball toward the goal. The Red guard tried unsuccessfully to intercept. Meanwhile Tish blocked another player from going to his team's aid. She was learning.

Tish rose in her stirrups as Graehm knocked the ball through Red Flag's goal. I cheered with her, admiring her strength and toughness and feeling her passion for the game. At that moment I might willingly have traded lives with her.

A whistle signaled the end of the chukker.

As they switched mounts I glanced up to see one of the Animal Freedom Fighters—Tina, who'd thrust the brochure at me the day Rowdy was injured—bearing down on me. She barely met my eyes as she thrust a flyer at me and swept past.

The flyer was of better quality than the earlier one. The heading proclaimed: THE WORST OFFENDERS: A SERIES.

Below this was a grainy picture of Ross.

The inside text theorized that slave drivers could be harassed into surrendering their evil habits. Ross was portrayed as an irresponsible abuser of horses who had committed murder to protect himself from discovery. The brochure failed to explain whether it referred to equicide or to the death of Umberto. It did, however, provide an address and phone number for anyone interested in harassing this particular evildoer.

They were my address and phone number, of course.

* * *

I left at halftime, hoping Ross hadn't seen me. He stumbled in around eight.

"You don't look very happy," I said. "How was the game?"

"We lost. What did you expect?" He pulled a beer out of the fridge and guzzled.

"I'm sorry." I didn't voice my opinion that everyone else on the team had played their best. Ross didn't even need to know I'd been there.

He shrugged, collapsing into a chair. "That's polo. It's not whether you win, and all that shit." It bothered me that he seemed to be getting used to losing.

"Then what's wrong? Oh, Ross, not another horse?"

"No, they're all fine. Those animal rights assholes were there again, with reinforcements." He looked at me with haunted, frightened eyes.

"What happened?"

He told me about the flyers. I pretended ignorance. "They can't blame you for what happened to Rowdy!"

"No? Those fuckers aren't living in the same world as you and me. Somehow they found out about all the bad luck I've had, the other horses. What Jaime did to Bella. And my threats against that goddamn Argentine." He finished the beer. His hands shook as he opened another one. "What the hell happened, Andi? I just wanted to play a little polo."

I remembered thinking Ross had changed when he first arrived—become more self-assured, comfortable with himself. Now I realized he'd gradually slipped back into the role he'd played when I knew him in school. Only I had changed. I wondered whether it was an improvement.

"They're a joke, Ross. Who cares what they think?"

"They carpeted the place with those flyers! I don't need anyone pointing out that I had a motive for killing Gutiérrez. Man, it's the last thing I need right now." He dropped his head into his palms, massaging his temples.

The skin stretched taut across his hands, thin and transparent as a rabbit's.

I sat on the arm of the chair and massaged his shoulders. "It'll blow over," I said. "These things always do."

Saturday morning the strain was impossible for Ross to hide. Clients and staff were sympathetic but wary.

We had driven to work together. We closed at two and were out of the clinic by three. Ross drove. Velcro rode in the back, home on a weekend pass.

Ross saw the damage before I did. I was chattering about the relative merits of various antibiotics when his quick intake of breath made me look up, two houses before mine.

"Oh, my God! Is that blood? Where did it all come from?" The tears would come later. I stared in shock at the front of my house, at my beloved Miata parked in the driveway.

Both were splattered with crimson.

The paint was almost dry. I ran for a bucket, splashed in detergent, and filled it with hot water in the kitchen. Velcro followed anxiously, ducking when hot sudsy water slopped over on him.

Don't think, I told myself. *Just wash it off. This is not Ross's fault. It's not.*

I began with the car, which had received special attention. Besides the random splatters, red block letters across the rear window spelled the word *murderer.*

"Damn them! Look what they did to my car! I'll never get all this off. Thank God I didn't leave the top down."

No reply.

"Ross?" He stood frozen, hands on hips, staring up at the front of the house.

"Are you going to help me clean up? Or do you plan to stand there and appreciate it all day?"

"God, Andi, how could they do this?" he said. "It's not my house. If they want to hurt me, why can't they just come after me? Why'd they have to do this?"

"Ross, dammit, just wash it off. While we still can."

He turned on the hose and directed the spray at the stucco. I looked at what was written there: BLOOD OF HORSES. The hose wasn't having much effect.

I was concentrating on scrubbing the paint off my Miata, so I never saw the car arrive. But I heard the unmistakable *pop-click-whir* of a camera. Ross must have spotted the photographer from the corner of his eye. I whirled to see a slender, brown-haired man standing in the driveway aiming a Nikon at us. He looked familiar but I didn't stop to wonder where I'd seen him before.

"Hey, come on," I said. "What are you doing?"

The man grinned and snapped a picture of my face. "Got a tip," he said cheerfully. He grabbed a shot of my car, where all but the last two letters were still legible, more grisly from my attempts to scrub them off. Then he turned toward the window of the house and adjusted his lens. "Aren't you the guy who offed that polo player? I'd like to get your feelings on this."

His face expressionless, Ross turned slowly toward the reporter with the high-speed garden hose in his hand.

Velcro barked gleefully and bit at the stream of water.

The reporter's smile vanished abruptly as he turned his back, shielding his camera with his body. "Hey! I'm just doing my job! I was going to get your story, too! Hey!"

Ross kept the hose trained on him until he fled to his tan Chevy and burned rubber. Ross aimed the hose after him until the car was out of sight, then calmly turned it off and stalked silently into the house.

I returned to my cleaning task, taking my anger out on the paint. By the time my car was almost back to normal, it occurred to me that I should have reported the incident to the police. If those pictures made tomorrow's paper, it would look bad for Ross. Even if it didn't affect his case, clients might begin to avoid him. In general, I thought, the less publicity the better.

I went through the breezeway into the house. Ross was

on the phone. I opened a beer and motioned for him to hang up.

"Yeah, I understand," he was saying. "Listen, I've got to go. Right. Talk to you later."

I took the receiver from him and tapped in the non-emergency police number. I explained the situation to a dispatcher, who promised to send someone out. As I hung up Ross scowled at having to deal with the police again. I ignored him.

Officer Steffani Tams of the graffiti task force showed up an hour later. By then it was dusk and difficult to see. See turned her spotlight on the house, took a few pictures, and accepted the Animal Freedom Fighters brochure handed to me by Tina Gering the week before. She took our report, chastised me halfheartedly for washing the paint off my car, and promised to look into it. She'd let us know, she said, if anything turned up. But don't count on it.

Early the next day I took a chip of house paint to the hardware store for a match. Armed with five fresh gallons, rollers, and pans, I mustered Ross up a ladder. He'd been outside the night before, scraping the window with a blade so that only the paint on the stucco remained. We barely finished one coat with what I'd bought.

Ross was in a surprisingly good mood, singing Beatles songs as he edged the window. Standing above him on a ladder, I spattered paint on him. "I can put up with anything but your singing," I laughed. He stepped aside, singing loud and off-key, "Singing in the paint . . ." and did a shuffle in the dirt.

When I climbed down to move the ladder, he ran behind me and slashed with his paintbrush, smearing my old black T-shirt with tan. I cussed and slashed an *X* onto his chest. He retorted with a *Z* and the fight was on as I chased him around the yard until we collapsed on the ground laughing. Then we were crying, arms wrapped tightly around each other's paint-spattered shoulders.

"I'm so sorry," Ross said. "God, Andi, this is such a mess. All I wanted to do was play polo."

"Don't worry; it's all right." What else could I say? "You'll make it up."

"No, Andi, you don't understand."

"What?" I leaned back, holding him at arm's length. Our paint had smeared and mingled into Rorschach designs on the T-shirts.

He shook his head. "Nothing. Just—I'm sorry about everything. And grateful. I can't believe anyone would do what you've done for me. And I'll never get the chance to repay you."

I shrugged, suddenly embarrassed. Ross sensed it and stood up. "Let's go. I'm sick of the smell of paint. Need some clean, fresh horse shit in my nostrils." His voice wasn't quite steady.

Chapter Twelve

The game was scheduled for one o'clock. I left Velcro in the backyard with the other dogs, cringing under the bougainvillea. He'd have to learn to get along if he was going to stay. Which he definitely wasn't.

Ross drove, and I spent the forty-five minutes trying not to talk about the murder, the damage to my house and car, or the charges against him. It was a quiet trip.

As we neared the back gate of the polo grounds, a riderless bay mare barreled out onto the street, tail streaming. Ross stopped the car in the middle of the road, and I was out the door, waving my arms to encourage the terrified animal onto the shoulder.

Ross jumped out and took a few steps toward her. She hesitated in midflight, then veered off the pavement. Hitting the soft sand, she extended her neck, pinned her ears, and settled into a serious effort. Dust and small gravel scattered in her wake as she headed north as if running the Derby.

As I watched, a black Honda tried to head her off, but she swerved gracefully around it and continued her flight.

We were in the car, ready to go after her when a chestnut gelding erupted from behind the tamarisk trees by the gate, turned south, and beelined for the date groves.

"What the fuck is going on?" Ross asked.

"I don't know, but we're not going to catch either one without a halter or something," I said.

He drove through the gate just in time to change a third

animal's course. The gray approaching at a trot veered right, where it would be contained by the fence.

Gaining sight of the stables, we gaped in disbelief. In the three hundred–plus pipe corrals only two or three horses remained captive.

People arriving for the one o'clock game either stood around shouting at one another or headed for the playing fields to recapture their horses.

"What the hell happened?" Ross demanded of a group standing nearby.

"It's those friggin' animal rights people. They oughta be shot after this stunt."

"How did they—"

"There was five or six of 'em. Wasn't no one else here, hardly. It was lunchtime. One of 'em stood over there by the trailer an hollered 'fire,' and when people went to help, the others ran down the aisles opening pens and whistlin' the ponies out. Shoulda seen the stampede."

I could easily imagine it—horses feed off each others' adrenaline. Once a few got loose, the rest would have willingly abandoned their stalls.

Ross collected several halters from the pen railings, and we went to help round them up.

Despite the shortness of the grass, several horses grazed peacefully in clusters of four and five, pulling up huge chunks by the roots. Most, however, associated being on the fields with running, which they now did with abandon. The temperature was cool—perfect weather for a good gallop. Herds of eight and ten flew wildly across the turf, bucking and snorting. Tails held high, they arched their necks and whinnied deliriously. Occasionally one reached over to bite another's neck or withers, or caught a companion's shoulder with a playful kick.

Grooms dashed everywhere, carrying halters and leads, but seemed generally mystified as to how to catch their charges.

"What are those bastards trying to prove?" Ross asked the air.

I pointed across the expanse of playing fields. The AFF van huddled under a grove of palm trees next to a half-familiar green Ford truck. As we watched, the van backed out and left. Everyone was too busy chasing horses to pay any attention, but I thought they'd have a hard time returning here.

"They've ruined the game," Ross said. "Not to mention God-knows-how-many horses. What are they trying to do, pulling a stunt like this? They think polo is cruel? They've injured more horses than a week of polo games!"

I recalled what Tish had said about the group's true aim. "They'll probably be arrested, drawing attention to themselves." Beyond that? I couldn't pretend to follow their logic.

I spotted Roger Dietrich standing in front of the clubhouse with a slender blond woman, older, classier, and more self-confident than the one he'd been speaking to the night of the party. He stared, slack-jawed, at the pandemonium on the field.

On the other side of the field, Tish haltered a brown mare. All over the green, grooms and players caught winded animals. Ross walked past a group of grazing animals and spoke to a bay mare that was slowing to a jog. She nickered at him and stopped, relieved to be caught. He strapped his halter on her head and ran a hand down each foreleg. Satisfied that she was sound, he draped her lead over his arm, collared another mare, and repeated the process with two more. He led them, two on each side, toward the stables.

I caught a mare at random and buckled on a halter. She held her head high and whinnied shrilly. I considered catching another but decided one was enough for me to handle.

Keyed-up thoroughbreds jogged and pranced beside grooms who struggled to return them to their pens. Most simply put any animal they caught in the nearest empty pen. Of course, there would be no game.

Walking beside Ross, leading the bay mare, I asked, "How will you sort them out? So many look exactly alike, and most of them are mares, so the sex won't be much help."

"The players know their own horses. Their shape and color, and no two horses' markings are exactly alike. I knew this was mine from a distance by the white on her face." He turned her head so I could see. She had a perfect diamond on her forehead.

"But they're not all so distinctive. Some don't have any white at all."

"If there's any real doubt, most polo ponies were race horses at one time."

"What's that got to do with it?" I closed the gate behind the mare and took one of Ross's while he penned the other three.

"Race horses are tattooed." He restrained the mare's head and turned back her upper lip. Underneath, there were some faded greenish black marks. "The letter tells you the year they were born, and the five numbers match the ones on her Jockey Club papers. So if someone tried to steal a horse in the confusion, the owners could dig out their records and compare."

Ross and I looked at each other. "Where's the foundered mare?" I asked.

He followed my train of thought. "Tish took her to her dad's farm in Coachella. I already checked, though. She isn't tattooed."

We headed back to the field for more horses. Graehm Block joined us. Roger Dietrich showed up at the barn and supervised. He introduced me to the blond woman, Debbie, his wife, whose voice I had heard on the answering machine.

The Hats Off Farm team arrived by van, and the players immediately sized up the situation and pitched in.

Tish had trailered in most of her horses, keeping only two in Ross's barn. One had been found. She scanned the fields and stables anxiously, looking for the other one,

Jojo. I hadn't seen her but couldn't swear I'd recognize her among so many look-alikes.

It took almost thirty minutes to round up all the horses, and another forty-five before most were returned to their proper homes. Grooms led the most winded up and down the road, cooling them off. Hal and the other four equine vets kept busy sewing up gashes and treating obvious injuries. Ross and I went over each of his horses carefully, noting swollen joints, cuts and scrapes, one badly bruised shoulder. Tish's brown mare had a deep laceration in her flank. With time and treatment—and some scars—all would heal.

Fandango was among the animals I examined, still on the grounds because she required daily bandage changes. Bella, completely recovered from her ordeal, was in the pen next door.

"What happened to Rowdy?" I asked.

"Hal arranged for him to go to a young girl in Desert Hot Springs. He'll need to rest for a year or so, and he'll never be any good for polo again. But eventually he might make it as a riding horse."

"That's great!" I'd been expecting much worse news.

"Yeah," Ross said. "She's a great kid. She'll take care of him."

Jaime walked by leading a sweaty, puffing thoroughbred. He and Ross exchanged macho eye contact—two stallions pinning their ears with no intention of fighting.

Suddenly there was a shriek from the road. "Is there a vet here? It's an emergency! Please, oh please!" Heads turned to see a dark-haired woman standing next to a black Honda, half sobbing and bouncing with anxiety.

"What's the problem?" someone shouted.

"There's a horse on the road. A truck hit it. It's horrible! Please, you've got to come right now!"

I glanced around. They were all busy. Hal shouted to Ross from the next row of pens. "You guys take my truck. Are the keys in your car? I'll come when I'm through here."

We hopped into the mobile unit, Ross driving, and followed the Honda. She turned north out of the gate. *That first bay mare,* I thought. We'd forgotten about her.

A distraught Hispanic man had climbed out of his pickup—the truck that had hit the horse, judging from the dented and bloodied front fender—and was trying to restrain her with his belt around her neck. The mare sprawled on her chest, gasping for air, making panicky efforts to stand. Blood pooled beneath her. Instinct told her to get up and run—the universal equine response to danger. But both front legs were twisted at vicious angles. Bone protruded. This mare would never run again.

Ross maneuvered the vet truck around several cars scattered along the road. One was an old VW van I knew only too well.

Ross approached the scene while I opened the vet pack to get the euthanasia solution. Mindful of the crowd, I locked the compartment and pocketed the keys. Armed with the bottle and a large syringe, I walked up to the mare. Ross had fastened a blue nylon halter over her head, and used it to keep her nose turned to her flank so she couldn't flail. The other man gratefully stepped back as Ross stroked the mare's forehead and spoke quietly to her.

"Any idea who she belongs to?" I asked Ross.

He shook his head. He wasn't looking at her. His hands shook violently, and speaking was an obvious effort. Poor Ross. He'd never learned to handle crisis.

"She's mine." We turned in the direction of the voice. There behind the truck stood Tish, tears streaming from her eyes. "It's Jojo."

"Oh no!" I looked more closely at the mare's face. I hadn't recognized her on the road or in her mangled state. But now I spotted the small triangular star, and even dulled with pain and shock, her wide-set brown eyes were familiar. She'd been patient with me. I owed her a quick, painless death.

"Do it," Tish sobbed, nodding at the syringe in my hand. "Hurry up. I can't stand to see her in such pain."

As I drew up the purple drug, a camera appeared in my face. The same young reporter who had been at my house the day before. He'd already taken several shots of Jojo, Tish, and the crowd.

"Bud Thorpe," he introduced himself. "Got a tip." He snapped one at close range, me with my mouth open to protest.

Tish relieved Ross at the mare's head, doing her best to soothe her panicked horse. Her own distress didn't help. Someone vomited, others whimpered or cursed. But one voice raised itself over the noise of the crowd.

"That's your solution to everything! Kill her. Kill them all. First you enslave them, then when they can't work anymore, you slaughter them like insects." Tom Gering was on stage.

I glanced up to see the AFF trio standing together. Two new faces, a tight-jawed, angry-looking woman and a scrawny, intense young man, stood close behind them. I assumed they were the new members Ross had mentioned. They all linked arms and began chanting.

"Killer! Killer! Killer!"

Bud Thorpe's camera clicked mercilessly.

Tish let go of the mare's head and stomped toward the AFF.

"You *bastards*! Stupid *idiots*!" she shrieked. "You did this to her! *You* did! She was my *friend*, you fuckers! Her name's Jojo. After what you did you're surprised she got hit? Didn't know what a truck could do to a horse? Well, take a look! *You* killed her. *Do you understand?*"

She ran at the leader, pummeling him with her fists. Several people yelled encouragement, moving back to watch. Tina and the new woman grabbed Tish's arms and continued shouting. *"Killer, killer."*

"She's not dead yet," Tom shouted in her face. "There's still time."

I paused, injection in hand, unsure whether to go to

Tish's aid. Even without restraint, Jojo was no longer struggling.

Bud Thorpe paused only long enough to change film.

Tom Gering stepped forward. Cords bulging in his neck, face flushed, eyes protruding slightly. "Only God has the power to take life. By rendering death to this creature, you hold yourself up to be God. But you are only a pawn of the Devil. God chose us to liberate these horses. These noble beasts have suffered enough at the hands of your kind. In the name of all that is fair and righteous in this world, I demand they be set free!"

The other members screamed. "Killer! Devil's Pawn!" Or maybe "Devil spawn," I wasn't sure. Tish's anguished shriek drowned out much of it, and other voices shouted epithets at the activists.

A few swarmed toward the demonstrators until I half feared a lynching. Tish didn't need me—others' hands freed her from the women's grip.

Gering's eyes held a lunatic's gleam. "Would you kill a black man because he broke a leg, just because he was a slave? Would you destroy your Mexican servant when she failed to speak your language? This mare's injuries are the result of human cruelty! Let not humans be her executioners as well!"

"It's not a person," someone shouted. "It's a horse! Don't make her suffer anymore."

Jojo's shock was so advanced, she didn't feel the needle I slipped into her vein. But as I did so my arm was wrenched backward, the syringe yanked from my hand. I jerked my gaze upward to meet the frenzied stare of Teri Gering, the one I thought of as at least marginally coherent. She held my syringe in her fist, the needle pointed toward me, a syrupy purple drop suspended from its tip.

"You should have listened to me," she growled.

My heart pounded, my hand trembled as I held it out to her. The syringe held a potentially lethal weapon—how manic was she? "Please," I said, "this isn't doing any good. She'll die soon anyway. Please don't make it any harder on her. I'm a vet, okay? She can't be saved. She can only suffer longer."

She brandished the syringe uncertainly, glancing at her brother for guidance. The crowd had fallen silent.

Her face hardened. "You didn't even try," she sneered, and lunged toward me. I jumped sideways, barely evading the needle.

The driver of the pickup truck stepped swiftly behind her. One of the members spotted him and tried to shout a warning, but too late. The man wrapped a powerful arm around her from behind and wrestled the syringe from her hand. He held it out to me, and I took it gratefully, turning to inject the contents into the now stuporous Jojo. I couldn't steady my hands and missed on the first try. Then blood flowed into the solution, and I pushed the plunger.

As Jojo's head slumped and her eyes gradually filmed, the keening of the activists rose in an eerie wave over the murmuring of keyed-up onlookers. Tish's wail joined theirs. I put an arm around her and led her toward Hal's truck. She kept sobbing, looking over her shoulder at Jojo's body.

An Indio police car pulled up, and people began to disperse. A khaki-uniformed patrolman got out and assessed the situation.

"Officer," I said quietly, "these people are responsible for the death of that horse. Also for a number of injuries to other horses. There were lots of witnesses." Several people agreed loudly.

"Nazis," Tom Gering spat. "Your laws have no bearing on the rightness of our actions. Because of those laws a nonhuman is dead. Better she should be imprisoned than me." He jerked his chin toward me but stood quietly while the officer cuffed him.

Ross was leaning against Hal's truck, staring toward

the stable gate, waiting for me. He was pale and sweaty. "Thanks, Andi," he said. "I couldn't deal with it."

How could anyone accuse this man of cold-blooded murder?

Chapter Thirteen

Hal arrived as I returned the euthanasia solution to its place. Ross got in his car and left. Tish headed back in the BMW, wanting to be alone for a while.

"How bad was it?" Hal asked as I gave him his keys.

I glanced to where Jojo's body lay in the road. Congealing blood brought flies swarming to a banquet meal. I shuddered, still fighting tears myself. "See for yourself."

"Jeez, Andi, I'm sorry you had to be there. I should have dropped everything and taken care of it."

"What do you mean, be there? Who do you think gave the injection? I'm a D.V.M., too, you know." I climbed irritably into the passenger seat of his truck. All I needed right now was a condescending male colleague.

"I only meant, since you do small animal work, it's just that—" He turned away, embarrassed, and spat tobacco juice on the sandy shoulder.

"It wasn't the last euthanasia I'll have to perform."

"Gosh, Andi, I know that. But it's my job."

Gosh? Jeez? After today? Where did this guy come from, anyway? "Forget it," I said lightly. "I'll send you a bill."

He glanced at me uncertainly.

"I'm kidding, Hal."

We followed Tish back to the polo grounds. Ross leaned against the pipe corral, holding a Coke can against his forehead. Whatever bug had made him sick the week before hadn't entirely run its course.

"That looks good," I said, meaning the soda.

"There's a whole coolerful in the tack room."

I took one and handed another to Hal.

Hal said, "Say, Ross, have you seen my twitch around? Last time I had it was the day that gelding bowed."

"Rowdy? That was a week ago. No, I haven't seen it."

Hal shrugged. "I hoped I'd left it here. Well, got to get back to work." He made no move to go.

"I imagine we'll be leaving soon, too," I said in Ross's direction. Ross didn't hear. He was staring toward where Dietrich stood in the aisleway, talking in low tones to Graehm.

"Ah, listen, Andi," Hal said, not quite looking at me. "Is there someplace I could get ahold of you?"

I hesitated. Pretending I didn't know he wanted to ask me out would be stupid. Pretending I wanted to go would be even stupider. But he was so damned nice, how could I refuse to give him my phone number? I got my purse from the car and gave him my business card without writing my home number on it.

Hal looked at it for a moment, then opened his mouth to protest my deliberate oversight.

I was rescued from the spotlight by Jaime's arrival in a late-model white Corvette. He pushed mirrored sunglasses up on his forehead and looked directly at Tish, who was on her knees rubbing the legs of one of Ross's horses. She wore dark glasses and hadn't spoken to anyone since the incident on the road.

"Nice car, Jaime," I said.

"Comes with the new job." He glanced pointedly at Ross.

Tish walked over and leaned into the car. He said something—"You okay?"—and she shook her head. He touched her face with genuine concern. Finally she got into the car beside him and they drove away.

Ross stared after them, then turned to me. "Andi, could you find another way home? I've got to look into something."

I frowned pointedly but he refused to notice.

"It's about the case," he said quietly.

Predictably, Hal spoke up. "I'd be glad to run her home, Ross. Don't you worry about a thing. Just go ahead and take care of whatever business you have. I've got a couple more horses to check on; then we can head out."

Ross might have known exactly what was going on. He avoided looking at me as he jumped in the Porsche and left without another word.

"A couple more horses" turned out to be about three hours' work. I held lead ropes while he tapped and prodded sore hooves, squeezed sensitive ankles, bandaged strained tendons. I led tired horses through the dust at a trot so he could evaluate subtle lameness. I drew up injections of Rompun and Banamine and penicillin until my hands hurt.

By the time we finally hit the freeway daylight was a memory. "Boy, ole Ross sure is having a rough time." Hal dribbled tobacco juice into an empty Coke can.

"That's putting it mildly. He could go to prison for life."

"Oh, yeah. That, too. I meant his horses. I never saw anyone have so many bad injuries in such a short time."

We rode in silence for a while. I couldn't think of anything else to talk about, and I was too tired to pretend. It was all I could do to stay awake, lulled by the highway and Dwight Yoakam playing on the stereo.

"Say, Andi, I'll bet you're hungry," Hal said.

Damn. Of course I was hungry, and so was he. But if I said so, he'd suggest stopping for dinner—another hour of tedious conversation. But no would be an obvious lie. Hal was annoying, but I couldn't bring myself to hurt his feelings.

"Actually," I said after too long a pause, "Ross cooked some chicken the other night. It'll go bad if I leave it in the fridge one more day. Think I'll just go on home, snack on that, and fall right to sleep. I'm beat." I stretched elaborately by way of proof.

"I love chicken," he said pointedly.

Won't this guy take a hint? "Sometime we can go eat chicken together," I lied. "But not tonight, okay? Take this exit."

He insisted on walking me to the door, and there was no polite way to avoid inviting him in. I offered him a beer, which he declined, and served him a glass of water instead. Then I opened the slider to let the dogs in.

Gambit, Romeo, Zeke, and Della tumbled through the doors, sniffed my shoes in passing, and went to investigate Hal. He wasn't intimidated by four big dogs and greeted them affectionately while they sniffed the cornucopia of odors on his boots.

I flipped on the outside light. "Velcro? Come on, boy, I'm home. Velcro? Bandit?" I used his old name, thinking he might respond to it more readily. No sign of him. I bent down to look under the bougainvillea that hugged the house and barely allowed room for a forty-pound dog to hide. Twin beams of reflected light shone in the darkness, and a whimper issued forth.

"Are you still in there? Come on out, boy. What am I going to do with you?"

I reached under and dragged him out by the scruff. He lay limp until I got him free of the bush, then plastered himself against me and tried frantically to climb into the meager lap I created squatting on my heels. I stroked him and touched blood.

"What happened, boy?" The bougainvillea had long thorns. I wondered if he'd impaled himself on one. But once I got him in the light, I saw his elbow had four punctures—two of which had torn, creating skin flaps. A similar set of wounds graced his flank.

"Damn, these are tooth marks. They've been fighting. Hal, can I borrow a little ketamine and some suture material?" For once I was glad he was there. Velcro and I entered the house, and Romeo, the Doberman mix, growled. Hal paused uncertainly.

"Is that a confession?" I asked Romeo. He glanced up sheepishly.

Velcro surprised me by growling back. Cowering against me, he turned a pseudomenacing expression on the others.

"Hal, could you help me get the others outside?"

I wasn't much use with Velcro doing his best to be part of my clothing, so Hal led the foursome out and closed the slider. Then we examined Velcro's side.

"Nothing I can't fix. How about that ketamine?"

"You betcha." He went out to get it, happy to be useful. I fought a guilty twinge over the way I'd treated him earlier. He returned with the bottle, a 3 cc syringe, cordless clippers, suture, and instruments. We sedated Velcro, clipped the hair away, and cleaned his wounds. There were four of them, with a lot of bruising, all deep but none extensive. As I sewed I told Hal the dog's story. He clucked sympathetically.

Velcro started to move his head before I finished, so Hal held him still while I put in the last few stitches. Then I grabbed a blanket from the sofa bed, spread it on the floor, and laid him on it to recover. I stood and walked with Hal in the direction of the front door.

I was reconsidering my previous rejection. I might even have been attracted to Hal if Ross wasn't in my life. But without Ross we'd never have met, so the question was moot. And at the moment I really wanted to be alone.

He paused in the doorway. "You sure you don't want something to eat?" he asked. "We could go out."

"Really, Hal, I'm beat. Thanks for your help." I held his equipment out to him and smiled apologetically, sincerely wishing he would just go away.

Suddenly he was kissing me, a wet, sloppy, one-sided smooch while his hands groped at my waist. The medical equipment clattered to the floor.

"Hey!" I shoved him back. "What the hell are you doing?"

"You didn't want me to?" he asked incredulously.

Where was this guy from? "I think you should go now."

"I thought you—I didn't mean—"

"Please leave, Hal." I ushered him out the door, my hands shaking.

I locked the door and watched through the peephole as he hesitated, turned miserably, and looked at the door, then returned to his truck, shoulders slumped. Could anyone be that gawky? Or was it me who was slow on the uptake?

I leaned against the door until my heart rate returned to normal. Okay, maybe his social skills lacked finesse. So did mine. Then I started laughing. "What a way to cap off a really rotten day."

But at least I finally had my house to myself. I kind of hoped Ross wouldn't come back that night.

Velcro whined and rolled ungracefully onto his chest. Honestly, what was I going to do with him?

Chapter Fourteen

Monday morning I showered, dressed in rust-colored cotton slacks and a matching shirt, took Velcro with me, and got to the clinic early. Which was just as well, since I had the day to myself. I'd gotten my wish—Ross hadn't come home.

Damn. Where could he have gone? I thought about his tearful apologies the day before and fervently hoped he hadn't done something stupid like go off after the real killer.

I should have asked more questions the day before. What "things" did he need to check out? Was he trying to catch Umberto's murderer? He could be that desperate.

There's no way he'd jump bail. No way.

To make matters worse, the picture of me standing over Jojo made the front page of Monday's paper. I looked slightly crazy holding the enormous syringe, and only Jojo's head showed—none of her horrible injuries were apparent. I read the brief caption with rising anger: "Palm Springs veterinarian Andi Pauling in a dispute with animal rights advocate Tom Gering over whether an injured polo horse should be humanely destroyed. Pauling eventually succeeded in putting the animal to death." Every client wanted the whole story. Once they heard the details almost everyone promised to write a letter to the editor complaining about the slant of the story. I couldn't help smiling. The *Desert Sparkler* didn't know what was in store.

Late that morning I was expounding on routine dental

care to a client whose Yorkie's breath smelled like something had died in the dog's throat when Sheila appeared in the doorway, her eyes open wide in astonishment.

"Dr. Pauling, you've got to come up front!"

I followed her without hesitation, expecting an emergency. Instead I found an acne-faced young man with a sheaf of papers.

"Are you Andrea Pauling?" he asked.

"Yes."

He handed me the forms and grinned. "You've been served."

I took them automatically. He vanished out the door.

I glanced at the papers, though some part of me knew what they were before I had them in my hand. My mind spinning, I carried them to my office and stared.

Mrs. Artimas was suing. Her attorney demanded one hundred twenty thousand dollars, plus the cost of a new dog, professional training, and a refund of all fees incurred both at Dr. Doolittle's and at the emergency clinic during Buffy's treatment. The enormous amount was apparently for emotional distress.

I struggled to think rationally. It was lunchtime. At least one more client waited, hopefully something quick. I picked up the phone and hit the two buttons that called Lara's number from the machine's memory.

"Not my field. You know that." Lara scowled at me over the forms spread out on the table. A corner of one page soaked up the moisture ring left behind by her iced-tea glass.

"I hoped you could offer some suggestion on how to proceed."

"Call your insurance agent; that's what they get paid for."

A long pause ensued while she studied my face and I studied the pattern of chili peppers on the plastic table cover.

"You *are* insured?"

"The premiums were due in July. You know how bad July was; I didn't even pay myself. I almost couldn't make payroll, and the drug suppliers wanted their money first. God knows I used little enough of their products."

"You're *not* insured."

"Now I am. As of this morning. But at the time this happened, no. *Damn* Ross. The check was made out when I loaned him the six thousand." The excuse sounded feeble to my own ears. Lawsuits have done for medical practice what AIDS did for sex. Ruth Artimas, who I'd thought of as a tragic figure the week before, was now an adversary. The suit accused me of being uncaring. As a result I could no longer feel even sympathy.

Lara concentrated on her chicken burritos for a few long moments, chewing with the same intensity she focused on cases.

"What exactly happened?"

"You mean with the dog?"

"Right."

I gave her the long version while she worked her way across her plate. My tostada resembled toxic waste as I pushed it around in its bowl-shaped tortilla.

"Everything seemed okay before you gave the anesthetic?"

"No, Lara, I'm in the habit of regularly anesthetizing animals I know are sick. Of course it seemed okay!"

She glared at me. "You want my help or not?"

"I want your client in my office so I can slowly peel the hide off his skinny butt." That made me feel better and I swallowed a bite of tostada to prove it. It got about halfway down before lodging like a hair ball. I gulped iced tea while Lara watched me through narrowed eyes.

"I'm not his mother, just his lawyer. He lives with you. You can't find him, why would I?"

"Who said I couldn't find him?"

"Know where he is?"

I discovered a fascinating bit of lettuce in my dish, an elaborate S shape, which suddenly demanded my full attention. When I looked up Lara was scraping the last of the cheese sauce off her plate.

Lara sighed heavily. "Look," she said, "the law only recognizes the value of the animal. Unfortunate for the owner but lucky for you. Was this a show dog?"

"No."

"Prolific breeder? Seeing Eye dog? Hearing ear?"

I shook my head irritably. "Spayed. Just a pet." My eyes returned to my fork, twirling aimlessly through the softening muck on my plate. "I checked before I came here to make sure. Ketamine isn't known to affect the pancreas. It can aggravate existing kidney disease, but a blood test showed that her kidneys were fine before I sedated her. She could have been treated, though. She might have survived. If she was hospitalized. If she was treated more aggressively." Ross had worked for me when he treated Buffy. The responsibility was ultimately mine.

Lara was vigorously shaking her head. "Wrong attitude. You did nothing wrong. Is this pancreas thing preventable?"

"No."

"Is it fatal?"

"Sometimes. In severe cases."

"Was this severe?"

"Pretty bad. At least the lab work looked that way."

"We'll emphasize that. Know where Ross is?"

"I haven't seen him since yesterday afternoon."

"I've got a conflict, since I represent him in the other thing. As your friend, I advise you to fire him immediately. You're doing everything in your power to make sure this doesn't happen again."

"But what if I fire him and he jumps bail? Lara, I could lose the clinic!"

"You'll have to decide which is the greater risk."

"I need to talk to Trinka Romanescu at the emergency clinic, find out what happened the night she put Buffy to sleep."

"Good. Do it today. Also, write a letter to the client's attorney. Tell him you're not insured; name me as your lawyer. Attorneys tend to lose interest when there's no one with deep pockets to go after. Offer to send the medical records to an impartial expert for scrutiny. Send a list of specialists. He won't know any, and you don't want it going to just anyone."

A corner of my depression lifted like a surreal eyelid as I formed a mental plan of action.

First I had to find Ross. Then I would decide what to do about him.

That afternoon I tried to write the letter: "Dear Sir." What went next? "A hundred and twenty thousand dollars? Are you out of your mind?" Not exactly the tone I was looking for. My mind wouldn't focus. I wanted to get busy looking for Ross. The letter remained unwritten.

I closed at six, hustled Sheila and Didi out the door, locked up, and went home. I'd considered leaving Velcro at the clinic, but he was so miserable in the cage, I finally relented. He followed me inside, and I'd have sworn he laughed when the other dogs whimpered and panted at the door. I filled their food dishes and left them outside.

Who might know where Ross was? Starting with the obvious, I dialed Roger Dietrich's condo. Spoke to the machine. Looked up Hal in the yellow pages, left my number with his service. Caught a frazzled-sounding Tish on her way out the door.

"Missing? Since when?"

"He took off yesterday, and I haven't seen him since."

"Me neither. You think he's all right?"

"Why do you say that?"

"He didn't seem himself all weekend. Kinda tired. I don't know. Not playing worth a shit. And he's lost weight. Is he sick?"

"Probably the stress of the murder charges."

"You don't think he'd, you know, try to do something to himself, do you?" she asked.

"Suicide? Not Ross." He couldn't, even if he wanted to.

"Think he took off? Jumped bail?"

"No way," I said too fast.

"What was he doing last time you saw him?"

I thought. "He was just standing in the barn and said he had some things to take care of or something. I'm afraid he might be trying to find the real killer himself."

There was a long pause that I finally felt compelled to fill. "I know not everyone is convinced of Ross's innocence. But believe me, he didn't kill Umberto."

"How can you be so sure? You weren't with him."

"I wasn't with you either, and I don't think you killed him."

When she didn't answer, I said, "If you hear anything, let me know, okay?"

"Sure. I gotta run. See ya."

I drummed my fingers impatiently on the coffee table, willing Ross to pull up in the driveway.

Several days' mail lay scattered on the table, some having been knocked to the floor by the animals. I leafed through it absently while trying to figure out where Ross might be. Car payment, MasterCard, GTE, some other bills.

I opened them, setting the envelopes and inclusions aside to recycle. Edison was down for a change, reflecting cooling temperatures. The phone bill usually had four pages, but this time there were six. I almost choked when I got to the final sheet.

"Four hundred dollars?" I said out loud.

Velcro glanced up from his nap at my feet.

"I don't need this," I muttered, rubbing the dog's ears. I scanned the pages. Lengthy calls to Kentucky, several different numbers, some lasting over an hour. Then there were all the calls to Indio. And clusters of third-party-billing calls to—

"Mexico? Who does Ross know in Mexico?"

I supposed it could have been a telephone company

mistake. Or someone using my number at random. But somehow I couldn't quite believe it.

Before this discovery, I'd been upset with Ross. Now I was really pissed. So much so that I almost forgot to call the emergency clinic before I walked out the door.

I dialed the number from memory and asked a technician to get out the Artimas chart and let me talk to Trinka. Twenty seconds of light rock later she came on the line with a harried-sounding "Romanescu."

I pictured her: a petite, intense woman a few years my junior who did three things at once and managed to do them all well.

"Hi, Trinka. Andi Pauling. Did you see Buffy Artimas last Friday night?"

"Barely. The woman came in demanding the dog be put down. She said you got a new doctor?"

"Ross McRoberts worked for me for a while."

"Hm." She sounded distracted. "Anyway, she said he'd diagnosed kidney failure. Seemed to think a lot of him. She declined lab work, just wanted the dog 'put out of its misery': her words."

"What was said about the fact that the dog was anesthetized on Monday?"

"She mentioned it and seemed to think it might have contributed to the kidney problem. It can happen, and I told her so. But this looked like pancreatitis to me."

I massaged my temples. "So you didn't specifically tell her the anesthesia caused the condition?"

"I didn't tell her anything. She did all the talking."

"Would you write all that down and mail it to me?"

"You gonna give me the juicy details?"

"Not right now. But next week I'll buy you lunch and tell you everything. Okay?"

As I set the receiver down I realized it would be fully dark by the time I reached the polo club. My mission was probably futile, but I had to do something.

I decided to leave Velcro on the breezeway in front of the house. It was the only place I could think of where he couldn't destroy anything, yet he'd be out of Romeo's reach. Dogs suffering from separation anxiety will often vent their frustrations on the last thing the owner touched, so I handled a chew toy before showing it to him. He ignored it, so I placed it on a blanket near his food dish. He clung to me until I squeezed out the door.

Chapter Fifteen

The Miata ate the distance from Palm Springs to Indio, glad for the exercise. I love my little red car's enthusiasm for the highway. Spyro Gyra jammed in the CD player. Movement and noise created an illusion of progress. By the time I pulled through the unlit back gate I actually felt I might accomplish something.

Lights burned in Talbot's house, and a dark Jeep Cherokee sat in the drive. I saw no other sign of human life in the stable area.

Two vehicles were parked in the gloom near the clubhouse. One, a late-model Nissan, leaned into a flat tire. Next to it was a now familiar gray VW van. No Porsche.

What were the AFF up to, parked here at night? More "activities"? Surely they weren't camping here. Then I realized they might still be in jail. Once out, there would be a restraining order barring them from the club. Maybe the van had been parked here by a sympathizer until they could claim it.

I got out of the Miata and wandered over.

A single floodlight behind the clubhouse illuminated the van's windshield, leaving the back in shadow. If practical, I could peek inside, maybe figure out their next move. The issues with Ross had distracted me, but I felt a gut-level revulsion for these extremists, with their twisted compassion, and the ignorant minority they represented.

I stood on tiptoe to peer in through the driver's side window. The ghostly shapes of a torn seat and wide steering wheel stared back. Similar view from the passenger side. Nothing of interest visible. The rear windows were covered from inside with paint or black paper. Why so secretive?

I tried to open the door. Locked. Driver's side, too. The big double doors in back, however, opened with a loud metallic crunch. A quick glance told me the lock was broken, and one hinge was questionable. The back of the van, which I'd had only the briefest glimpse of the first day, held a mobile office.

Heart pounding, I returned to my car for the small flashlight I carried for emergencies. I took a deep breath and climbed into the van. The springs groaned loudly, as if calling for help. I hesitated, stuck my head out, and glanced around to see if anyone had heard and was coming. Nothing moved that I could see. Finally I turned resolutely to the task at hand.

I sat on one of two small stools that were fixed to the floor. On one side was a fifteen-inch platform that served as a desk top. A series of slots beneath it substituted for drawers. One was crammed with tracts like the one Tina Gering had handed me the day Rowdy was injured. Others held the flyers called the "worst offender" series. I wondered whether Tish knew she, too, had been singled out.

Across from this was a bank of file cabinets. Four drawers in stacks of two, old and gray like the van.

None were locked, but neither were they well organized. The top right drawer contained folders crammed with tracts from various advocacy groups. Many represented strident animal rights leagues; others had nothing to do with the movement. In fact, some seemed contradictory. There were pamphlets for Operation Rescue and similar antiabortion groups, as well as children's rights advocates and environmentalists across the spectrum of extremism. The collection also held brochures from paranoid survivalists, The Moral Majority, and another religious fundamentalist society calling themselves The

Right. I'd thought animal rights extremists belonged on the far left. What did they have in common with these others? Publicity tactics? I stuffed a few at random into a pocket of my jeans.

The next drawer down contained several years' back issues of a magazine called *The Animals' Quest.* I only glanced through a couple. They were filled with sappy, emotional articles that seemed to group farmers, physicians, cosmetics manufacturers, and fur trappers into a single group called "Them."

So that's how we all think of each other. How had they left veterinarians off the list?

The top left file drawer held clippings: folder after folder crammed with articles cut from newspapers and magazines from all over the country.

The sound of an approaching car separated itself from the almost subliminal noise of occasional street traffic. I tensed and leaned out the back of the van, standing on tiptoe and craning to see over its top. A pair of headlights glided toward me from the horsemen's entrance. I held my breath. They turned into the stable area, stopped, and the lights went off.

I breathed again. A groom or trainer, making a last check on his ponies before turning in. The beams were too high and too far apart to belong to Ross's Porsche. A pickup truck, probably.

What the hell am I doing? But I couldn't tear myself away. There's something perversely satisfying about spying on people you despise. Besides, given recent events, I had to consider their possible motive in Umberto's death. Ross certainly would have; therefore, it followed that they might know where Ross was now.

I glanced through the clippings in the file. Unsurprisingly, many were local snippets of the Animal Freedom Fighters' activities, going back only a few years, with much more press the past month than ever before. Most bore the byline of Bud Thorpe.

Interesting.

Other animal advocates made cameo appearances, and there was a great deal on an international federation calling itself the Animal Liberation Front. I found several photocopies of a recent *People* magazine interview of "Valerie," a pseudonym for the organization's leader. The larger, British-based group prided themselves on violent spectacles, including, according to the article, firebombing a meat truck and setting fire to several businesses they deemed antagonistic to their cause.

The AFF were wannabees.

Some small part of my mind acknowledged the departure of the car or truck that had driven into the barn area earlier. Then all was quiet again.

I moved on to the second folder, arbitrarily plucking out a couple of articles. A pebble skittered outside and I tensed, half-consciously shoving the papers into my back pocket as I flicked off the flashlight and listened. Another pebble, and the faint *whoosh* of a boot crushing grass. Someone approaching on foot. From which direction? One of the AFF, or the Nissan's owner? I thought of my own Miata parked next to the van, its telltale license plate proclaiming ANDI DVM.

Which way did that come from? Should I make a break for my car? If I stayed, I was trapped, but I stood paralyzed.

A key in the driver's side lock galvanized me. I leaped out the back and slipped around the passenger side. As soon as the newcomer saw the yawning doors, he'd be on my tail.

I jumped in my car and frantically twisted the key. The motor caught immediately, and I took off across the sidewalk. Glancing back, I saw the spindly young recruit from the previous day running after me, shouting something that was lost in the noise of spinning tires and the jazz that started with the motor. I left him eating dust kicked up by the Miata's heels.

By the time I hit the road behind the polo club, adrenaline churned in my veins like a caged tiger. My hands shook so badly, I could hardly steer. I desperately wanted to pull over until my system settled down, but if the van came along . . .

I kept moving. Ahead was The Tenth Goal's garish neon sign, the rider's mallet perpetually pounding the motionless ball. It was Monday night, and business at the honky-tonk was almost nil. My tires crunched on gravel as I wheeled into the nearly empty lot, killing my lights as I pulled around the building's side into a shadowy alcove. The engine died as I lurched to a stop. I sat hunched over the wheel taking great gulping drinks of anemic air, which churlishly refused to fill my lungs. My heart beat spasmodically against my ribs, threatening escape at any moment. Medical training does no good at such a time. This was a pure, elementary response to terror.

Damn, what if he calls the cops? I could picture the headline: LOCAL VETERINARIAN QUESTIONED IN ANIMAL RIGHTS VAN BREAK-IN. With Bud Thorpe's byline. No, thanks.

So what was I doing back there? What was I thinking? *Am I nuts?*

When I thought my legs would support me, I went into the bar. I scanned the lot as I approached the door, but there were no Porsches, vans, or any other familiar vehicles in the lot.

"Coors Light," I told the bartender as I slid onto a stool. He limped to a cooler and produced a bottle, followed, after a brief hesitation, by a glass. I waved it away and reached for the bottle. The rush from the cold beer was immediate.

I made myself drink the second one more slowly.

"You were a man I'd say you look like you had a run-in with a jealous husband," he said, taking my second three dollars. "Or was it *your* husband?"

I looked him over, noticing him for the first time as something other than a means to a beer. Fortyish, with thick gray-blond hair brushed back from a high forehead, square features, crooked nose. Hands that moved with the assured grace of a good polo player, but his left leg was withered and crooked.

"Horse fell on me," he explained in a practiced offhand tone when he saw me looking. "What's your story?"

I couldn't tell whether he was being rude or merely curious. It wouldn't have mattered. I needed to talk.

"Animal Freedom Fighters after me." I immediately regretted the words. They sounded ridiculous to my own ears; I could imagine how they sounded to this friendly stranger.

But he only nodded. "They're a weird bunch," he said. "Heard they paint-bombed some player's house last week. Made it look like blood. Yesterday they set every horse on the grounds loose. Three had to be put down." He shook his head: *What's the world coming to?* "What'd you do to piss them off?"

"One caught me in their van."

"Find anything interesting?" Merely curious, nothing more.

"That reminds me." I felt in the back pocket of my jeans for the clippings and spread them out on the bar.

He craned his head to look, and we squinted at the pages in the dim light of the bar. There were two articles, one from *Time*, the other from the *Desert Sparkler.* Both pertained to the murder of Dr. David Gunn in Florida at the hands of rabid antiabortionist Paul Hill.

Death in the name of life. Much as the bay mare had died as a result of being "liberated" by the Animal Freedom Fighters. Yet enormously different; I had put the mare out of her agony while they demanded she die slowly and miserably.

How far would these people go? Did they kill Umberto?

Ross had accused the Argentine of sabotaging his horses. Three polo ponies out in a week did seem like a lot. Even Hal had commented on it. Several people saw

Berto hit the ball that blinded Fandango. Surely no one was accurate enough to do that on purpose, but what if he'd meant only to injure her, not caring where? Maybe he'd even meant to hit Ross.

What was Berto doing in Ross's barn that night, carrying the mysterious vial and syringes? Was it something deadly he planned to inject into another of Ross's mounts? Why? I needed to ask Lara whether the police had had their contents analyzed, but if the extremists thought he was doing something harmful it might justify—in their minds—the use of extreme measures.

Ross believed Umberto had switched the mare he sold him with a crippled look-alike. Maybe his pride needed to believe it, since he'd done the prepurchase exam himself just days before she came up lame. Or maybe he was right.

Or maybe I was succumbing to the same paranoia that affected Ross.

Why would Berto do such a thing?

I remembered Ross telling me two horses had been poisoned in Lexington but that Berto hadn't been in Kentucky. Also, could one induce a bowed tendon? It didn't seem possible that Rowdy's injury fit the pattern. And there was Bella. If overworking her was deliberate, it meant Jaime was in on it, too. I couldn't believe that. I was sure Jaime's distress had been real.

Two coincidences and two acts of war? Delusions of my stressed and overworked imagination? How could I find out?

Where the hell was Ross, anyway?

Chapter Sixteen

Resisting the siren song of a third beer—and maybe a fourth—I skulked to my car like Tweety watching for Sylvester. Then I made my way home in a decidedly less anxious Miata. It's my belief that cars, like horses, pick up on the emotions of their navigators.

Velcro greeted me ecstatically, interfering with my progress into the house. No damage done tonight, but I couldn't stand to keep him isolated on the porch. Maybe I'd try leaving one of the friendlier dogs with him next time. He followed me to the kitchen, where I satisfied my interest in another beer, through the living room—no Ross, but what did I expect?—down the hall to the bedroom.

The red answering machine light flashed like a dim beacon. Blink, blink, blink: three messages. I flicked on the overhead light and ghosts vanished into their corners.

I hit the play button. "Andi, this is Hal. I'm really glad you called. Would you like to go out sometime this week? Maybe dinner and a movie. You name it. Call me back when you get this." And a number with an Indio prefix. Damn, I wished I hadn't called him. How would I get rid of him now? I should at least have mentioned I was looking only for Ross.

Speaking of whom. Ross's voice. "Andi? Are you there? I need your help. Where are—I'll call you back."

Damn. The whole night had been a bust, and now I'd missed Ross's call.

And finally Lara's terse missive: "Someone call me!"

I glanced at the clock: 9:45.

Lara answered on the second ring. "Barrett." Her office calls are forwarded to her house.

"Me. Have you heard from Ross?"

"Hasn't turned up yet?" More irritated than concerned. "When he shows, tell him to check in. I'd like to assure the court he's alive and hasn't skipped bail. Most clients bug me constantly."

"I think I'll hear from him soon." I told her about the recorded message.

"Save it; might be useful. And let me know if you hear anything else from the Artimas woman or her attorney."

I had to write that letter. "Dear Sir: Your client is out of her mind. She killed her own dog to punish me." Not fair. Ross had given Buffy a poor prognosis. Maybe she'd even done the right thing. "What did you find out?"

"First off, the mallet was Ross's. Gutiérrez's blood on it. Ross's fingerprints all over, some of yours. No one else's."

"So? The killer obviously wore gloves."

"Wait, there's more. Got the medical examiner's report this afternoon. Interesting. Lethal blow killed him, but the wound didn't fit a polo mallet. The actual weapon was smooth and roughly cylindrical but too long and thick for the mallet. Also, the angle wasn't right." She was euphoric.

My mind reeled. The polo mallet was the natural weapon of anyone who might be a suspect, especially Ross. Besides, it was there. "They can't tell what it really was?"

"Who cares? Point is, the killer left the mallet behind to frame Ross. Touched it to the wound and everything. This is great news. It'll help at the preliminary hearing. Might even get the case thrown out."

Lara finally believed in Ross's innocence. If only we could find him to tell him. "Will he have to be at the hearing?"

"Yep. Three weeks away. He should turn up by then."

"Is there any real chance of getting the charges dropped?"

"Not impossible. Prelim's when the D.A.'s got to prove there's enough evidence for trial. But bail could be revoked if he doesn't show."

"He'll show," I said, wishing I felt as confident as I sounded. "Did you get the analysis of the stuff in the vial and syringes they found with Umberto's body?"

"Doesn't ring any bells. Important?"

"Might be."

"I'll check it out."

"If you want to find out who really killed him, maybe you should interview Tom Gering and his sisters Tina and Teri. They're animal rights fanatics; call themselves the Animal Freedom Fighters. They may be in jail right now in Indio." I told her about finding the articles in their van. She remained disapprovingly silent while I spoke.

"Can't hurt to interview, I guess. Want to come along?"

"Sure. When?"

"Let you know tomorrow." She hung up, leaving me more alone than I'd felt in a long time. I missed Ross.

I wasn't lonely enough to call Hal back, though. If he knew anything about Ross I'd find out later. The fact that Ross had called relieved me tremendously.

Had I really believed he would cut out on me? I'd felt betrayed when I saw the phone bill, but to be fair, Ross hadn't seen it yet. Still, how did he plan to pay for his share—which was most of it?

I'd put myself in a very uncomfortable situation by signing over my clinic to cover Ross's bail. But that was my fault, not his. I hadn't given him a chance to stop me. So what did I expect? Abject gratitude?

Still, he could check in more often.

The dogs were whining to come in. With trepidation I opened the slider and they tumbled through, leaping ecstatically over one another as if I'd been gone for days.

Romeo and Velcro bared their teeth and rumbled menacingly in their throats.

Velcro slept on the water bed again. The others didn't approve, but it was the only way to keep them apart and still have relative peace in the house. Four of the cats ignored him and spread themselves along my other side. It's amazing how small a king-size bed can seem with only one person in it.

Around five A.M. the phone jarred me awake. I clung to the bones of a dream about horses galloping through a vast oasis of virgin sand—probably something Freudian here—and pushed Velcro off the extra pillow so I could reach the receiver. "Hello?" Expecting Ross.

"Dr. Pauling?"

The brisk, authoritative voice on the other end brought me to a state more approximating consciousness. "Yes, who is this?"

"This is Yolanda, from Tight-As-A-Drum Security. We have a report of an alarm at Dr. Doolittle's Pet Care Center. Police have been called; they're on their way now."

Now I was fully awake. "Damn. Should I go there?"

"Not yet. Stay on the line while I verify with police and let them know you didn't set off the alarm. Who else can enter the building?"

"This time of night? Nobody. The only people with keys are myself and my staff. And my associate—" Suddenly I felt positive this had something to do with Ross. "Tell the police I'm on my way."

I hung up on her protests and grabbed my clothes from the night before. I dressed on my way to the door, shoved the dogs out back and Velcro out front. I made record time getting to the clinic, normally only five minutes away. Palm Springs is a daylight kind of town, with almost no traffic in the predawn hours.

The back door into Treatment gaped open, three blue-and-whites parked outside it, lights flashing with that cool blue that's supposed to discourage panic. It wasn't working tonight. I squealed to a halt behind them, leaped out, and ran inside.

Smack into the muzzle of an enormous gun.

Behind the weapon loomed the terrified face of a very young cop. "Freeze!" he shouted redundantly.

My hands shot up of their own accord—that's body language for "no problem." "Don't shoot!" I squeaked.

"Who are you?" demanded an older, calmer policeman who scooted around the doorway from the hall, his back against the frame. He held his weapon with both hands at hip level, pointed at the floor.

I opened my mouth but couldn't speak. The gun, unwavering despite the rookie's apparent fright, was two feet away and pointed directly at my chest. It looked about a yard long, and I wondered irrelevantly how it fit in his holster.

"Why are you here?" The other man asked.

"I—the alarm—Yolanda called me," I managed. "This is my clinic."

"Friedler, relax, okay?" The younger cop lowered his gun, and I gulped a lungful of air. I appreciated that breath more than any I'd taken in a long time, though there was something decidedly odd about its quality. I sniffed.

"What's that smell?" Stupid question. Now that my attention was free, I saw bottles smashed on the floor, the open cabinets having been relieved of their pharmacy. What I smelled was the combined fragrance of injectable vitamins, antibiotics, and various disinfectants.

"You own this business?" he asked.

I nodded with relief. "Yes."

"We'll need you to remain outside until we secure the building. Please get in your car and lock the doors until we're ready to talk to you."

Quaking like an epileptic poodle, I did as they asked. A few minutes later another uniformed man appeared from within the building, holding a German shepherd on a tether. The three conferred briefly, then the K9 handler put his dog in one of the cars, got behind the wheel, and took off.

"All clear?" I asked, opening the door.

"Yes, ma'am."

I locked the Miata and approached them apprehensively. I'd stopped shaking but was still edgy. "What did they take?"

"We'll need some information, ma'am. I'm Officer Cranston. You've met Officer Friedler," he said wryly, indicating the younger cop. Both men had holstered their weapons, which now appeared much smaller than I remembered.

"Fine. What do you want to know?"

"Why are you here?"

"The alarm company called. I had to see."

He rolled his eyes. "Who was the last authorized person in the building?"

"I was."

"And the premises didn't look like this when you left?"

I blinked. "Hardly."

"Who has access when you're not here?"

"Two employees have keys, and they know the combination to the alarm. And the other veterinarian has a key." I couldn't remember giving Ross the code for the security box inside the door, but I must have done so.

He took down all three names. "What time did you leave?"

"Around six."

"Are you certain the building was secured when you left?"

"I locked up like I always do."

"You own this business?" Cranston asked again.

"Yes." Me and a bail bondsman named Chuck.

"Would anyone else have reason to be here after you closed?"

"No. May I look in the other rooms? Is it all like this?"

The two exchanged glances.

"Do you keep narcotics on the premises?"

I saw where this would lead. "Nothing with much abuse potential. The few legend drugs are locked up."

"Could you show us please, ma'am?"

We passed through the hallway, where I stole a quick glimpse into Pharmacy—it looked like six wild cats had been chased through it by a pit bull—and I led them into the office. A metal lockup cabinet was bolted into the office closet. Smocks hanging in front of it were undisturbed, and the room in general was no more a disaster than I'd left it. The computer sat untouched in its corner. I retrieved the keys from my desk and opened each of the two locks as the policemen watched.

"Do you always keep the keys so accessible?"

"The staff need to be able to get them." I pulled the inside door open. "Looks like everything's here. I have ketamine; I hear that's got some street value."

Officer Friedler picked up the small vial and examined it. "This is a cat tranquilizer?"

"Right."

"Very hot on the streets right now. The kids call it Special K."

I blinked at him, suddenly nervous. "I have a little Valium, some phenobarb, apomorphine—"

His eyebrows arched.

"To induce vomiting. Not a lot of fun. And this is euthanasia solution. I guess someone might try it, but only once." My attempted joke earned me a blank expression. "Anyway, you can look at the records. It's all still here." I handed Officer Cranston the controlled substance log, which tallied every dose of every legend drug we'd given since I first went to work for Philip. He glanced through it and handed it back.

Officer Friedler reached for one of three unopened bottles of euthanasia solution. "Euthanol? What's in this stuff?"

"Pentobarbital. Very concentrated."

"What a name." He grimaced but held the bottle, staring into its dark and lethal depths. "This is to put animals to sleep?"

"Right."

"How much would it take to kill a person?"

"An average-size man, probably fifteen or twenty milliliters. Half an ounce or a little more."

"So if I took this, how long would it take me to die?"

His face betrayed only mild interest. Some of my clients were fascinated by this, too. "Depends on the route and the person's health. If you drank it, you'd probably vomit before it worked. Injected intravenously it numbs the brain until the diaphragm is paralyzed. Death in minutes from asphyxiation. But of course you'd be in a coma by then and wouldn't know."

"Is there an antidote?"

"Not exactly. If someone caught you before permanent damage was done they might give artificial respiration until it wore off. It would take days, but theoretically you could recover. I don't know if it's ever been done outside the lab."

He shuddered visibly and carefully replaced the bottle on the shelf. We all have our fears, I thought, eyeing his gun.

I locked the cabinet and put its keys in my pocket, recalling my own early response to a drug whose sole purpose was to render fatality. It came with names like Terminol, Beauthanasia, Sleepaway. In the morbid humor of vet school, students gave it more colorful titles: Purple Passion, Blue Juice, Enditol, Last Call. No matter the name, its purpose was the same—quick, painless eternity as an alternative to lingering illness or prohibitively expensive therapies. A better option than we offered ourselves in the same circumstances, and a common choice among veterinarians bent on suicide.

Friedler and Cranston followed me from room to room while I took inventory. I told them about the attack on my house and mentioned that Officer Tams had the AFF brochure.

I noted with no small relief that the few animals in the ward and the boarding wing were fine. The gas anesthesia machine had merely been overturned, not damaged. X ray and Lab appeared untouched. More than half my pharmacy was lost, but I already considered myself fortunate.

My sense of invasion and personal affront was worse than the actual monetary loss. Insurance would cover most of it—the blanket policy, not the liability coverage I'd just renewed. But this on top of the assault on my house only four days ago—well, five, the sun was rising in pastels—made me ache for revenge.

"Are you through in here? Don't you need to dust for fingerprints or something?" I asked as we reached the door.

"With the number of people that come through here, prints would be pretty useless. I hate to tell you, but since nothing seems to have been taken and no one was hurt, this crime won't rate a high priority." Cranston shrugged apologetically.

"I figured. Thanks for coming out. No telling what might have happened if not for that alarm and your quick response."

"We'll keep an extraclose eye on the place for the next few nights. I should mention, there's no sign of forced entry." He indicated the lock and the doorjamb. "It looks like someone used a key to get in."

Chapter Seventeen

I retrieved what I could from the jumble of tablets and capsules that lay among the broken glass and spilled liquids in Pharmacy, documented the rest, and swept up the mess. I'd started on Treatment and my third cup of coffee when Sheila walked through the back door. It was seven-thirty.

"Dr. Pauling, what are you—Ohmigod, what happened?"

"Some . . . *bastard* broke in last night." I explained about the alarm and the police. I'd long since gotten over the shock, and with every wasted antibiotic capsule moved beyond anger toward a listless frustration rooted in helplessness.

"What did they take?"

"Nothing, that's the weird part. The cops think they were looking for drugs. By the way, do you still have your key?"

She showed it to me and went up front, still in shock. Moments later her voice came over the intercom.

"Everything seems okay up here. The cash is still in the drawer and the TV and VCR are fine."

I'd already checked that and been as mystified as she was. There was about twenty dollars in the drawer, undisturbed. We kept a series of educational videotapes in the reception area so clients could learn about dog behavior or feline urinary problems while they waited. The video equipment and the untouched computer were things I'd expect a thief to steal. With the alarm screeching in their ears, why take time to search the clinic, even for drugs? No, the "burglar" had been after something specific.

They'd used a key. They'd trashed the pharmaceuticals. In some ways it *looked* like they'd been searching for narcotics, but this didn't stand up to scrutiny. Then why?

I hoped the Animal Freedom Fighters were responsible—revenge, at least, I could understand. They knew I'd been in their van. At least one member was at large. But where would they get a key? If it was Ross's key, how did the burglar get it?

Where the hell was Ross?

Didi arrived just before eight, quickly recovered from her shock, and pitched in cleaning up. She, too, had her key.

Sheila brought the mop, and Didi carried a bag of trash to the Dumpster. I found eight or ten bottles of injectables that appeared intact, and swept up twice as many that were broken or cracked. They'd simply been swept off their shelves, not thrown or deliberately smashed.

It was plump, unexcitable Didi, refilling spray bottles of disinfectants from the larger gallon jugs beneath the sink, who realized what was gone.

We kept all scheduled drugs in lockup, with one exception. An open vial of Euthanol stayed under the sink in Treatment, readily accessible. The abuse potential was so low, we thought nothing of it. I'd opened a new one last week; there should have been half a bottle left.

I racked my memory, trying to recall a stinking purple puddle among the mess I'd cleared. It hadn't been there.

Fifty milliliters of euthanasia solution was missing from my hospital. What would the Animal Freedom Fighters want with that?

I washed my face and arms in the back bathroom and changed into surgical scrubs. I longed for a hot shower and ten hours' sleep, but this would have to do. After several failed attempts to make my hair behave I pulled on a paper surgical cap and went to see clients.

Ironically, business sparked. I wrote prescriptions for drugs I normally dispense and made a desperate midmorning call to my distributor to order steroids and antibiotics, the staples of medicine. I called Officer Cranston to let him know what I'd found, and reported the stolen drug to the DEA lest they inspect my records and decide I'd used it on myself. An anonymous voice promised to send the appropriate triplicate form.

Lara called around nine. "The Gerings are scheduled for arraignment tomorrow morning," she said. "They'll most likely be released on their own recognizance."

"But right now they're in jail?"

"Unless they've escaped."

"When do we go talk to them?"

"Five-thirty?"

I wouldn't even have to shuffle appointments. "I'll meet you there."

At lunchtime I collapsed into my chair, hoping for a nap. The intercom buzzed and Sheila called me to the front desk. Last time she did that I was served with litigation papers. This time I asked what she wanted.

"There's a reporter up here. The same one that was looking for Dr. McRoberts last week. I told him he's not here, but he wants to talk to you."

I sighed, considering my options. Finally I asked Sheila to escort him into my office.

I didn't stand up when he came in. He looked around with obvious curiosity before speaking.

"Bud Thorpe," he said unnecessarily. "Freelance reporter. I was working on a story for the *Desert Sparkler*, about the polo club, when that player got himself killed. Now it looks like book material." He plopped down in the leather chair that had been Philip's, later used by Ross. I could have warned him it was an unlucky chair but decided to let him take his chances.

"So, you got burgled last night, eh? What'd they get?"

"How did you know?"

"Sources." He fished in his shirt pocket and came up with a crooked Camel, which he stuck in a corner of his mouth.

"I hope you're not planning to light that? There's oxygen in the next room. I haven't checked for leaks. You could blow the whole place up and kill us all." Actually, that was one of the first things I'd checked.

He looked at me uncertainly, then put the cigarette back in his pocket. "Right. What kind of losses you take, anyhow?" He settled back, crossing an ankle over a knee.

"Too early to say."

"You think it was those animal rights guys again?"

Now, why would he ask that? "That's for the police to decide."

"How does it feel to be victimized twice in one week?"

Why had I let this worm into my office? "No comment."

His hand migrated toward the cigarette. Irritably he caught himself as the fingers dipped in his pocket. "Listen, Doc," he said. I hate being called Doc. "I could sue your friend for assault, turning that hose on me the other day."

I stared slightly past him, showing him just how little he intimidated me. I was so tired, this was easy. He met my gaze only sporadically, his own eyes moving restlessly behind me. He fidgeted in his chair like a child forced to sit still. Neither of us spoke for most of a minute.

"If that's all . . ." I stood up. "This is my lunch hour, and I have a lot to do."

He rose and followed me out.

We met Sheila and the locksmith in the hallway.

"The perp had a key?" Thorpe's interest quickened. "Sure he did, else how come you'd have a smith out so quick?"

"He could have broken the lock."

"How do you know it's a he? Or just one person?"

"You're right. I have no idea."

I kept silent until we reached the front door. Thorpe handed me a business card and said, "Call me if you come up with anything else." I watched until he got in his Chevy and backed into the street. The card said "Bud Thorpe, Independent Journalist." It smelled of cigarette smoke.

The phone rang as I closed the door. It was the back line. Sheila was busy with the locksmith, so I answered it.

"Dr. Doolittle's Pet Care Center."

"AT and T operator. Dr. McRoberts is calling collect. Will you accept the charges?" The monotone voice asked.

"Thank God! Put him through."

"Andi? It's Ross."

"Hang on. Let me go to the office."

I put him on hold and walked quickly to my desk. By the time I picked up the phone my relief had given way to anger. "Where are you?"

"I'm at a pay phone. Listen, Andi, I need a favor." He sounded weak and desperately tired.

"Only one?"

"Uh, yeah. What's wrong?"

"I wouldn't know where to begin. Let's just say I'm not inclined to do you any more favors. Where the hell are you?"

"I need you to meet me at the polo club."

"Why? Where's your car?"

"I'm sick, Andi. I can't drive. And I think they're looking for me in Palm Springs. They might even be watching the clinic."

"Watching my clinic? Who's looking for you? Ross, what—"

"I can't talk now. Just get out here, okay?"

"What's going on? Are you okay? You're supposed to check in with Lara; she's afraid you've skipped bail. I can't cover for you if you don't tell me what the hell is going on."

"I know. I'm sorry, Andi, I haven't been fair to you. After all you've done . . . I'll tell you everything when you get here."

"Do you have your keys with you?"

"My keys? Sure, why?"

"Someone broke in here last night, and it looks like they had a key."

"Broke into the clinic? What did they take?"

"Nothing much. A bottle of euthanasia solution."

"Fuck. How soon can you get here?"

"I haven't said I'll come at all."

"Andi, come on!"

"Settle down. I'm thinking. I have appointments all afternoon. Then Lara and I are going to interview Tom Gering in conjunction with your case." I paused to let this sink in. "It will have to be later. I'd say no earlier than seven."

"Shit. You've got to come earlier."

"That's it, Ross. Don't press your luck."

His breath in the phone sounded like he'd been running. I wondered out loud what all the secrecy and urgency were about.

"I'll meet you at the barn," he said. "You're wasting your time with those sheep fuckers. I know who killed Gutiérrez."

The line went dead.

The Indio jail was immensely depressing. An overweight, burned-out-looking bailiff took our purses, passed a metal detector up and down our bodies, and left us in a dingy, austere room with cement block walls, a scarred table, and four folding chairs. The oppressive odors of stale cigarettes and old sweat and timeless fear pervaded the room, and already I couldn't wait to leave. A few minutes later the bailiff led Teri Gering in and stepped out of the room.

"I thought we were going to talk to Tom," I said to Lara.

"You got me instead," the sister said.

Lara placed a tape recorder on the table and turned it on. After introducing us she asked, "What's your name?"

"You don't know my name?"

"For the record, please."

"Teri Gering."

"What do you know about a break-in at Dr. Doolittle's Pet Care Center?" I demanded.

Lara was shushing me before I finished. "I'll ask the questions," she hissed.

Teri's eyes widened but she didn't speak.

"You are aware I'm the attorney for Ross McRoberts, who's been accused of murdering Umberto Gutiérrez?"

"Uh, when they said you were a lawyer—I thought you were here to offer us your services."

"Did someone tell you that?" Lara asked sharply.

Teri shrugged, back in control. "We've been expecting someone." She bit her lip as if afraid she'd said too much. I wondered what the big secret was. Did hiring an attorney imply they weren't willing to serve enough time to be martyrs? Maybe the reality of jail dampened their fervor.

"Are you willing to speak to me about Umberto Gutiérrez's death?" Lara asked.

"I didn't know him; none of us did. He was a fascist slave trader, and we're not sorry he's dead. But none of us would have killed him, if that's what you're getting at."

"Do you have any idea who might have?"

Teri rolled her eyes like it was the stupidest question imaginable. "Most likely your client. He did get arrested, after all."

Lara glanced at me. I shrugged. She continued. "I understand you were at Las Palmas Polo Club on the night Mr. Gutiérrez was murdered. Did you see either the victim or my client near the stables at or around eight o'clock?"

Teri's eyes suddenly narrowed, swiveling from Lara to

me and back. "Why should I talk to you, anyway? You're on their side—you're a vet, aren't you? Vets experiment on animals, you hypocrite. What are you doing here, anyhow?"

I sighed, thinking this hadn't been such a good idea after all. "Ross is my friend. I'm just trying to help him out. Let me ask you something, though. Not about the murder."

She squinted at Lara, then turned off the recorder. "What?"

"Why do you do the things you do?"

"You mean try to save the horses? Because they can't save themselves. They don't even know they need saving."

"That seems like a fair statement," I said. The irony went right past her.

"God created all beings equal. God never built a fence or a wall. Horses are His creation, meant to run free and unfettered on the earth." She was gazing intently at me now, gauging her effect. Trying to conjure a vast wild herd, thundering hoofbeats, manes and tails streaming.

"Even in the wild, they have to stop running sometime," I said. "Do you really think these pampered thoroughbreds would be better off foraging for food, starving, and being hunted by scavengers? Is that really the life you have in mind for them?"

"Hardship makes everyone stronger. Some of them would survive, and the next generation will be tougher." I suppressed a smile, wondering how she thought a bunch of mares and geldings were going to reproduce. "These animals should never have been born," she said earnestly. "They're the artificial result of man's intervention."

"Have you ever spent time with a horse? Or a dog, a cat, even a gerbil? Did you ever consider what they might want?"

She sat back and glared at me, disgusted. "You'll never understand."

That much certainly was true.

* * *

I was later than I expected getting to the polo grounds. Tom and Tina had refused to speak to us, but it was almost seven before the unhurried bailiff handed me my purse and I said goodnight to Lara, reluctantly declining dinner at a Chinese place she recommended near the courthouse.

On the way I wondered what I'd say to Ross. Should I fire him right away or wait till I got him home? He'd sounded both terribly ill and truly upset on the phone. Maybe this wasn't the time to add stress. What he was going through made my little lawsuit look like the territorial squabble between Romeo and Velcro.

Ross this isn't working. I'm sorry, you're just not cut out for small animal work. I've got to look out for myself—if I don't who will? Maybe they'll let you remain free on bail. . . .

Which was contingent on his remaining employed.

I'm sorry but what can I do? My business is all I have.

Except my business was already at risk.

I tried to convince myself that my own concerns had to come first, that Ross had proven himself unreliable multiple times already and in no way deserved any more chances. But my problems paled against the threat of his being thrown in prison for a murder I knew he didn't commit.

I wondered briefly whether he really knew who'd killed Umberto, and found I lacked the energy to care. How the hell had I gotten so deeply involved in his problems?

Fire him tonight.

Could I do that?

Is it fair not to tell him?

My hands clenched around the wheel as I entered the back gate, determined to tell Ross he no longer worked at Dr. Doolittle's. The clock in the dash said 7:14. Ross would be either angry or humble. His mood would determine mine.

As I entered the stable area a Ford pickup nearly side-swiped me on its way out. I couldn't tell its color in the dark. I honked and cursed under my breath, taking some of my anger out on the anonymous driver.

I drove slowly, scanning the stables for my classmate. There, in a far corner, half hidden beneath a tamarisk tree 300 feet from Bob Talbot's trailer was the Porsche. I drove across the loosely packed sand and parked next to it. Ross slouched in the driver's seat.

He didn't even look at me when I pulled up. Asleep? Now? Damn him! I got out and tapped on his window. He didn't stir.

Muttering under my breath, I yanked at his door handle. Locked. I pounded on the window. Nothing. With a vague but mounting sense of unease, I ran to the passenger side. That door was also locked, but peering through the glass I saw the problem.

Ross's right hand lay palm down across his thigh. A line ran from the wrist upward. Hanging from the rearview mirror was something I recognized instantly.

I'd found the missing bottle of Euthanol.

Chapter Eighteen

I grabbed a football-size rock and smashed the window, groped for the handle, yanked the door open, and reached in to jerk the IV line from Ross's right hand before anything else. Drops of sticky poison fell on my skin as the needle raked my palm.

How much did he get?

I touched his throat, leaning my elbow on the horn. Felt the faintest quiver of carotid pulse, a cat's breath against my fingers. Reached across to open the door, and we fell in a heap.

I stretched him on his back between our cars and began CPR. Five rapid chest compressions and a breath. *It works at brain level,* I reminded myself. If I could keep oxygen moving, maybe he had a chance. *Pump, two, three, four, five. Now breathe.*

Too late, too late, the refrain echoed in time to the cadence of my crossed hands thrusting at Ross's sternum. *Too late, should have come when he asked.* His heartbeat was nearly undetectable. After several minutes I reached into the car again and leaned on the horn. I returned to my efforts.

"What the hell? What is it?" Bob Talbot shone a flashlight in my eyes.

"Get an ambulance!" He'd broken my rhythm: Was that two pumps or three? *Screw it, throw in an extra.* A rib cracked beneath my hands.

"What happened?"

I could smell the booze on his breath from where I knelt. *"Call the fucking ambulance!"*

"All right, fine, just gimme a minute."

Babs had followed him out. "What's going on, Daddy?"

"Get back in the house. I'll take care of this." He hustled her toward the trailer.

"Call an ambulance now!" I shouted, hoping my urgency would affect Babs more than it had her father. *Three, four, five, breathe.*

And on and on. My arms felt disconnected from my body, my lips numb and swollen. I disassociated my mind, let my body work by rote; it was easier to ignore the aches and the absolute lack of response. Easier not to blame myself for being too slow.

I never heard the approaching ambulance. Suddenly the whole area was awash with light—glaring white headlights, pulsing red beacons of alarm. Merciful relief for my throbbing shoulders and arms as a paramedic took over with a mask and an ambu bag. They started an IV in his left arm, opposite where the Euthanol had gone in.

I explained the problem, pointing out the bottle still hanging from the rearview mirror of the Porsche. They radioed the information in: barbiturate overdose. They gave drugs to stimulate the heart and breathing as ordered by the doctor's voice. Finally they whisked him into their van, through the gate, into the night. The lights never stopped swirling.

An Indio patrol car—more flashing lights—pulled in as the ambulance left. A single uniform got out, the tall black officer who had taken Dietrich's and my names the night of Umberto's murder. Briar? No, Bryant. He hitched up his khaki pants and strolled over, glancing at the two cars parked side by side, facing opposite directions. The strobes turned him into a negative image of himself: white skin, black teeth. He leaned over to look inside the Porsche. His light picked out the bottle of

Euthanol still hanging from the rearview mirror, whatever remained of its contents soaking into the leather seat.

"Who called it in?"

"I did," said Bob Talbot. He stood away from the scene in the darkness, as if to make it clear this was none of his affair. "She was here, gave him the kiss of life. I knew that one was trouble. Good riddance, I say."

Officer Bryant glanced at him. I wondered what Talbot meant. Me? Ross? Trouble how?

Bryant turned to me. "Can you tell me what happened?"

I thought for a minute, beginning to shake. Where to start? I decided to keep it simple, told him who Ross was and that he'd asked me to meet him here earlier but this was the soonest I could come.

"Can you describe what you saw when you arrived?"

Then my knees, those trusty parts of anatomy that had carried me well for most of my thirty-two years, suddenly refused to support my weight. The ground lurched up and caught me on one hip. I bit my tongue and the pain, or something, brought hot tears, which I blinked into submission. I sat cross-legged on the ground, resting my forehead in my hands and breathing in ragged gasps. *Oh my God, what if I'd been five minutes later? Or five minutes earlier.*

After a few moments I became conscious of Talbot's agitation and Bryant's curiosity. I took a few more greedy breaths and forced myself to look up at the policeman, whose steadying hand was on my shoulder.

"I thought he'd fallen asleep waiting for me. His door was locked, so I went around. It was locked, too, but I saw the bottle. . . . I broke the window and tried to resuscitate him."

He made some notes, then shone his light on the inside of Ross's car again until it rested on the hanging bottle. The label was partially obscured by a piece of white tape that held a loop of baling wire from which the bottle dangled. The spike from an IV set had been forced through a stopper meant to be pierced only by a thin needle.

"What's in it?" he asked.

"Euthanasia solution. I think it was stolen from my clinic last night. This morning, I mean."

This earned me a curious glance. I explained about the break-in, and he asked me to sit in the back of his car. Then he radioed for investigators. I asked him to leave the door open.

Two more uniforms arrived, along with Detective Braun. His amazing eyebrows expressed, more than any words could, how interesting he found my presence at yet another mysterious night scene at the polo club. He listened to Bryant's report, took a look in the Porsche, and moved away for the photographer. The lab tech awaited his turn.

Babs invited me in for a cup of cocoa. I accepted gratefully, ignored a halfhearted protest from Bryant, and followed her up the plank stairs through the front door of the mobile home.

The place was spartan and none too neat. Back issues of *Polo* magazine and a few videotapes decorated the flimsy wood veneer coffee table and stained sofa. I sat on the only piece of furniture in the room with character, a sturdy oak rocker polished by time and many broad bottoms. Babs brought cocoa for each of us. Her father had apparently decided to remain outside to keep an eye on the cops.

"You think he'll be okay?" Babs asked.

"I don't know."

She stared into her cup, holding her hands around it as if to warm them. I realized I felt cold, then noticed my own hands wrapped around my mug the same way. Neither of us drank.

"What happened?" she asked.

I wondered how much she'd heard. "I don't know."

"I liked Ross," she said. "He was nice to me."

I stared at this plump, homely young woman in her

too-tight jeans and baggy sweatshirt. She'd thrown herself unashamedly at Umberto. I'd assumed she, like everyone else, thought Ross had killed him.

"Nice?" I asked.

"Yeah. Not like . . ." She stared at her cocoa like it held the answer to her life. "You know."

"The other players."

"Yeah. They're all after one thing." She patted her belt buckle. "But Ross was different. He was . . ." A shrug.

"Nice."

"Yeah. Sometimes he'd come out here at night and sit in his car. Not do anything, just sit there. Later he'd get out and stand in the barn, and I'd go out and talk to him."

So that's where he'd gone. What else didn't I know?

"How could this happen?" she said.

Which, of course, I should have asked myself. And would have, eventually. I remembered the pickup I'd passed on my way into the barn area.

"Have you been home all night?"

"Yeah. Me and Daddy. He's pissed with me right now." She shrugged again, giving me the impression this was a standard situation between her and "Daddy." She wouldn't meet my eyes.

"Who was here just before I came? Someone in a pickup truck. A Ford, fairly new, but I couldn't tell what color."

She stared into her mug. "I didn't see anyone tonight."

I felt sure she was lying but hated to destroy our rapport by calling her on it. "What about last night? I was up by the clubhouse and someone drove in. It looked like a pickup, too."

"I know the one you're talking about." She was suddenly animated. "It's a supercab. It parked for a while and I figured someone was checking on their horses. I watched from my bedroom window, but they just sat in the truck for a few minutes. Then one of them got out, and the other one drove away."

"That was last night?"

"Yeah."

"There were two people."

"Two guys." Trust her to notice that. "The driver was a heavy-set dude with a gut. He barely got out of the truck. I think he's a *patrón*. The other one was sorta skinny." She thought a minute. "He was shorter. When the one guy drove away, the skinny one started walking up toward the clubhouse. I told Daddy, but he said to mind my own business as long as they didn't bother the horses."

The new AFF member who'd caught me in the van. He'd gotten out of a Ford pickup. The driver's description didn't match any of the members. Who was he? What did he have to do with Ross? I remembered the man in the baseball cap who'd threatened Ross. Who was he? "What about tonight?"

She gazed into her cocoa as if reading her fortune there. "Come to think of it, I might've seen the same truck tonight."

Bob Talbot appeared in the doorway. "Cops wantcha," he said to me, glancing irritably at his daughter. Babs got up and walked me to the door. I was glad to leave the suddenly oppressive trailer.

By now it looked like a tristate cop convention outside. The horses danced nervously in their pens, snorting and nickering to each other. I wondered whether the police had found anything, or were out in force only because Ross was a murder suspect. As I approached Braun, two marked cars drove away, shut off their lights, and left.

When Braun saw me he held up a plastic bag containing the now empty Euthanol bottle. "How do you know this is the same one that was stolen from your clinic this morning?" he asked.

"I assumed. The circumstances—"

"There's a number on the side. Is it some kind of serial number?"

I took the bag and held it up to read it. The weird light made it tough. "That's the expiration date. The other one is a lot number. If you'll write it down, I'll check to see if it matches the others in my safe, but I still can't prove it's the same because the lot would have been broken up and sent to several clinics. It would have my fingerprints on it, though."

"Can anyone besides vets get this stuff?"

"Not as far as I know." I shrugged. "Researchers maybe."

"But the other vets around here would have it?"

"They might. Although there are a half dozen different brands, and none has any particular advantage over the others. I generally buy whichever one's on sale."

He retrieved the bottle. "Would McRoberts have had access to this prior to tonight?"

"Yes, but I doubt he touched it." I couldn't explain my classmate's aversion to Euthanol and what it represented.

"You can come by the station tomorrow and make a statement. In the meantime, you're free to go."

I was surprised. "It didn't take long this time. Not like when Umberto was killed."

He looked at me over his shoulder as he walked toward his car. "That was murder. This was attempted suicide."

Chapter Nineteen

"Suicide?" The word hung between us, foreign and irrelevant. "No way."

He raised an eyebrow in mild surprise. "What'd you think? He might have wanted you to stop him when he called. A cry for help, like the shrinks say. Look at the facts." He held up his hand, tallying points on his fingers. "He's a vet. He knows how to put a needle in a vein, right? And he knows about this stuff, this—Euthanol."

"Anyone who works with animals knows. That doesn't—"

"We still have to check it out, but if the bottle came from your clinic, which he had access to—"

"But the alarm—"

"Let me finish. He's facing trial for murder. He had good reason to be depressed. Depressed people do this sometimes."

"Did you find a note?"

"Notes!" He waved his hand dismissively. "People don't wrap everything up with a neat explanation. Who could understand anyway? Take my advice," he said gently, "don't think about it too much. You'll make yourself crazy."

"He said he knew who killed Umberto."

He clucked, shaking his head in a pitying gesture. "McRoberts killed him. They all claim they're innocent."

"Ross couldn't—"

"The physical evidence clinches it. He's not big, but he's gotta be pretty fit to play polo. Someone tried to put that stuff in my arm, I'd fight like hell. There's no sign of a struggle, except where you broke the window. Unless the assailant was Hulk Hogan, there's no way it could be anything but self-inflicted. I know it's hard to face, but that's the way it is."

"But what about the murder weapon?" I meant whatever Umberto was killed with, not the Euthanol.

He ignored me, slipped into his unmarked sedan, and drove off, no doubt congratulating himself on closing the case so quickly. The last two units followed, leaving me alone in the darkness. After a moment I got in my own car and left.

I could add a lot to Detective Braun's argument, things the cop didn't even know about. Ross's behavior the past few days backed up the depression theory. I'd be despondent in his position. Charged with murder, abandoned by Jaime, treated as a pariah by other players. Dietrich was probably less than thrilled. Winning meant a lot to Ross, and he'd been losing at everything. Knowing I was angry with him—though he didn't know just how angry—he must have felt he had no friends left anywhere. Then I was late meeting him. Sure, suicide made sense from that standpoint. And euthanasia solution was the suicide weapon of choice among veterinarians. But.

But not for Ross.

He couldn't inject Euthanol into a chronically ill horse. He was innocent of Umberto's death. And this afternoon he'd been as manic and controlling as ever.

To my mind the scene looked staged: the bottle hanging from the rearview mirror, its contents dripping slowly into Ross's arm through the temporary butterfly catheter.

Oh, really, Andi? How would you do it?

The way the bottle was rigged—was that something a veterinarian would do? A syringeful of the stuff, given rapidly, would be far more efficient.

But anyone injecting himself by syringe took a chance of passing out before he got enough to kill.

Which lent credence to the suicide theory, but I still wasn't convinced. To me it still looked like a clever setup.

The break-in had taken place the night before. Ross didn't know I was angry until that afternoon. And he'd been agitated when I spoke to him. Frightened, even, now that I thought about it. Afraid for his life?

Ross claimed he knew who had killed Umberto. Was that just bluster, or had the real murderer discovered that Ross was on his trail? Someone who could hit a vein, who knew how to make a veterinarian's death look self-induced?

But Detective Braun was right. How do you hold a grown man down to put in an IV and then keep it in long enough to hang up a bottle? I pictured the IV set—probably also stolen from my clinic; I wouldn't have missed one—wedged into the rubber stopper of the injection bottle, the connection wrapped with tape. Obviously prepared ahead of time. Okay, but say you had the whole thing already connected, you'd still have to get it in the vein—without much light, unless you brought your own—then take a hand off your victim long enough to open the line.

Two people working together? In the front seat of a Porsche?

With these thoughts spinning through my brain I drove the back roads to Indio General Hospital. I bypassed the busy emergency receiving area, assuming that Ross would have been processed and admitted to the Critical Care Unit by now. I parked, caught the door behind someone who was leaving, and approached the front desk. The foyer was deserted except for myself and a volunteer who looked about to depart.

When she saw me she glanced at the clock above the desk. It was nearly eleven. "Visiting hours are—"

"I'm Dr. Pauling," I ad-libbed, hoping I didn't look too frazzled. It wasn't a lie, exactly. I was still wearing the surgical scrubs I'd put on that morning, but the knees were caked with dirt and one had a tear in it. "I'm here to see Ross McRoberts. I was the one who found him," I added by way of explanation. I tried to look like a regular visitor, called in to see patients at all hours.

"Oh, Doctor, I'm sorry!" She was suddenly eager to help, trained not to question doctors' appearances. "We don't usually get family physicians at this hour but I suppose . . ." After a quick once-over she consulted the computer monitor behind the desk. "He's in Neuro three thirty-seven."

"What can you tell me about his condition?"

Her eyes narrowed slightly. "Nothing, except he's critical."

I shouldn't have asked. Medical records would be off-limits to front-desk volunteers. I thanked her quickly and strode purposefully toward what looked like the elevators.

"Doctor, are you new here?"

Her voice stopped me, and I turned, arranging my features in a puzzled frown.

"'Cause the elevator to the third floor is over there." She pointed in the other direction, to a red-painted door clearly marked CRITICAL CARE.

"Right," I said, cramming a smile onto my face. "I am new. Pretty obvious, huh?" Thankfully, the elevator opened as soon as I pushed the up button. I stepped inside and grinned idiotically at her as the doors closed.

On the third floor I wandered the hallway, trying to look like I belonged while surreptitiously reading the CCU ward signs. Cardiac, Medical . . . ah, Neurology. I turned in there. Tried to anyway, but met a pair of doors with no knobs and no glass to peek through. I stopped short, frustrated and dismayed.

A male voice spoke from the wall. "Can I help you?"

"I, ah . . ." I looked for the source of the voice. "I'd like to see Ross McRoberts. He's a patient here."

"Are you a relative?"

A-ha. The sound came from a box on the wall behind

me, which also held a keypad like a Touch-Tone phone. A miniature video camera watched me from above the doors.

"I'm Dr. Andi Pauling. I'm a friend of the patient's." I was getting nervous about pretending to be a "real" doctor, but when the doors swung open I stepped through.

"Dr. Pauling? I'm Ken O'Grady." A nurse approached me, offering his hand to be shaken. He stood a few inches taller than me, slender and confident in a blue-gray scrub suit with frayed edges. His sandy hair curled under at the nape, disheveled but clean.

I shook his hand, glancing behind him. The Neurology Critical Care Unit consisted of an octagonal central work space, with the door to a patient room on each wall. About half the rooms were occupied.

The central area looked well used but clean and smelled vaguely of antiseptic. Two female nurses, both heavy and blond and wearing similar faded blue scrubs, lounged in the center of a large open control station encircled by work surfaces, one end of which consisted of a bank of monitor screens. A fourth nurse exited a room in which a tiny, ancient woman sat crying softly by a bed. The patient presumably lying there was hidden by a proliferation of tubing and machinery.

"I'm glad someone came," Ken O'Grady said. "We don't have much information on the patient. His ID says Kentucky, but the phone's been disconnected, and there's no indication of insurance or next of kin."

"I'll try to call his father tomorrow," I said. "And I may be able to reach his ex-wife. How is he?"

"It's too early to tell for sure. We got blood pentobarb levels and a panel, but that's it until tomorrow."

"What about brain function?"

"His EEG is consistent with deep coma, but we didn't need the machine to tell us that. He's a one or two on the Glasgow scale." He gestured toward the third glass door on the left, number 337, which like most of the others hung wide open. I guessed the patients didn't mind. As far as I could tell they were all unconscious. "Tomorrow he'll get a scan."

I paused in the doorway, staring in. The face was recognizable as Ross's, but he looked much younger in sleep. A respirator tube protruded from his mouth, and ventilator noises dominated the cramped space. His chest rose and fell beneath the white blanket with each mechanical *whoosh.* Three intravenous lines led to a catheter in his neck, a nasogastric tube was taped to the tip of his nose, a half-full urine chamber hung at the foot of his bed. Various other lines and wires descended beneath the blankets. A monitor screen glowed with squiggles and numbers, only a few of which looked familiar.

The lights were off, shadows within shadows turning the life-support equipment into monklike robots in silent prayer. Ross's eyes were wide and staring. I shut them gently, but they slid open again as soon as I lifted my fingers. Presumably the nurses put drops in from time to time to prevent the corneas from drying out. But the sight of them, vacant and uncomprehending, shocked me into seeing how close Ross was to death.

I sat in the armchair, leaning to reach for a tissue on the small bedside table as fat, sluggish tears paused on my lashes and plopped on my shirt. *Dammit,* I thought furiously, *he doesn't deserve this. No one deserves to be this helpless.* I couldn't shake the guilty feeling that he might have been better off if I hadn't shown up when I did.

Cut that out, Andi. He's not one of your patients, he's a human being.

A sudden whine arose from one of the monitors outside. Seconds later a speaker erupted: *"Code Blue, Neuro three-thirty-nine! Code Blue!"* Alarmed, I glanced at Ross's screen: no change. I looked out as the nurses dragged a crash cart into the room where I'd noticed the old woman at the bedside. I stood in the doorway for a moment, watching as they began frantic resuscitative efforts on the invisible patient while the tiny woman continued her weeping, unheeded. Then I returned to my chair.

I found myself thinking about a case Ross and I had shared in school. Maybe it was the environment, the Critical Care ward, but I remembered a terribly sick foal that had been my case and had baffled me completely. Horses in general frustrated me, with their inherent fragility and the logistical problems in their manipulation, but this colt's will to survive drew me in from the start. The resident in charge was facing board exams and was less than absorbed with her patients. For two days I struggled to keep the foal alive while it steadily faded.

The last day of the rotation the resident wanted to euthanize the foal. Grades were in, it was a bitterly cold day, and most of the class left early. Ross came up after rounds as I sat staring into the hospital stall in utter frustration, sure the foal would die that night one way or another.

"What antibiotics is he on?" Ross asked me.

"The usual. Penicillin and Amikacin." What the resident had prescribed.

He studied the chart for a long minute, then got out the X rays and stared at them. "Try Erythromycin and Rifampin."

"Just like that?" As a student I wouldn't dare thwart a clinician, and this particular resident was known for her wrath.

Ross didn't share my trepidation. "It's worth a shot. The kid's done for otherwise. I'll stay awhile if you want."

"But the party . . ." That night was the traditional bash the students threw at the end of each rotation. Ross never missed it.

He just shrugged. "Someone's got to stay with him."

We both did, all night. The foal gradually improved and by four in the morning began to look like a survivor. Later Ross convinced the resident it had been her idea to switch antibiotics. I got an A in the course—my first. Ross got a B and he never stepped up to take credit for saving the foal's life.

"Damn you, Ross, what were you thinking?" I mumbled. "Why did you have to go and play Perry Mason? I know you didn't do this to yourself. Now I've got to find out who did."

I left twenty minutes later. The woman in room 339 was still there, sobbing quietly. The tubes had been removed, and the patient's blanket now covered his face.

Chapter Twenty

I'm out of my mind.

What was I thinking, promising to find out who'd injected Ross? I urged the Miata down I-10 toward home.

Andi Pauling, vet detective?

What did I know about tracking down killers?

Okay, so forget it. He's comatose, didn't hear me anyway.

Let them write it off as suicide? Could I live with that? Knowing they were wrong, that I might have made things right but didn't? Ross's near death would go down as self-inflicted, and only a killer and I would know differently.

I realized I was already assuming Ross would never be able to stand up for himself. He could die anytime. Worse—and no less likely—his coma might be a permanent state of limbo.

If I'd done more to help prove he didn't kill Umberto, or if I'd gone to meet him when he asked, this wouldn't have happened.

Stop that. He might recover. He might.

If the killer doesn't get back to him first.

The car swerved, tires grabbing shoulder. I wrestled it back onto pavement.

Whoever did this is still around. Does he know Ross isn't dead? If he thought he might wake up, identify his attacker . . .

The Indian Avenue exit loomed ahead. I took it too

fast, squealed to a halt at the light, burned rubber when it turned.

Who says it's a man?

I'd been assuming a lot. Bad habit.

How long since I'd had a full night's rest? My brain was running on fumes. The road blurred and swam, my arms hung from my shoulders like lead—they would ache in the morning. But objects glittered and shimmered in my vision, and part of me actually looked forward to the search ahead. How often does one get the chance to right a serious wrong?

Damn, I thought I'd left the front light on. I parked in the dark driveway, not bothering with the garage for the few remaining hours before the clinic opened and I had to act alert.

A shadowy form darted off the breezeway. I had a brief impression of a slender man, average height. Dark clothes and hair, pale face, no hat. He ran across the yard, vaulted the neighbor's oleander bushes, and the darkness swallowed him.

"Hey!" I shouted. "Dammit, come back here!"

He didn't.

A burst of adrenaline carried me to the hedge, but he was gone. I couldn't see creeping around the neighborhood after some weirdo. Better to see what he'd been up to.

Velcro didn't greet me. As I entered the breezeway the coppery scent of blood shocked me. I couldn't see the dog. Glass from the broken bulb crunched under my shoes. I unlocked the door and flipped on the inside light. He was a lump in the shadows, a twisted mass of fur, the dull sheen of fresh blood.

That rotten son of a bitch! I knelt to examine him—still warm. "Velcro? You all right, kid?" Stupid question. Blood ran between my fingers from an open throat wound. At my touch he whimpered softly. Still alive, but not by much.

I dashed into the house for a towel and wrapped it

around his neck to staunch the bleeding. All I could think was that he'd protected my home as his own. Now I hoped I could save his life. I scooped him up, laid him on the passenger's seat, and flew to the clinic. This made two such early-morning races in as many days. And two close calls with death in one night.

I hoped these things didn't come in the proverbial threes.

As I carried the dog inside I was breathing hard, but from fear rather than exertion. With a bright light directed at his throat I removed the makeshift bandage, then quickly replaced it.

"Knife wound. The bastard. Thank God he missed your carotid." But he'd nicked the jugular, and minutes counted. I started an IV, hung glucose, went to the fridge for blood. As the transfusion dripped I grabbed a suture pack and rolled the anesthesia machine over, the automatic actions returning control to my movements.

I stroked the dog's head by way of apology. He licked my hand as I pushed the anesthesia mask over his face.

It would take some doing, but he was going to be okay.

It took me more than an hour to stitch Velcro's wound, finish the transfusion, and assure myself he was stable. He woke smoothly but a little slowly from the gas, then slipped into a natural, healing sleep.

I left Sheila a note to reschedule morning appointments and call me at nine. I drove home carefully, not trusting my reflexes, showered away the day's grime—and Velcro's blood—and stretched out on the water bed. A crescent of dawn peaked through the skylight. The next thing I knew, my phone was ringing and morning intruded in the form of Sheila's cheery voice.

The indicator light on the answering machine was blinking, a single message that turned out to be from Hal, the night before.

"Andi? Haven't heard from you. How about Monday

night? You can pick the restaurant. Around seven? See you at Las Palmas this weekend. Bye."

I groaned, trying to keep my eyes open. The lids felt like sandpaper, and repeated blinking failed to produce lubrication. I made my way to the shower by sense of touch.

I couldn't imagine sitting in a restaurant with Hal. *So, Andi, do you think you'll keep working after you get married? Say, how's that Ross doing? Are they still gonna press charges since he's brain damaged?* Please, God, no.

As coffee brewed I called the police to report the attempted break-in. They promised to send someone to take a report. They knew the address. In the meantime I went to the hardware store and bought new locks for the outside doors. I suspected whoever had keys to the clinic would also have a set for the house, and had only been prevented from entering last night by a scruffy, friendly mutt who thought he lived here.

On the way I picked up the morning's issue of the *Desert Sparkler.* Thorpe's byline topped a brief story on page three: VET CLINIC BURGLARIZED. The text portrayed me as an active opponent of animal rights and implied the break-in was an attempt by the Animal Freedom Fighters to release impounded animals.

Impounded? At my clinic? What was Thorpe up to?

The locks switched easily. With a towel to shield my hand I changed the broken yellow bug light for a new, brighter white bulb. As I finished sweeping up the glass, a young Chicano police officer arrived. I explained what happened, pointed out some fat drops of blood the stranger left as he ran away—probably Velcro's—but I hoped he'd bitten the creep and it was his blood instead.

He took down a description and expressed skepticism that the interloper was an animal rights advocate. I could see his point, but he hadn't met these guys.

I'd already taken what steps I could to prevent anyone's gaining entry later on. As far as I could tell, the intruder had not returned after I left with Velcro the night before, but I couldn't swear to it. The officer promised to contact me if anything turned up. He didn't sound optimistic. Before he left he said, "Good thing you weren't home. Who would've sewn you up?"

Unbelievably, the thought hadn't occurred to me. Was this a message from Ross's would-be killer? A warning to stay away? Or a serious attempt on my life?

I made it to the clinic a few minutes late for my eleven o'clock, stopping to check on Velcro first. He was awake and anxious to escape the cage, so I disconnected the IV and let him follow me. His enthusiasm had not been dampened by his ordeal.

Bud Thorpe was in the waiting room. The lay-in-wait room, I thought irritably. He tried to follow me into my office. Velcro growled menacingly from between my calves. The reporter stared in alarm, though it might have been all those stitches.

"Hold it, Thorpe. What is it this time?" Velcro was difficult to restrain, since he couldn't wear a collar until the wound healed. I'd never seen him act like this. Maybe he knew how much I disliked this weasel.

"I hear McRoberts tried to off himself last night. With dope you supplied."

"Excuse me. I have work to do."

"You know who burgled your house last night? What'd they get?" He followed me down the hallway.

I picked Velcro up and whirled to face him. "You mean the bastard that almost murdered my dog?" *How does he know about that?* "You seem to know as much as I do. Now, if that's all, will you please leave the building?"

I turned my back to him and quickly put the closed door of my office between us. I set Velcro on the floor with relief.

For some reason I felt energized, and seeing cases through my lunch hour barely fazed me. At any rate, it kept me from thinking.

I even managed to write the letter Lara had told me to send Mrs. Artimas's attorney: "Dear Sir: Your client's assertion surprises me in light of the fact that Buffy was euthanized only due to her insistence. . . ." I affixed Lara's card and a list of southern California referral clinics, addressed it, and gave it to Sheila to mail. I opened a file containing the papers served on me, a copy of my letter, and the medical record. Wanting it out of sight until I had to deal with it, I stuck it in the back of the cabinet containing bills and tax forms.

A bill from a supplier I rarely used caught my eye. It was for nearly four hundred dollars. I couldn't remember ordering from them recently. My invoice file offered no explanation. Finally I called the toll-free number at the top of the bill and explained to a cheerful, anonymous voice what the problem was.

"On October twenty-fourth you ordered two bottles of Nizoral two-fifty milligram tablets. . . ."

"No, I didn't. I script out those drugs because I hardly ever need them and they're too expensive to stock."

"Do you want to return them?"

"I don't have them. I'm sure because I just went through the Pharmacy yesterday." Of course, they could have been stolen along with the Euthanol, but I doubted it. Antifungal drugs, no matter how expensive, had no abuse potential at all.

"Our records indicate the shipment went out on the twenty-fifth. You should have received it the following day."

"Does your record indicate who actually placed the order?"

"A Dr. McRoberts?"

Damn Ross. He must have ordered them for one of his horses. "Never mind. Sorry to have bothered you."

That afternoon I tried to reach Ross's family. I'd brought the phone bill, our vet school yearbook, and a class newsletter from six months after graduation, a time when Ross and Kelsey were still locked together in something resembling matrimonial bliss. It listed addresses and phone numbers of everyone who'd written to report on their new lives as actual doctors of veterinary medicine. Several had declined to write.

Ross's name was there, with a long paragraph about how great life was starting an equine practice in Lexington, Kentucky, that mecca of horsey folk. He described driving the winding, two-lane highways from one landmark thoroughbred farm to the next, delivering the foals of champions, and injecting the knees of the next Derby winner. I remembered being the tiniest bit jealous reading it the first time, since I was struggling along on the twenty-four thousand a year Philip paid me, facing student loan payments, expressing anal sacs, and trimming toenails. Now, looking at the words, all I felt was pity. They were so glowing, so forcefully positive, so *Ross*, they simply couldn't be true.

I dialed the home number, hoping Kelsey had kept it. A woman with a pleasant southern drawl answered. I explained who I was and asked if she knew Ross McRoberts or his ex-wife.

"No, I'm terribly sorry. I've had this number for over three years and there's been no one here by that name. Would you like me to look him up?" The offer was almost an invitation, her voice was so musical.

"I hate to impose. . . ."

"Nonsense. You're calling from so far away, it must be important. Now, let me see. . . . There's a Virgil McRoberts, and a B.K., but no Ross and no R, and no Kelsey or initial K."

"He's a veterinarian. Would it be too much trouble to check the yellow pages?" I searched my memory for Kelsey's maiden name. She was from Lexington and surely would have stayed after the divorce. Something like suitcase. Satchel? Baggage? No.

"Well, there are an awful lot of vets here, but the only ones under *M* are Chauncey Madison and J. Putnam Morris."

"Damn, he definitely said he practiced in Lexington. When was that directory published?"

"March of this year."

Sheila stood in the doorway, hands on hips. She'd already put a client into an exam room. People were waiting.

"Thank you so much for your time," I said. "You've been a great help, really." *Attaché? Portmanteau? Come on, Andi.*

"Well, it doesn't seem like it. You be sure and call again if there's anything else I can do for you, all right?"

"I sure will, and it's been wonderful talking with you." I started to hang up, then remembered. "Oh, wait!"

"Ye-es?"

"Vallice! Ross's ex-wife's name was Kelsey Vallice. She was from Lexington. Would you mind looking one last name up?"

A brief, whimsical laugh. "The Vallice name is well known around these parts. The numbers are unlisted of course, but I do happen to have them in my little book. Here it is. Richard and Amy, daughter Kelsey."

I scribbled the number. "Thank you so much."

"Oh, not at all." She paused, waiting for me to give her the juicy details. My part of the bargain. I sensed this was the most interesting thing to happen to her all day. I felt like a heel as I thanked her again and hung up the phone, on my way to look at a shih tzu with a corneal abrasion.

By the time I got another break, it was a quarter to five in California, nearly eight in Kentucky. I dialed the Vallice number as Sheila's head reappeared in the doorway. She frowned, gesturing for me to see another client. An answering machine with a southern drawl answered. I declined to leave a message.

This patient was a blue-and-gold macaw with a bald breast. The bird was obviously plucking himself from loneliness or boredom, but at the owner's insistence I drew blood for a panel before prescribing Valium to add to his water. It wasn't a perfect solution but few things are.

I sat down again at a quarter to nine Kentucky time, about as late as I felt comfortable calling. The Vallice number again yielded a machine, and I still didn't want to leave a message. This was too complicated to explain to a tape.

I realized I should have called Roger Dietrich first. But it was long past bank closing time, and I didn't have his Lexington home number. I tried Ross's work number from the newsletter and got a convenience store instead of a vet clinic. The teenager who answered had never heard of Ross. Big surprise.

I spread the phone bill out across my desk. Ross had called his father last Monday. A short call. There, one of the last entries on the bill. I looked up the area code—Nebraska, where I knew Ross had lived prior to attending school in Missouri.

On the third ring a creaky male voice said, "Hello?"

"Hello, is this Mr. McRoberts?"

After a suspicious pause he said, "Who wants to know?"

"I'm a friend of Ross . . ."

"Who?"

"Ross McRoberts. Aren't you his father?"

"Never heard of him."

"But he called this number last Monday—"

"We get a lot of wrong numbers here." The line went dead.

Bizarre. Ross had definitely spoken to someone after calling this number. I double-checked to make sure I'd dialed correctly. The digital display on the desk phone matched the listing on the bill. No other calls were made around that time.

I wasn't going to solve the mystery tonight. One of the Kentucky numbers undoubtedly belonged to Dietrich, but there were several and I couldn't tell which was which.

Velcro got up to follow when I picked up my purse. With his face, right flank and shoulder, and now his entire neck shaved down to bare skin in various stages of healing and sutured here with nylon, there with horse-strength Poly-Fil, he looked like a crazed patchwork quilt. Didi had hacked the rest of his coat to an inch-and-a-half length the first day, but she's not a groomer and the job was pretty choppy. It would be hard to find a home for him now, and I was no longer sure I wanted to.

At any rate, I could hardly leave him in the kennel after what he'd been through, so I let him out and he accompanied my right leg to the car. He hopped in and took up his usual place in the passenger seat, sniffing curiously at the bloodstains.

"How will I get those out?" I asked him. He cocked his head as if considering the question.

I wondered again about the motivations of the bastard who'd stabbed him. Any reservations about pursuing Ross's attacker vanished in a storm of self-protection. I would do whatever it took to find the creep. Under no circumstances would I end up like Ross.

Chapter Twenty-one

I put Velcro on the breezeway again, and Gambit with him. I left the other three in the house in case someone tried to get in through a window, and did something I almost never do—locked the wrought-iron door to the breezeway.

How could anyone stab a dog? It made no sense. If this person wanted to get in my house, why? After trashing the clinic, stealing my euthanasia solution, and almost murdering Ross, what was left? Me? Was I really a threat? He couldn't know I planned to investigate. I hadn't even made up my mind at the time. Speaking of which, how should I go about that? The only mysteries I dealt with were the medical kind.

So pretend that's what it is. Got to start somewhere.

In a challenging case—the sick dog sort of case—I'd look at history and physical findings first. Then I might run some tests. Was this so different? For coughing, scratching, vomiting, diarrhea, substitute motive, means, and opportunity.

Okay, here goes. Motive: Who wanted Ross dead and why?

That was easy. Whoever killed Umberto. Assuming Ross was attacked because he knew the killer's identity. Which was like saying the dog scratches because he's got an itch. Who wanted Umberto dead? That question lay at the heart of the problem.

Heart problem? *Stop it, Andi, you're being goofy.*

I didn't know enough about Umberto to speculate.

So run some lab tests, take an X ray. Get a better history. Look a little closer at the patient. In other words, find out.

Good, a plan. *Who had opportunity?*

Everyone in the valley, it seemed. Certainly anyone who'd been at the postgame party could have killed Umberto.

Specifically, who? History: the scene *before* the murder scene. Babs flirting with Umberto; Tish fighting with Jaime. Bob Talbot entering then leaving with Babs in tow. Jaime stalking out; Tish following. Ross accusing Umberto, storming out. Umberto leaving. Hal with "a couple more horses to look at." Who could say where he went? Where was Roger Dietrich at the time? Why did he leave his car at the barn? And don't forget the Animal Freedom Fighters were on the grounds.

Instant suspect list. Who among them had opportunity to attack Ross? I could check that out. This wasn't so tough.

Oh, right, we're making loads of progress. How about means?

Did any of these people have medical experience? Hitting a vein took practice. Hal could do it easily, but why would he kill Umberto? He would think of Euthanol as a murder weapon, though. He definitely bore further consideration.

But no matter how sick Ross was, he wouldn't hold still while Hal wormed a needle into him. The biggest question was how. And the hardest to answer. If I knew how, I thought I'd know who.

Another angle: Keys to my clinic—who had access to those? *Does that count as means or opportunity?* Who cared? The keys were Ross's; they had to be. The police would have them now. Ross had them the night he was attacked. But who used them to break in and steal the Euthanol?

What about the Animal Freedom Fighters? The guy at my house could have been the kid who caught me in their van. But would an animal rights activist stab a dog? I needed to talk to them. Their brochure listed a mail drop for donations. Where could I get their real address? Thing was, I wanted them to be the bad guys—an enemy I could despise. I felt threatened by this fringe group.

Careful Andi. You have no proof at all, not even any evidence. Don't treat the kidneys without testing the pancreas.

I entered Indio General with more questions than I'd had when I left home. But at least I had the beginnings of a plan.

Ross's condition had not changed. I sat on the visitor's chair and rested my chin on one knee, staring at him as if he might open his eyes at any moment and explain everything. The mechanical persistence of the equipment pressed in on me. This was a place for dying, and a sense of hopelessness pervaded everything.

Ken O'Grady spoke to me with a certain diffidence, unsure how to treat me. He called me Dr. Pauling, but hesitantly.

"Did you reach his family?" he asked.

"No, I may have better luck tomorrow." I looked around. "How easy would it be for someone to get in here?"

"In the CCU? Only relatives are allowed."

"You let me in."

"And family doctors."

"I'm not—" I shut up too late. "I'm the only person Ross knows in the desert. I am his family until I get hold of someone else. I'm not even sure where his father lives, but I may have found his ex-wife. Tomorrow I'll try his partner." Dietrich.

His eyes narrowed. "What sort of work did he do, anyway?"

"'Did'?"

"Sorry. *Does* he do?"

I decided not to pursue that. "He's a veterinarian."

Tumblers snapped into position behind his eyes, and his features relaxed a little. "You?"

"Me, too."

"You shouldn't be in here."

"Are you going to kick me out?"

He seemed to consider it. "I guess not. Everyone should have visitors."

I doubted Ross could tell, one way or the other. Tonight's visit was for me. "Would you mind if I look at his chart?"

He hesitated, then shrugged and handed me a three-ring binder packed with varicolored pages. I leafed through it, trying to make sense out of the system. Gold sheets for doctors' notes, green ones for the nurses'. Daily chem panels and serum pentobarb levels. Initial blood alcohol .05 percent, opiates and cannabis negative. Hepatitis and HIV tests pending. I flipped to the next page and caught my breath. The results had come in that evening. Ross was HIV positive.

Click. "Damn." I pointed to the entry, thinking that on some level I'd known all along.

"I figured you knew. He's got Kaposi's on his feet."

"He's got what?"

"Kaposi's sarcoma." He flipped the sheet, exposing Ross's legs. Fleshy purplish masses grew there like a fungus. "It's a marker for AIDS. See these scars? He's had some lasered off."

"So he's not just HIV-positive, he's got full-blown AIDS."

"Probably for several months at least."

Oh, Ross. Oh no. "He lived in my house. I gave him CPR. What are the chances . . ." I stopped, ashamed. *Think, Andi. You know how the virus is transmitted. Semen, blood . . .*

Oh, shit.

I stared at the palm of my left hand: a tiny scratch, swelling in reaction to the trace of Euthanol left by the needle as I yanked it from Ross's hand. So minor at the time, hardly noticeable.

Ken shrugged. "Get yourself tested in six months, and don't have unprotected sex before then. And try not to worry." I thought I heard disappointment in his voice, a loss of respect. But this was AIDS we were talking about here.

"Damn him. He could at least have told me."

"You'd have been eager to invite him into your house then."

The sarcasm, however well deserved, rankled. "He never said anything. How long has he had it?"

"There's no way to tell for sure, but probably eight to ten years, maybe more. That's the average time lapse between infection and onset of AIDS."

So he'd carried the virus through vet school, most likely been infected before I even met him. Maybe before the virus had even been isolated. All those years. When did he know? What first caused him to suspect?

"Shouldn't he have been on medication?"

"Probably was. Antispasmodics, Bactrim for pneumocystis—"

More incidents fell into place. "My Di-Trim was gone. It's the veterinary equivalent of Bactrim. He took what he said were vitamins all the time. And he ordered Nizoral on my drug account."

"He must have had a bout of thrush, then." Yeast infection in the mouth and throat. He scribbled in the record. "Plus most AIDS patients take an antiviral drug, if they can tolerate it. AZT, 3TC, Crixivan. And some of them get hold of foreign drugs like Compound Q. Do any of those sound familiar?"

"No. He's a very private person." I stared at my hand.

"Look," Ken said, setting the record aside. "Try not to worry. AIDS is a lot harder to catch than most people think. You're a much greater danger to him than he is to you. With his suppressed immune system, bugs you wouldn't even notice could put him in bed for days. He's getting over an episode of severe diarrhea now."

Ross looked desperately vulnerable with his pale, tumor-ridden legs protruding from beneath the white blanket, and I covered them. I realized I'd never seen him barefoot or even in shorts when he lived in my house. The night he'd fallen asleep and I'd helped him undress, he'd pushed me away. I swiped at suddenly teary eyes. That was the same night I'd almost climbed into his bed. He'd have told me then. Wouldn't he?

"How long before you assume he won't come out of the coma?"

"Depends. Several days, anyway. His doctor is reducing the cerebral edema slowly. Sudden changes can be harmful. The edema might explain part of his condition."

"Why would his brain swell?"

"Tissue hypoxia, cell damage. He wasn't breathing when you found him, right?"

My fingers traced the scratch on my palm. It was beginning to itch. "Brain cells don't regenerate. If they were oxygen-starved long enough they'll die, won't they?"

"It's not that black-and-white. Don't you have these problems in animals?"

"Probably. Not many clients will sustain a comatose animal; it's too expensive and the odds are so bad. CT scans and MRIs are considered exotic for pets. Neurology in veterinary medicine is sort of a premortem phase of pathology."

A smile flickered across his face at the old vet-school truism. I glanced from him to Ross and wondered fleetingly which of our patients got the better deal. Was it possible this really was a suicide attempt? Could I be that far off base?

No. I was badly shaken to learn how much I didn't know about my friend. But it all fell into perspective. Nothing would convince me he'd done this to himself.

"Well," Ken said, "the cells don't regenerate, but

they're pretty tough cells. And he's got billions of them, so even if some die, he may still be functional."

"What do you mean, 'functional'?"

"It depends on the permanent damage. He could remain vegetative or recover completely. More likely he'll wind up somewhere in between. Maybe paralyzed, or he might lose speech or his memory. But if he can learn to take care of himself and hold down a job, then we consider the treatment successful."

I swallowed a bolus of nausea, imagining Ross learning to brush his teeth, stumbling awkwardly across the room, struggling to pronounce my name. Considering his HIV status, who would put effort into his rehabilitation? Did he even have insurance? Maybe we vets had the right idea: a quick, painless injection, permanent oblivion. But who decides for someone like Ross?

Quit that. He might recover. "How did he get it?"

Ken shrugged. He knew I meant the AIDS. "Any of the usual ways."

A polo accident requiring blood transfusion? Could Kelsey . . . ? No, both would be much too recent. Something that happened before I'd even met him.

Was it possible . . . No way. Ross wasn't gay. I'd know.

Of course you would, Andi. After all, you were so quick to pick up on the AIDS.

But he was married. He made a pass at me. Which proved nothing at all.

Was the attack connected to this? A sex partner who thought Ross had exposed her (*him?*) to the virus and wanted revenge? Except no one who knew would place a needle into his vein.

Unless his attacker had nothing to fear from the virus because he was already infected.

Otherwise, maybe I could use it for leverage somehow.

After he went to such lengths to keep it quiet you'd blow his cover?

"Tell me, Ross," I said. "What should I do?"

He lay unresponsive, not even breathing for himself. Hypnotically I traced the scratch across my palm. Fluids dripped in, urine dripped out, and a woman named Melanie came in to hang a bag containing the bright green liquid that comprised Ross's dinner. She connected it to the nasogastric tube and left. Then Ross's bowels moved, Ken hustled me out of the room, and I decided it was a good time to go home.

Home was undisturbed, the dogs fine. Hal had left another message: "Call me soon. I've been trying to reach you for days." If I didn't disillusion him soon, he'd come next Monday to pick me up for that date. I'd have to call him back tomorrow.

I dreamed I treated a dog who'd been hit by a car. Among other things, he'd broken a leg. The owner wanted immediate surgery, but I tried to explain there were internal injuries we had to address first. "The leg won't kill him," I kept saying. "The bleeding might. We've got to consider the whole patient."

The whole patient. The whole murder?

What was I missing?

Chapter Twenty-two

I missed Ross, missed waking to the smell of coffee, missed his casual cynicism and compulsive neatness. He was easy to be with, as long as certain subjects were avoided. I wished I could discuss the murder with him. How had he become such an integral part of my life in so short a time?

As I made coffee my eyes strayed often to the scratch across my palm.

I went to work early, figuring it would be easier to make my calls from the clinic. Velcro followed me closely as I poured another cup of coffee and carried it and the morning paper into the office. I spread the *Desert Sparkler* out on the desk.

Velcro's bloody body looked back at me. The photo near the bottom of the front page was poor-quality black-and-white, but the headline removed any doubt. LOCAL VET'S DOG INJURED IN BURGLARY ATTEMPT. The story rehashed Ross's murder indictment and apparent attempted suicide. It wasn't much of a story, but the picture gave it impact.

How did he get that picture?

His card lay on the desk: "Bud Thorpe, Independent Journalist." He answered on the first ring.

"Thorpe here."

"Who gave you the picture?"

"Dr. Pauling, I presume? Sorry, babe, can't reveal my sources."

"You son of a bitch! You're protecting someone who

knifed a defenseless dog and then documented it! Tell me who!"

"Can't do that. Sorry." He didn't sound sorry. He sounded delighted.

"Why are you doing this?"

"Just going where the story is."

I slammed down the receiver before I gave him anything he could use. I crumpled his card, then thought better of it and dropped it into my purse. I waited until I'd calmed down before dialing Roger Dietrich's number.

I went through three underlings before they let me speak to the man himself. He came on the line with a hearty, "Well, hello, little lady, what can I do you for?"

Great, he's like that sober, too. "Mr. Dietrich, I hope . . ."

"That's Roger to you, little lady. Any friend of Ross is a friend of mine!"

"Um, okay. That's what I was calling about. Ross has a . . . a pretty serious problem, and I hope you can help."

"Not another horse? I can loan him one, I guess, but that's gonna leave me without a spare."

"He won't be playing polo any time soon." I told him the whole story, at least the public-consumption part. I didn't mention AIDS or my dawning suspicions as to how he acquired it.

When I finished he said quietly, "How can I help?"

"Do you know about his family? His father or his ex-wife?"

"Seems like he told me he was *ess*-tranged from his folks. Never said much about that little gal he was married to. Kelly?"

"Kelsey."

"That's her. Played around on him, din't she? Not much point gettin' aholt a her. Let me check with Debbie on that other and have her get back to you. She's in the desert this week."

"Your wife knows Ross's family?"

"Heck, only reason I know him is Debbie and his ex's

ma were real tight. We went to the wedding, had an intro, and I invited Ross to stick-and-ball one day. Surprised the hell—oops, the *heck* outa me when he accepted. Never thought we'd be playin' together in the Springs. Jes' goes to show, I guess, eh?"

This man managed other people's money? "So Debbie would have kept in touch? It does seem like I should let her know. Kelsey, I mean."

"Yeah, I s'pose you're right. We don't see 'em much anymore, but Debbie sends a Christmas card. Dad's name's Dick, ma's Abby, Angie, something. I han't got the number handy, but Deb's got it in her little book. I'll be sure and have her call you with it."

"Would that be Amy? Richard and Amy Vallice?"

"Sounds right. You know 'em?"

"No, it's a pair of names I got from someone. Thanks. I appreciate your help." I hung up wondering why he wouldn't know the names well. Surely he moved in the same social circles?

I called the number I'd written down the day before for Richard and Amy Vallice. It was picked up on the second ring.

"Ye-es," sung the voice of an aging belle.

"Hello, is this Amy Vallice?"

"Yes, it is. Who's callin', please?"

"My name is Andi Pauling. I hope I'm not disturbing you?"

"Not at all. What is this in regards to, if you don't mind my askin'?"

"I went to school with Ross McRoberts, who married a woman named Kelsey Vallice. Are you her mother?"

After a cool pause she said, "We don't speak that name in this house any more."

"Kelsey? Maybe you could tell me—"

"Not Kelsey's name. That other one. That . . . snake disguised as a man."

"Oh, I see." And maybe I did. "Well, I thought I

should tell her he's in the hospital. In a coma. It might be fatal."

"I'm sure she won't mind. I'll certainly let her know. Thank you so much for your call." She hung up gently, too polite to slam down the phone.

Interesting. I wondered what had really happened between Ross and Kelsey.

I saw clients until Debbie Dietrich called at around nine-thirty. I had to keep her on hold while I finished explaining the difference between rabies and distemper shots to a first-time dog owner. After escaping from the exam room I trotted to the office and grabbed the receiver.

"Mrs. Dietrich, are you still there? I'm sorry for keeping you."

A pleasant chuckle. "Don't be silly, you must be terribly busy. If I'd known you were at work, this could have waited till later. Please, call me Debbie. I'm quite sure I have some of the information you've been looking for, and I'm delighted to be of help. Now, you just ask away."

"I just spoke to Amy Vallice. She was . . . a little cool toward Ross."

"I imagine she would be nowadays. Since the annulment they haven't spoken to him, or even *of* him so far as I know. In fact they hardly speak to me, since Roger and he play together."

Annulment? "Isn't that a little extreme? I admit Ross was pretty hostile when I brought up Kelsey's name, the first night he was here. But after all, she was unfaithful, right?"

"Oh, my goodness, where did you hear that? Wait . . . it might be better if we met for lunch. We have a great deal to discuss."

I could make time. "Can you come to Palm Springs?"

"Certainly. I have shopping I can do there. Where shall we meet?"

I considered and quickly rejected El Burrito and settled on Riccio's. She promised to be there at twelve-fifteen.

After hanging up, I got the directory of the American Veterinary Medical Association out. If I could find Ross's practice—if he had a practice—maybe a staff member would know what was going on between Ross and his father.

He wasn't listed. I looked again, both in the alphabetical section and under Lexington, Kentucky. No Ross McRoberts. Weird. Virtually everyone with a D.V.M. belonged to the AVMA. All of my classmates joined on graduation. Why would Ross drop out?

Suddenly nervous, I looked up the Board of Examiners in Sacramento, the organization that oversees veterinarians in California. I asked to verify that a certain vet was licensed. They'd never heard of him.

Damn. I'd taken his word, never thought to check. A big strike against me in the impending lawsuit. What other ugly truths lay waiting for my discovery?

My fresh anger at Ross might have caused me to drop the whole search were it not for my lunch date with Debbie Dietrich.

She was waiting when I arrived, cool and sophisticated in winter-white leggings and a jeweled pullover, her blond hair tied back in a short ponytail.

We made small talk until our food came. She seemed nervous, but I didn't know her well enough to say for sure. I was still wondering how to tell her Ross had AIDS. Under the table my fingers traced the scratch on my palm. Finally, as Debbie toyed with her salad, I asked her why he and Kelsey had broken up.

She studied me for a moment before answering. "She caught him in bed with a jockey. A man," she said flatly, then watched to gauge the impact of her statement.

The room tilted. I took a few deep breaths, waiting to speak until I trusted my voice. *It's okay, I can deal with this.* "He told me *he* caught *her* with a jockey." *What else did he lie about?*

"Ross has his own way of looking at things."

"Why did your husband team up with him, knowing he was, well . . ." I assumed middle-aged southern gentlemen were overwhelmingly homophobic. *Careful with those assumptions, Andi.*

"Don't be silly," she said. "Roger doesn't know. He'd drop him like a hot stone. Ross probably told him the same story he told you. And don't you dare tell him any different, you hear?" She took a small bite of lettuce and sipped her iced tea.

"I don't understand. Why do you protect Ross from your husband, knowing how he feels?"

She sighed, setting her fork down on her plate. She wore a diamond bracelet on her right hand. Now she played with it. "That's a long story, and really quite personal. But I suppose you deserve an explanation. My son, Ricky—he'd be thirty-one now." She blinked and looked at the wall, the table, the carpeted floor. "He had the same . . . problem? Condition? I thought he could overcome it, sort of a passing phase, a . . . choice? I begged him to change. My reasons . . . God help me, I wanted grandchildren." She shook her head, obviously struggling against tears.

"Ricky died six years ago of AIDS, but he shut me out of his heart long before. Lord, it took a long time to accept. Maybe I still haven't, quite. Ricky had no more control over that aspect of his life than I did, and I only made it more difficult by assuming he did. Unfortunately, I understood this too late to mend fences with my son." She blinked furiously and dabbed at her eyes with her napkin, smearing her mascara.

"Didn't your husband go through the same thing?"

She smiled sadly and shook her head. "Ricky wasn't Roger's son. He was from another marriage, when I was very young. He and Roger never did see eye to eye. I always blamed it on Roger's resentment of my first husband, but I think he somehow knew, even before Ricky did. Roger despises homosexuals. Ricky's death almost ruined our marriage."

Her tone, despite the tears, was calm and neutral, far removed from the content of her words. I had lots of gay clients, many of them my favorites. But as far as I knew, none of my close friends qualified. Except, I now realized, Ross. Was that deliberate, even if unconscious? Like Debbie, I would have to work at this for a long time.

"How could I not see it?" I asked, not expecting an answer. "Why didn't I know?"

She reached over and squeezed my calloused right hand with her soft, manicured fingers, and my own eyes filled. We smiled at each other in a moment of empathy. But the fingers of my left hand traced the scratch on my palm. *Would she touch me if she knew?*

"Andi," she said, "it's not your fault, or even your responsibility. We see what we expect to see, what others want us to see. You were Ross's last chance to live what he thought of as a normal life. He didn't ask your permission. He used you. You can either let him continue doing so, or you can move on. But at least make a decision with your eyes open."

Wow. I'd be working on that one for a long time. "What it must be like for you, protecting Ross from your own husband. After what happened, wouldn't it be all over town?"

"Of course there have been rumors, but Dick and Amy hushed it as much as possible. They gave him a good filly to keep him quiet, but even that wasn't necessary. Ross categorically denied he was gay. He claimed it was a onetime thing, that they'd both been on drugs. He fought his homosexuality, though I understand his and Kelsey's relationship was never quite, well, normal. Amy told me. She had to talk to someone. My knowing destroyed our friendship."

"There's something else Kelsey needs to know." I took a deep breath and rushed on. "Ross has AIDS. They can't tell how long he's had it, but he was probably already infected when he married Kelsey. She needs to be tested."

"I'll try to let her know. If I can find a discreet way." Her eyes said she saw the urgency and would tell her, somehow.

"What about Ross's father?"

"I haven't seen him since the wedding."

"I think he lives in Nebraska." I told her about the strange phone conversation. "Directory Assistance gave me the same number. Damn, I'll bet the Vallices know. I hate to ask, but do you think you could . . ."

"Of course. Let me get back to you. Better yet, I'll see you at the polo club this weekend. But I'll say this. If Ross's father is anything like Roger, and he learned that Ross is gay, he'll have disowned him completely. It would be the worst possible blow to his personal manhood. He'd have to pretend it didn't exist."

"Pretend the son didn't exist, you mean." She nodded as we got up to leave.

We hugged briefly in the parking lot, and I drove back to the clinic with my emotions in a tangled net. The dominant feeling was sympathy for Ross, but close beneath it lay self-pity. Why me? Why AIDS? I didn't want to die, not now and not in ten years. I'd been trying to help.

But if you'd just gotten there sooner, he'd have been fine.

I really had to quit thinking like that. Deal with the situation that exists, not what might have been. That could drive me around the bend if I let it.

What's it like, I wondered, discovering you're gay? How old had he been? How did he know?

I recalled thinking, when Ross first arrived, that he seemed at peace somehow, like a man who'd come to terms with himself. I was thinking in terms of the day-to-day weaknesses we all face. But I now realized that what I'd seen was a man who knew he was dying, had accepted the inevitable, and was making a final grand gesture toward the life to which he'd always aspired.

"Polo," I said out loud. "That's my Ross."

Did anyone know the real Ross? His whole life was a lie, so why should he balk at lying to me? The image he carried of himself was strong and tough, cool and respected. Anything that failed to meet this expectation he simply ignored. Unfortunately, that seemed to encompass most of the truth.

As soon as I entered my office, Sheila was on the intercom. "Could you come up front for a minute?" Her voice was agitated.

"Whatever it is, Sheila, deal with it."

Seconds later she appeared in the doorway. "Mrs. Artimas is here, and she wants her medical files. She's getting, like, real belligerent."

Damn. Of all the people I least wanted to see, that woman topped the list. Velcro, who'd been left in the office all morning, seemed to sense my anxiety. He whined and glued himself to my leg, tagging along as I followed Sheila.

"Hello, Mrs. Artimas. I'm sure you know we shouldn't communicate without our attorneys present."

"I certainly had no intention of speaking with you. Where's your partner?"

"If you mean Dr. McRoberts, my *associate* is ill. Please have your attorney contact mine if you want something." I turned to go.

"I fired my lawyer. The new one wants the record. That file belongs to me, young lady. Now you just tell your secretary here to hand it over, or I'll sue the pants off you."

"I'm afraid I can't give it to you."

Velcro sidled over to her and curled himself around her knees, wriggling his back end and grinning up at her. Traitor.

"I'm not leaving without that record. It's mine."

"No, it isn't."

"It is. I know my rights."

"This isn't one of them."

"Young lady, you give me that file or I'll come back there and take it!"

Velcro's head swung back and forth as we parried, and his tail stub wiggled indecisively. A dull ache began in my temples.

"That file is a permanent legal document, and the law requires me to keep it for three years," I told her. "I mailed a copy to your other attorney. I'm sure he'll forward it to the new one." *May this one have a better grasp of reality,* I silently prayed.

Velcro whined with pleasure as Mrs. Artimas reached down absently and rubbed his right ear. She glanced down at him.

"Buffy always liked that. What's your name, sweetie?"

"Velcro, come here," I said sharply. The little scoundrel ignored me.

"Velcro, eh? For the stubble, I bet. What happened to you, anyway?" She addressed the dog while clearly expecting me to answer. I rolled my eyes at Sheila, who was doing her look-up-through-the-bangs routine.

"He had a series of accidents," I said harshly. "The last one with a knife."

She gasped and I quickly corrected myself. "Someone tried to break into my house. He got in the way. Barely survived." Apparently she hadn't seen the morning's *Desert Sparkler.*

"Oh, dear! You poor, brave baby!" She bent over, holding his face in her hands. He gazed soulfully back, thumping his short tail against the floor. "What are these other stitches?"

I gave in and told her the whole story while a couple of other people in the waiting room listened with amazement. Clients were arriving for their afternoon appointments, and I wanted her out before she said anything else.

"I'll get you a photocopy of that record," I said. The

file was in my office. Sheila led a client into an exam room, leaving Velcro in the lobby with Mrs. Artimas and a man with a sick Amazon parrot. I copied as fast as I could and hurried back with the sheaf of pages in a brand-new folder.

She took the file, and I tried to pry Velcro away from her.

"What a sweet thing that was, taking him away from that awful woman! You really do care about animals, don't you?"

I gave her my professional smile, biting my lower lip to prevent myself from answering that question my usual way: *It's a pretty stupid way to make a living, otherwise.*

"So you understand how I feel about losing Buffy due to your incompetence. And why I have to sue you."

Great, I thought, glancing at the last client in the room. *Why don't I just hang a sign out. The woman actually expects me to agree with her.*

"Mrs. Artimas, if that's all . . ."

"And now he has a happy new home."

"I'm not sure what I'm going to do with him. He doesn't get along with the other dogs."

"Well, of course you'll keep him!" Her command sent guilty ripples over my conscience.

She frowned at him, then at me, probably changing her mind about my compassion. I grabbed Velcro just before he darted out the door by her side. He gazed anxiously from me to the closing door.

"Honestly," I said to him, "what am I going to do with you?"

Nobody in the room had an answer, not even the parrot.

Chapter Twenty-three

The phone rang shortly after six. We were officially closed, but I hated to disappoint a client. I switched off the answering machine, picked up the receiver, and impersonated a receptionist.

"Dr. Doolittle's, may I help you?"

"I'd like to speak to, ah, Dr. Pauling." The soft, feminine voice bore the same unmistakable southern inflection as Debbie Dietrich's but was considerably more hesitant.

"This is Andi Pauling."

That peculiar kind of pause ensued that only happens long distance. I could almost hear AT&T rubbing their hands together as the charges accrued, but they were someone else's charges, and I sensed my caller needed time to gather her thoughts.

"This is Kelsey Vallice. We met several years ago?" Her voice, a powdery contralto, conjured an image of the woman I vaguely remembered: poised and slender, unobtrusive, with perfect hair—brown, I thought, or a deep auburn; memory missed a step here—and makeup that never smeared.

"Of course, Kelsey. I'm sorry I missed the wedding." Maybe mentioning it was a mistake. "Anyway, I'm relieved that you called. Did you speak to Debbie?"

"Yes. Thank God. My mother's . . . I heard her, when you phoned? That was you? I wanted to speak to you when I realized what it was about but, well . . ."

"What did she tell you?"

"I understand there's been an accident, and that Ross is in the hospital?"

"He's in a coma. The prognosis is still uncertain." I didn't say, "and gets worse every day that there's no improvement." She would know that soon enough if she didn't already.

"I'd like to come down."

"Here?"

"He isn't in Palm Springs? Perhaps I misunderstood. . . ."

"No, no, he's here. I'm just surprised. I thought you never wanted to see him or even hear his name again."

"That's my mother. I'll explain when I see you. Can you recommend a good hotel near the hospital?"

Should I invite her to stay with me? She'd have to sleep on the foldout so recently vacated by her ex-husband. What did etiquette dictate? Screw that. I couldn't handle the idea. "Let me make a reservation for you, and I'll meet you at the airport. Call when you know your arrival time." I gave her my home number and said good-bye. Her voice had reflected only concern for Ross. I wondered whether she knew about his having AIDS.

I swiped another chew toy from the display and took Velcro home. He was growing accustomed to the routine and seemed content to go on this way. Still, I felt guilty for locking him up on the breezeway, even with Gambit for company. I left them both gnawing contentedly, and went to visit Ross.

Ken was off but he'd left instructions for the other nurses to let me in. An orderly or nurse's aide wearing scrubs, gown, cap, mask, eye shield, shoe covers, and latex gloves was bent over Ross's bed when I arrived. He looked like a pale blue mummy.

All that to protect himself from Ross? I trailed my fingers over the innocent-looking scratch on my palm for the hundredth time that day. It itched slightly, beginning to heal. I paused at the work station to scan his chart before going in.

"Any improvement?" I asked one of the female nurses I remembered from the first night.

She ran a hand through shoulder-length blond hair. "His EEG showed some new activity this afternoon, and he's begun to move his hands. Nothing purposeful yet, but . . ."

A high-pitched squeal emanated from one of the monitors. She glanced up irritably, clearly expecting the trouble to be mechanical rather than medical. Then she ran into Ross's room, ignoring me when I followed.

"Code Blue!" she yelled over her shoulder. Another nurse picked up a red telephone and spoke into it: *"Code blue, Neuro three thirty-seven."* She repeated it and hung up while a third nurse wheeled in the crash cart. It held drugs and fluids, a defibrillator, and a litter of plastic-wrapped items I couldn't identify.

I stood, horrified, wedged against the tiny sink, as they slammed drugs into his IV line, pumped frantically on his chest, and applied the defibrillator paddles.

"Stand back!"

The charge jolted Ross's body, and they stared at the monitor screen waiting for a response. I watched helplessly as the white line danced a tortured jig across the screen, relaying activity that bore no relation to that of a functional heart.

"Okay, again."

The ventilator continued to force oxygen in and out of his lungs, but the heart refused to deliver it to his body's starving tissues. A third jolt was no more effective.

Then the doors flew open and God walked in. Six and a half feet of confidence and surgical garb, he crossed the work space in three strides and snapped a second layer of latex over already-gloved hands.

The nurses practically tripped over each other in their haste to get out of the way. The doctor glanced at the monitor and barked a few questions at the nurses, instantly assessing the situation. He held out a hand, and a nurse placed a scalpel in the palm. With no hesitation, he opened Ross's chest.

The complex incision took all of three seconds. Skin parted like butter; a tiny saw split the sternum. Then a huge gloved hand descended into Ross's thorax and massaged his flaccid heart.

I leaned against the sink and willed away a sudden, violent nausea. I would *not* create a distraction by passing out. I looked away from the spectacle on the bed and up at the monitor.

Ross's oxygen saturation crept slowly up from less than 50 to a life-sustaining 82 percent. The pulse wave, still uneven, at least registered on the screen. The doctor continued to call for drugs. Nurses hung IV bags like Christmas ornaments.

Finally a nurse opened a pair of delicate sterile paddles for the doctor, who placed them inside Ross's chest. The cables were connected to the defibrillator. Everyone stepped back as an electrical charge jerked the heart. Then five pairs of eyes traveled upward, and we stared at the monitor screen.

The line jiggled and hopped off its baseline in what resembled an R wave. This was quickly followed by a spiky T, then a few more drunken complexes. And it began to stabilize. I glanced down to see the rhythmic wobble of Ross's heart within his gaping thorax, before the ventilator-inflated lungs obscured the opening.

"All *right*!" said the nurse who'd first called the code.

"Yes!" Another leaned against the far wall. Even through the masks I could tell everyone in the room was relieved and a little giddy. Except for Ross, of course, whose only job right now was to keep his heart beating while the doctor packed his suddenly bloody chest cavity with sterile saline dressings and covered him with a green drape. I blinked away tears of relief, watching his sats climb into the nineties.

"Let's get him to the O.R.," the doctor ordered. "Get

me a panel. And gases. *Now!* I want to know why this happened."

A nurse drew several vials of blood from Ross's arm and a syringeful from an arterial catheter in his thigh. She labeled them and rushed out while another nurse phoned the lab and the third produced a gurney. A couple of orderlies appeared and helped the nurses transfer Ross. He was switched to a portable ventilator, and the IV bags were transferred to a hanger attached to the gurney. The complicated monitor was disconnected, a portable pulse oximeter substituted. They pushed him past me toward the unit's swinging doors, moving quickly but without desperation.

The doctor had removed his gloves and stepped out of the room. I followed hesitantly.

"Who are you?" he demanded, turning to me so suddenly, I gaped mutely for a moment before I could answer.

"A—Andi Pauling. I was visiting when he, when the arrest—"

"You his wife?"

"No, I'm his classmate, ah, friend."

"What are you doing in CCU?"

"Visiting. I'm the only person Ross knows in the desert."

"Out," he commanded, stripping off his cap and mask and tossing them into a bag at the side of the cart. His bald head gleamed, and I wondered if he polished it. "Relatives only."

"But I . . . Who was the man in here when I arrived?" I followed him as he left the CCU and moved into the hall, in the direction Ross had been wheeled.

"Who?"

"When I got here, someone in blue scrubs, full gown, and mask was in Ross's room. I assumed he was bathing him or something, so I waited until he left. Ross coded very soon after that, but the man had disappeared."

He tossed me a scornful glance. "A man wearing

scrubs and a mask. You've just described fifty percent of the staff here. The other half are female."

"Why did he go into arrest?"

"That's what we're trying to find out." His long legs moved purposefully; I had trouble keeping up. "The lab report will be faxed to O.R. prep. You can't go in here."

He swept the door out of his way and stepped through. The sign said SURGERY PREP—AUTHORIZED PERSONNEL ONLY. I stopped as the doors swung shut behind the doctor's arrogant back.

He had to close the incision under sterile conditions. How long could that take? I waited, pacing the corridor.

He emerged some forty-five minutes later, carrying a sheet of paper in his right hand.

"How is he?" I asked, falling into step beside him again.

"You're still here? He survived the procedure. That's all I can tell you."

"What did the lab work tell you?"

He handed me the page he'd been carrying. "See for yourself."

I tried to scan it and keep up with him at the same time.

"You going to follow me into the men's room, too?" he asked.

Glancing up, I stopped short of going in. I waited outside, studying the report. When he emerged, wearing chinos and a button-down shirt, a maroon tie dangling around his neck, I was ready for him.

"His potassium's nine-point-six! That's twice what's normal! High enough to stop the heart if it happened suddenly."

He stopped and turned to me. "What do you know about potassium levels?"

I'd finally gotten his attention. "I'm a veterinarian. Andi Pauling." I offered my hand, and he shook it automatically.

"So you are." He wasn't impressed, but I could tell he

hadn't expected me to know anything about the lab report, either. "So you tell *me* why it's up."

He was waiting, and I sensed this was a test. I chewed my lip, staring at the blurry numbers on the fax paper. In dogs, the most common cause of high potassium levels is kidney failure. Ross had good urine production, and his BUN was normal. I didn't know much about blood gas interpretation, but the pH seemed fine, too. I half shrugged. "I don't see any explanation here."

"Sorry to hear that. I hoped you'd have it all figured out." He threw the comment over his shoulder as he walked away.

"Wait," I said, hurrying to catch up. "That's what I was trying to say earlier. That person in his room earlier—someone may have tried to kill him."

He stopped so suddenly, I almost crashed into him.

"That's it!" he said, slapping his forehead in mockery. "Who wouldn't want to kill him? He's an obvious threat to world stability, lying there in a coma."

His sarcasm cut me, but I persisted. "Whoever failed the first time might have tried again."

"I don't think he was in a position to try it again. I understand this was self-inflicted."

"Only the police think it was attempted suicide."

"But you're too smart for that."

"You'd have to know him. He couldn't do it. They're wrong."

"You believe someone tried to kill him."

"Twice."

"Here, in my hospital."

"Um . . ."

"Impossible." He turned and started walking again. I was getting tired, and I hadn't just finished surgery. This man's energy level matched his arrogance. Thankfully, so did his skill. Because of him, Ross was still alive. More or less.

Just then a scrub-clad nurse jogged up to him from the direction of the O.R. and handed him a new report.

"The post-op results on the open re-suss," he said, and trotted away.

As unobtrusively as possible, I looked over the doctor's elbow as he studied the page.

"Six-point-eight now. That's a pretty steep drop," I said.

He glanced at me irritably. "More likely the first set was erroneous."

"Injecting undiluted potassium into the IV could stop the heart." I knew my persistence irritated him, but I was tired of his bullying. "With rapid fluid administration, such as with resuscitation, it would be diluted quickly."

We stared at each other for a minute, until he blinked and looked back down at the page. His fingers massaged his upper lip as if expecting to find a mustache. He started walking again, back toward the CCU, but this time he motioned me to come along.

"What else can you tell me about the person you saw?"

I struggled to call up the image. "I didn't get a good look. I assumed it was an orderly, or a nurse's aide."

"White? Black?"

"I'm not sure. His back was to me. He was slender, I think, but with the bulky gown . . ."

"Are you sure it was a man?"

I looked up, surprised. Under all those layers, from outside the room, I couldn't swear to anything. "I guess not."

"Hair color?"

"Couldn't tell. It was all covered by the cap."

"All of it? Usually there's enough sticking out at the bottom to identify color. And the caps themselves aren't opaque."

I shook my head, frustrated. "No, I'm sure the hair was completely covered. It was a hood-style cap, wrapped around his chin, like yours. That's why I thought it was a man, possibly with a beard."

"Maybe he was bald." One hand massaged his own smooth scalp while the other tapped a few buttons on the code pad outside the door to the Neurology Unit. His earlier scorn was replaced with an ironic wit and genuine curiosity.

As we entered the unit the nurses looked up.

The doctor said, "Anyone here let in a gowned man or woman just before three thirty-seven coded?"

One of the blond nurses shook her head. The other said, "I thought I saw a woman. She came in behind Melanie."

"Get her."

We waited while the nurse dialed and asked for Melanie. The doctor took the receiver and inquired whether she'd come in alone. Then he asked whether someone had come in behind her. He waited, then hung up abruptly.

"Someone followed her in. Her impression was a man, from the way he moved, but she's not sure, either. She thought it was an orderly who'd forgotten the code. Goddammit!"

"Who has access to all that garb?"

He glanced at me, frustrated. "Almost anyone. It's readily accessible so staff can gown up in an emergency." He gestured toward one of the ubiquitous tall carts, which held sterile linens, absorbent pads, bandage materials, and, yes, disposable protective garb.

Anyone who'd been in a critical care unit, either as a patient or a visitor, would know this was available. Polo players were injured regularly. I hadn't narrowed the list down at all.

"Will Ross recover from this?" I asked.

"Can't tell. He already had brain dysfunction. This will set him back, to say the least. Who'd try to kill a comatose patient?"

"I wish I knew. What are we going to do about it?"

"*We* aren't going to do anything. I'll get hospital security." He reached again for the phone.

"Wait," I said. "They can't be with him constantly. I

may know a better way to prevent this from happening again."

"What are you talking about?"

"Let Ross die."

Chapter Twenty-four

I rummaged through my purse for a rumpled business card: "Bud Thorpe, Independent Journalist." Then I explained.

The doctor's eyes narrowed as I spoke, and he continually stroked his upper lip, resting one elbow in the other hand. I learned his name, Wesley Hostettler. He was a thoracic surgeon, not Ross's admitting physician. That explained some of the arrogance, I supposed. And the skill. He'd simply been available when the call went out. As I described my plan, his eyes gradually took on a gleam of excitement.

"We sometimes alter the identity of gang members," he said slowly. "When there's a threat. Even those involved in the patient's care might not know who he is. I can't see why this should be different. A patient of mine died in Cardiac tonight, a transfer. Your friend can borrow his identity for a while."

We spent the next half hour fiddling with medical records.

I dialed the number on the card. It was picked up on the first ring.

"Thorpe here."

I tried to sound grief-stricken. "This is Dr. Andi Pauling. I thought you'd like to know that Ross McRoberts passed away tonight." The words came out bitter and accusing. Perfect.

"Hold on! What—"

I hung up, knowing he would call the switchboard for confirmation.

Kelsey's flight arrived Friday at four forty-five. I jogged through the front doors of the small airport at five-thirty feeling guilty and inept, castigating myself for not just telling her to take a cab. I'd been delayed by an illegally kept ferret with hormonal bone marrow suppression whose owner, after arriving unannounced, feigned shock at the cost of an emergency hysterectomy. It was the only condition I knew how to treat in ferrets, and I was looking forward to it. She took up an hour of my time before agreeing to the procedure. But it had gone well, and I expected a full recovery.

Then Sheila caught me as I was getting in my car. Lara was on the phone. I grumbled my way to the front desk and reached across the counter to grab the receiver.

"I'm already late; what's another ten minutes?" I said.

"Won't be that long. Got the analysis on that vial from Gutiérrez's pocket. Something called streptokinase. Mean anything?"

I called up a dim memory from sophomore pharmacology class. "Streptokinase. It's a proteolytic enzyme—"

"Pro-*what*?"

"An enzyme that breaks down proteins. It's used to dissolve blood clots in human heart attack patients. It's ungodly expensive. Thousands of dollars a dose." What was Umberto doing with a vial of it in Ross's barn late at night? I wondered what it might do if injected into a horse. "What about the syringe?"

"Isopropyl alcohol."

"Rubbing alcohol? Weird. Whatever Umberto had in mind that night, I'll bet it would have cost Ross another horse."

I was still wondering how as I scanned the small airport foyer. Kelsey sat alone with a copy of the local paper. She looked severely shaken and incapable of even such a simple task as hailing a taxi.

"Kelsey, I'm sorry. . . ."

"Why didn't you call me? My God, why did you let me find out this way?" She held up the paper, and I saw the headline I'd been too busy to look at before.

"No, wait, he's not dead! Damn, I never thought . . ."

"He is. He's dead. Didn't you see it? Look." She pointed to the article. On the front page, under Bud Thorpe's byline: MURDER SUSPECT DIES IN HOSPITAL FOLLOWING SUICIDE ATTEMPT. Ordinarily the death of a critically ill patient in the hospital would warrant little notice, but the circumstances were fairly unusual here, and it had been a slow news day.

"I should have found some way to warn you. Come on. Let's get in the car and find a place to have a drink, and I'll try to explain." I touched her shoulder. She visibly stiffened, and in that instant my paranoia kicked in. *She knows I've been exposed to the virus.* Then she stood, and I saw that her tension was unrelated to me and my personal concerns. The paper fell to the floor and I retrieved it.

I was surprised she brought only a carry-on bag. I'd pegged her as the type to bring three suitcases for a weekend stay.

If I remembered right, Kelsey was twenty-six or -seven now. She had aged dramatically in five-plus years. Her deep auburn hair showed no gray, but the skin around her eyes was punctuated by lines even Clinique couldn't disguise. She'd put ten pounds or so on her gaunt frame, which would have looked good except she wasn't keeping in shape. Her shoulders slumped, possibly from the combined effects of a long plane trip and the shattering newspaper article.

I drove to El Burrito because it was close and familiar, though probably not the sort of place Kelsey expected to encounter in a town with such an elegant reputation.

"This reminds me of some of the racetrack bars," she said as we sat down. "I think I'll have a beer."

I hid my surprise and said, "I knew we had something

in common." I ordered two Coors Lights and took a minute to scan the paper, relishing the embarrassment Bud Thorpe would experience when the true facts came out. By then I hoped Ross would be out of the killer's reach.

I told Kelsey the whole story. Horror, concern, skepticism, and outright disbelief chased each other across her wide-set green eyes, each displayed at exactly the right moment. She was an easy person to tell a story to.

When I mentioned the HIV she winced and nodded but expressed no concern for herself. "I was tested last year when I went to work for my father's company and applied for medical insurance. I wouldn't be worried anyway." She flushed crimson, staring fixedly at her beer, running her finger around the edge of the glass. Was she telling me she was married to the man for nearly a year and they'd never had sex? Or didn't she believe the virus could be transmitted that way? I couldn't bring myself to ask. Absently I traced the scratch on my palm.

"Could we go to the hospital now?" she asked.

I drove to her hotel first. We dropped her bag in the room and headed for Indio General.

Dr. Hostettler had left instructions that Kelsey and I be allowed to visit "his" patient, Ivan Aronson, whose records indicated that he had been moved to Cardiac CCU the night before, following transfer from another hospital and an emergency thoracotomy, with resulting anesthetic complications. Ross's records had been credibly confused by repeated passage through the intrahospital fax system, his new identity superimposed. According to the chart, Mr. Aronson was a forty-year-old accountant and a heavy smoker with a history of epilepsy. Hostettler had assured me that Ross's neurologist was a close friend, and care would continue uninterrupted. Once started, the good doctor had proven himself exceedingly skilled at duplicity.

Ross, unfortunately, couldn't appreciate the efforts made on his behalf. Whatever improvement he'd shown the previous day was completely negated by the cardiac arrest. He lay oblivious to visitors and attendants alike.

Kelsey let out a short cry when she recognized him, and slumped into the bedside chair. She clutched his hand, which lay flaccid and unresponsive in hers. "He's cold," she whispered.

A glance at the monitor showed his temperature at a steady 98.5. I showed her the parts of the display I'd been able to decipher.

"Andi, thank you for taking care of him. He doesn't have anyone. He's always been like that, so independent. If not for you, he would have died. I'm sure of it."

I still wasn't convinced I'd done Ross any favors. We both stared at the screen for a while; the ventilator made the only sound in the room.

"Why did you come?" I asked quietly.

"He was once my husband. I do love him, as much as he allowed anyone to."

An interesting choice of words. "Your mother said—"

"My mother doesn't speak for me, no matter what she may think. She finds the whole affair desperately embarrassing." She spoke with a bitterness that clashed with the soft inflections of her voice.

"Do you want to tell me what happened between you two?"

She gazed at Ross for a moment, as if willing him to wake up and tell the story for her. I refrained from mentioning his version. What good would it do?

When she spoke, the words seemed to come from far away and blended with the cadence of the respirator that continued to fill Ross's lungs.

"We met at a student horse show. I was a senior, at Clancy Equestrian College?" She squared her shoulders briefly, giving me a quick glimpse of her pride in this fact. I'd known this, and it was one more thing I held against her. Clancy was an elite private college attended almost exclusively by women from wealthy families. We university students had always regarded it as a late-twentieth-century finishing school.

Kelsey continued. "Ross was one of the vet students who volunteered to monitor the show? I spotted him right off." She smiled wistfully. "He was so good-looking, and the other students seemed to look up to him. Like he was their leader."

"Ross?" I couldn't hide my surprise at her take on Ross's bossy detachment.

She glanced at the form on the bed as if afraid Ross might hear, then smiled self-consciously. That smile reminded me of the poised beauty Ross flaunted the last month of school. No one had seen him with a woman other than me before. They watched to see how I'd react, and I knew I hadn't done well.

"And there I was," she went on, "totally inept at anything but riding. I couldn't imagine what he might see in me." She glanced from Ross to me. "I was taking this class, in self-assertiveness? I went after him, sort of as an exercise. I talked a friend into introducing us."

Our eyes met and we both laughed out loud. I wondered if she knew that Ross's classmates perceived her as a hopeless snob when she failed to make friends among them or their spouses. I recalled feeling distinctly inferior, besides being jealous.

"Well, anyway, it worked," I said. "The time he spent in Lexington during senior year—was that with you?"

"I was still in Columbia, and we weren't that serious yet." She blushed. "But he wanted to make connections there, so I made some calls for him. And I went back a couple of times—he was in Kentucky over Christmas."

How well I remembered. I'd received an impersonal card and a note: "Love Bluegrass Country. Think I'll stay." Throughout a miserable holiday on ICU duty, I'd tortured myself wondering whether I should have responded to Ross's advance the night before he left. But it was a viciously cold New Year's, and by the time classes resumed, I was firing off résumés to every southern California hospital advertising for help. He'd gotten married so quickly—it could easily have been to me. Pushing Ross away that night turned out to be one of the most important decisions in my life.

Kelsey had fallen silent, staring at the monitor screen. She was unconsciously breathing in time with the ventilator. I studied her profile for a minute.

"What about the breakup?" I finally asked.

She sighed deeply. "Ronny DiBartolo broke my filly's maiden. He's this tiny man, about my age but he looks older, the way jockeys always seem to? God, he can ride."

I let the silence linger until she continued.

"We all went out to celebrate that night. Ross and I had our problems, but that night everything was perfect. Then Ronny said he had to get up the next morning to work a horse. Ross asked him for a ride home since I wasn't ready to leave. I was thinking he might surprise me with—it sounds silly now, but I hoped he'd find a private way to congratulate me. Anyway, the party broke up about thirty minutes later and I left alone.

"When I got home Ronny's Ferrari was in the driveway. I was going to ask him to move it so I could put my car in the garage. They weren't in the living room, so I called their names. They didn't answer but I heard . . . I went back and they . . . they were there . . . together. On the bed." She was breathing faster, but her voice remained soft and somewhat detached. "I don't know who was more shocked, though he must have expected me home. He said they were drunk, he didn't know what he was doing, blamed it all on Ronny. As if a hundred-pound man could force him.

"It explained so much," she finished.

"I'm sorry I asked. It really isn't my business."

She waved my apology away. "I thought everything was my fault. Things were never right between us. He could never—I used to buy clothes so I'd look more feminine, sexier. What a joke. I always thought there was something wrong with me."

"He let you think that, rather than admit the truth."

"What is the truth for Ross? It was awful for me, but it was a hundred times worse for him. With the way his father brought him up . . ." She looked me in the eye. "He despises himself."

"You still care, don't you?"

"Of course I do. I told you, I love Ross. I just couldn't be married to him."

I wanted to ask about something more pleasant. "Tell me about the Alydar filly?"

"She was mine. Ours, but Daddy meant her for me. He had four racehorses, and he gave me this gorgeous two-year-old, for a wedding present. You should have seen her: She was this glowing chestnut, golden red with no white anywhere. The sun would glint off her back. . . ." She shook her head sadly.

"I'd never quite . . . approved of racing before, I suppose, but Daddy adores it. He never misses when one of his colts runs. I think he gave me the filly to show me, you know, what it was like? To be around the lifestyle. And Ross was busy; he said he was building a practice. So I decided to train my own filly." She tossed me a defiant glance, as if expecting me to protest.

"Sounds like fun," I said truthfully.

Her expression relaxed and she continued. "The trainer worked with me, and I broke Cash from the start. She was a fast learner. And we had this rapport—"

"What was her name?" I asked more sharply than I'd intended.

"Hm? Oh, Cash was her nickname. Her registered name was Alyourmoney, one word like that. It's a play on the name Alydar. A lot of his babies get names that start with *Aly*. And her mama was by a horse called Ante Up. Daddy called her Alyourmoney because he swore that's what Ross was after: the trust fund Grampa left for me to inherit on my wedding day."

All your money. *Alyourmoney.* The man at the polo grounds hadn't been demanding cash, he'd wanted *Cash.* Who was he?

"So your parents never approved of the marriage?"

"Daddy didn't, and my mother always agreed with him, even when she didn't. Oh, but don't think . . ." Her brows furrowed.

"Don't worry about what I think. I'm glad you came, and I'd like to hear the rest. Please go on."

She gave a nervous, relieved smile. "Anyway, when they saw I would marry him no matter what, they pretended to go along with it, for the sake of appearances. They always told me I'd be sorry."

"Were you?"

She appeared to think this one over for a long time, staring alternately at her ex-husband's slack features and the shapes dancing across the monitor screen. Then she looked at me.

"No, I never regretted my involvement with Ross. It's the only time in my life I felt . . ." She groped for a word. "Real."

Chapter Twenty-five

Kelsey patted Ross's arm and stared at him while she spoke.

"Ross has his problems, and I guess a lot of them are related to his sexual identity. He's very manipulative—I guess you know that—and not just with people. He sees things the way he wants to. But Andi, please try to understand." She placed a hand on my wrist for emphasis. "He *does* things. He gets his hands dirty; he takes what he wants. He . . . he makes things happen. After he passes through, your life isn't like it was before. Nothing matters in Ross's world but Ross. Do you know how fascinating that is when you've always put yourself last? That's how I was raised, like a good southern lady." Once more the bitterness in her voice contrasted with her soft facade.

"You had the strength to defy your parents and marry him," I pointed out.

"Only because he gave it to me. He was always there for me, always knew what to say to make me strong. Sometimes I hated him, because he made me hate myself, but I always realized I was only seeing my true self. He was showing me how to change."

Looking at her, I saw what Ross must have seen: a lovely, vulnerable woman with a stainless-steel backbone she herself barely knew existed. "What you describe comes awfully close to emotional abuse," I said gently.

Shock swept her features. "Oh no! Ross never abused

me! He only—oh, how can you understand? You've always been so strong. He *needed* me. No one had ever done that. I was important to him, and he meant everything to me. So I became important to myself, because I was valuable in his eyes." Her expression pleaded with me to comprehend.

I thought I did. "You never lost touch with him, did you?"

"No."

"Did you send him the money for bail? And attorney's fees?"

"Of course. Sixty thousand dollars. It was a loan. I knew he could never kill anyone, and when it was all over he'd pay me back."

He had fifty thousand when he had to make bail. He gave me another six. What became of the other four thousand dollars? "Had he borrowed money before?"

She tossed me an exasperated glance. Of course he had, and nothing would be gained by pushing the point. "He always paid me back."

Of course he had. As he did my six thousand. Ross wasn't above lying to get what he wanted, but he hadn't cheated me despite the cost of repaying me. And he'd paid Kelsey money he'd borrowed in the past, though I was pretty sure she wouldn't have pressed him. So, what about the man who'd appeared in his barn the day Rowdy was injured? He'd implied that Ross had swindled him on a horse sale.

"What happened to Alyourmoney?" I asked.

Her eyes filled with tears. "She died. That was the last time I spoke to Ross until just lately. He called me about four months ago. He knew how much she meant to me. He sold her, and the day before the buyer came to get her, she twisted an intestine and died."

He told me he had sold her. So where did he get all that money to start his polo team? "How did he sound?"

"Distant. At the time I thought he was uncomfortable speaking to me, and maybe that was part of it. But it might have been the disease. He didn't have health insurance. If he was selling Cash without giving me a chance to buy her back, he must have needed money."

"What's a mare like that worth?"

"Three or four hundred thousand dollars, depending on the buyer. She'd had two promising foals, but none racing yet."

"Wow. Did he have any other horses?"

"Maybe a few polo horses. They aren't as expensive, but polo is considered such an elite sport. Ross likes prestige. And money. Daddy was right about that, but it wasn't the only reason he married me."

No. Camouflage had something to do with it. But I suspected Ross loved her besides. His sexual preference hadn't prevented him from caring for someone who happened to be female—obvious from his ties to both Kelsey and me. "Who's covering his practice while he's gone?" I asked innocently.

"His what?" She looked at me as if I'd asked about some peculiar and private part of his anatomy.

"His practice. He told me it was covered, and I assumed he'd leased it or hired someone to work it until he returned." But I can't find any record of its existence.

"You're joking, of course. Ross hasn't tried to practice for almost four years."

I thought so. "What has he been doing?"

"Most recently he operated a lay-up. Lived on the property and took care of things."

"A lay-up?"

"Sure. Where they turn out racehorses that have been injured or just need some time off to rest. Sometimes he'd take in mares to foal. The farm belonged to a . . . a friend of his."

"Earlier you said he was building a practice, and it kept him away from home for long stretches."

"*He* said that's what he was doing. He bought some equipment, with money his daddy gave him for graduation. He even had a few clients. He did okay with the day-to-day stuff, the breeding and some of the sports medicine. But one day at Keeneland it all fell apart." She gazed at her hands, twisting the strap of her mocha leather purse into knots in her lap.

I wondered if I should say something or whether she would continue when she was ready. Finally she looked up.

"There was an accident. A colt he took care of, for one of the small farms. It collided with another horse in its first race. The owner had big plans, went into debt to buy and train him. He trusted Ross. The colt broke his front leg; it was horrible. Oh, God, that poor horse. I can still see it. He kept trying to run. Like he didn't understand what had happened, but he knew he was out there to race and was determined to finish no matter what. Ronny was the jockey. He had some injuries, but the paramedics were attending to him. Ross just stood there. The owner was in shock; he kept yelling at Ross to put the colt out of its misery, at least give him a tranquilizer, something. But Ross stood there in front of the whole crowd, shaking like a newborn foal. And then he ran. He turned away from that man who'd been so good to him—the one time Ross really was needed."

"Because the colt had to be euthanized," I finished for her. "The one thing he never learned to handle."

"You know, then."

I nodded.

"There was more to it than that. The colt had been lame. Ross X-rayed him the week before the race and said he was fine. Later another vet looked at the films and found a hairline fracture Ross missed, in the exact spot the bone broke. If he'd seen it to begin with, the colt wouldn't have raced, wouldn't have died. The man blamed Ross, and that was the end of his practice. He sold all his equipment to pay the man off and avoid a lawsuit. My daddy gave him some money then, too."

I debated how to ask my next question. Directness was best. "Do you believe he tried to kill himself?"

"Of course not." She watched me as if to see whether this was the right answer, then lowered her eyes. "He couldn't do that. He may have wanted to, but he just couldn't. Any more than he could kill that colt."

"Will you help me find out who did try?"

"The same person murdered that polo player, didn't he?"

"Yes, I think so."

"Then, by solving one mystery we'll also be able to clear Ross's name?"

"Yes. If you'll help me."

She nodded slowly, reached over, and solemnly squeezed my hand. "No one else will do that. It's up to us."

I had an ally. At least one other person cared what happened to Ross.

The Porsche was still at the polo grounds, so I took Kelsey there first, and she followed me to her hotel. I drove home, went directly to the phone, and dialed the emergency clinic. I asked for Trinka Romanescu, who caught me singing along with a Muzak rendition of "Leavin' on a Jet Plane" when she came on the line a minute later. She sounded out of breath.

"Did I catch you at a bad time?"

"That depends. Are you sending something out?" She was asking whether I wanted to transfer a case.

"No, I want a favor. A big one."

"What?" Her voice was guarded. I pictured her, built like a jockey, tousled new-age hair in a different color every month, probably scribbling in a medical record while she talked to me on the phone. Trinka was three years out of school and ran the emergency clinic like she had an M.B.A. instead of a D.V.M. She was also a highly competent veterinarian, a rare combination.

"Can you fill in for me tomorrow?" I asked. "I need to be somewhere else, and I hate to close the clinic on a Saturday."

After a long silent moment, during which I became convinced she would refuse, she said, "On one condition."

"Name it."

"Give me the whole story about this McRoberts character."

I laughed. "Once it's over, I'll buy you lunch *and* fill you in."

"You got a deal!"

I picked Kelsey up at the hospital at twenty to ten the next morning. She wore huge sunglasses and had pulled her hair into a bun. She'd selected a loose-fitting pantsuit both modest and flattering. I wore a teal sweater and blue leggings. We made it to the polo club just as the first game started, which featured two teams I'd never heard of.

The weather was pleasantly nippy. We bought coffees from the golf cart concession stand and sat on the patio to watch the people watching the game. Most were dressed in black or other dark colors, and a few fur coats stood out ostentatiously.

Babs spotted us first and wandered over just as the ball was thrown in to begin the first chukker. She cast questioning eyes toward Kelsey. I introduced them. Babs examined her sneakers.

"I'm sorry about Ross."

Kelsey's mouth twitched slightly, then formed a solemn line as she stared past the other woman's left shoulder. "Thank you," she said quietly. Exactly the right reaction.

"No Animal Freedom Fighters today," I said. "That's a relief." I nodded toward one of the fur-bearing women.

"Daddy got an injunction or something," Babs explained. "They can't come on the grounds for six months. That's past the end of the season. Next year, who knows?"

She stood with us for a minute, looking increasingly uncomfortable, then left. We watched the action for a while before Debbie Dietrich approached from the clubhouse door.

"Kelsey, it's so good to see you!" The two embraced. "I wish it were under better circumstances. I was so sorry to hear about Ross. Did you arrive in time to see him?"

Kelsey, downcast, shook her head.

"Oh, what a shame. Though I don't suppose he was . . . coherent? That's some small comfort, I suppose."

Kelsey nodded slightly. "Thank you for your sentiment. We've been apart for such a long time, but I do feel somehow, I don't know . . . so much we never got to say to each other—" A tear slid beneath the frame of her glasses. The emotions were real.

"Did Roger find a substitute for Ross?" I asked.

"No, he thought it best to fold the team, at least for the season. Under the circumstances."

"I understand. Did you reach Ross's father?"

She bit her lower lip, glancing at Kelsey. "I'm afraid he has refused to concern himself with his son's affairs."

We all turned at the sound of shouting on the field. The captain of one team was chewing his *patrón* out loudly and colorfully. Debbie blushed.

"Honestly," she muttered. "Polo used to be so refined. Roger would kill any employee who spoke to him in such a way. Especially in front of a crowd." Then she put her hand to her mouth. "I didn't mean . . . not *really*, of course."

An angle I hadn't considered. "Who sponsors the Hats Off team?"

"That's the name of Jackson Crawford's farm in Lexington."

From the corner of my eye, I saw Kelsey open her mouth to speak, and then shut it, frowning hard.

Jackson Crawford. I'd heard that name recently. "They're playing next. Could you point him out for me?"

Debbie shook her head. "Jack doesn't play anymore since his accident. A horse fell on him and crushed his hip several years ago. He needs a cane to walk. He simply sponsors an all-pro team now."

Of course. The man who accosted Ross the day Rowdy bowed his tendon, and before, the day of their practice game. He drove a Ford pickup, like the one Babs saw the young AFF member get out of the night I searched their van. Like the truck I saw leaving the stable area the night Ross was attacked. A green one.

He'd accused Ross of cheating him. How had Ross put it? *He bought a horse from me, and now he's changed his mind. Everyone wants something for nothing.* And now he kept popping up in the investigation of Ross's murder.

There was something definitely not right about Jackson Crawford. Surely no one actively involved in polo could sympathize with the Animal Freedom Fighters. So why hang around with one of their members? If, in fact, it was him.

But surely he wouldn't kill his own high-goal player in the middle of a tournament.

Unless he had a motive more important than winning.

Chapter Twenty-six

"By the way," Kelsey said after Debbie left, "who's taking care of Ross's horses?"

Damn. How could I not have thought of that? "Let's go check on them now."

We walked. As we passed the trailers and vet trucks parked along the edge of the field, Jaime Alegro pulled up next to the Hats Off Farm twelve-horse vans. The Corvette stood out, even among the BMWs and Porsches. Behind his sunglasses, Jaime looked uncomfortable when he saw me.

"Hello, Jaime," I said as neutrally as possible.

"*Doctora.*" A minimal nod.

A fair-skinned, athletic-looking woman got out of the passenger's side, and he turned to her. She leaned back in to extract a child, whose age I guessed to be around two.

"Jaime, this is Ross's ex-wife, Kelsey."

"Jaime Alegro." He shook her extended hand, automatically running his eyes down her body. "My sister, Graciela. And my nephew, Carlos. Berto's funeral was this week, and she came back to get his things."

"Where was the funeral?" I asked. I hadn't heard anything.

"Argentina, of course," he said. "That was his home."

Kelsey cast a wan smile of empathy toward Graciela. The boy, Carlos, was dark and solemn-eyed, his father's exquisite bone structure already visible in his chubby face. No doubt he would grow up to play vicious polo and break fair maidens' hearts.

But he would grow up without a father to teach him how it was done.

I felt uncomfortable but couldn't pass up the opportunity to get some information. "When did you arrive?" I asked. "How was the flight?"

Her English was heavily accented but fluent, her attitude polite but cold. "We came last evening. The flight was . . ." She shrugged. "Normal."

"Jaime, were you able to make it back for the funeral?"

"He was my sister's husband. Of course I went."

"When did you leave for Argentina?"

His head came up, spine straightening defensively. "What is this? Why should you ask that?"

Testing for opportunity. Where were you last Tuesday night? And last night? "I wondered if you heard what happened to Ross."

He looked momentarily nonplussed. "I heard. I left Monday morning, but it's all people were talking about when I got back."

Graciela glared at Kelsey. "It is only right," she said. "Your husband caused the death of mine. I am sorry you must suffer, but, you see, Carlos has no father now and I am a widow."

"I'm terribly sorry for you. Your loss is greater than mine," Kelsey said graciously. "But I'm making it my business to prove Ross had nothing to do with your husband's death. Nor his own."

I interrupted a disbelieving comment before it could escape Jaime's lips. "Will you be okay now?" I asked Graciela. "Did Umberto have insurance?" It was a stupid question, but all I could think of. I expected a cold reply, but not the one I got.

"He left me very well, thank you," she said, flipping long, glossy hair behind her shoulders and shifting Carlos's weight on her hip. "Just before he died, my husband sent me enough money to put a down payment on an *estancia* in Argentina. He wished to breed horses there, perhaps to become a *patrón*. He will never see it, but Jaime and I have vowed to make the *rancho*. It will be a tribute to my husband. He was a great man."

I wondered if she knew her husband had cheated on her as casually as he might hit a ball with a mallet. Where would he suddenly get enough money to buy a ranch? He was a good player, but that was a lot of cash.

"Is land cheaper in Argentina than in America?"

"Our *rancho* is not . . . *cheap*!" She spat the word.

A ranch that would now belong to his brother-in-law. . . . *Motive, maybe, but no opportunity. You can rule out Jaime; he was thousands of miles away. His sister, too.*

Jaime looked at Kelsey. "By the way, I might want to buy that one-eyed mare of Ross's, maybe one or two of the others. You gonna sell them all?"

"I doubt the decision will be mine. We weren't married, after all, when he . . . when he died." She had obvious difficulty with the last word, but Jaime didn't appear to notice.

Kelsey and I continued toward the stable area.

Hal's truck blocked the aisleway of the Bluegrass barn. Had I been alone I might have turned away, but I couldn't explain that to Kelsey without sounding churlish. We walked silently around the front of the Ford, surprising him as he finished giving a penicillin injection to Fandango.

Startled, Hal jumped, fumbled for the syringe, and jammed the needle into the base of his right thumb. Fandango tossed her head, and he let go of the twitch on her nose. It swung wildly, clipping his ear before it fell to the ground.

"Oh . . . *darn*!" he groaned.

Darn? He'd just impaled his hand on an eighteen-gauge needle, then been hit on the ear by a heavy piece of wood. *Darn?*

"Hello, Hal," I said. "Sorry if we spooked you. This is Kelsey, Ross's ex-wife."

"Nice to meet you," he said, holding his right hand tightly in his left. Neither offered to shake hands.

"New twitch?" I picked it up and hefted it. The handle was shorter than the one he'd lost. The old one would have made a lethal weapon in the wrong hands. I looked at Hal with renewed suspicion. He'd have the knowledge necessary to place an IV; he'd naturally think of euthanasia solution as a murder weapon—potassium, too. But why steal mine? Wouldn't he use his own? And I couldn't think how he'd gain access to Ross's keys. "Ever find the original?"

"No. It was better, too." He rubbed his ear, oblivious to the fact that a longer handle might have knocked him unconscious.

"How's Fandango?" I asked. Her face was uncovered, the first time I'd seen it without a bandage since the day of the accident. Was that only three weeks ago? The right side was caved in, and at some point the remnants of her eye had been surgically removed.

"Oh, she's got a little infection, nothing serious. Did you get my messages?" He bent down to retrieve his syringe, carefully capping the needle before leaving the pen. As he took the twitch from me, he made sure his hand touched mine.

I fought an urge to wipe my palm on my jeans. "Yes, but it's always too late to call you back. I've been spending a lot of time at the hospital, that is until . . ." I cast my eyes downward, hoping I wasn't overdoing it.

"Oh, yeah, I was sure sorry to hear about Ross." He glanced at Kelsey, who smiled bleakly. "Seemed like a nice guy."

"Actually," I said, "I tried to call you Thursday night. The night Ross died." The lie slid easily off my tongue. "Your service said you were out."

"Working, I guess. You know how it is. So, where do you want to eat Monday?"

"About that. I can't make it, Hal. I've just got too

much going on." I smiled weakly. "Trying to catch up; you know how it is."

His shoulders sagged. "But I was looking forward to it!"

"Sorry about that. Please don't count on me for anything in the future without asking me first. And waiting for an answer. Okay?"

He scowled at the ground, sulking. Then his lean face broke out in a radiant smile, tobacco-stained teeth on full display. "If that's how you want it, Andi. I'll do whatever you say!"

He moved toward his truck, placing the heel of his injured hand in his mouth. I stepped back as he passed. Either Hal wasn't tracking right or he was way too nice for me to deal with. I didn't have the time to focus on him. But I did need his help. He was the only equine veterinarian I knew who was conscious.

"Hal, are you familiar with a drug called streptokinase?"

"Streptokinase. It's an enzyme, isn't it?"

"Does it have any use in equine medicine? For instance, what would happen if you injected it into, say, a horse's muscle?"

"Jeez, I don't know. It might just digest it. In fact, I think it's an ingredient in the spray I use for proud flesh. It might have some use in research."

Proud flesh, I recalled, was when a horse's wound, instead of healing, bulged with raw tissue. The technical term was "exuberant granulation tissue." I could see how a digestive enzyme might help.

"Could you find out for me? Soon as possible." I gave him my nicest smile, feeling like an absolute heel.

"Well, sure, Andi, I'd be glad to. I've got to go do alcohol blocks on some quarter horses when I leave here, but I can look it up after that."

"Alcohol blocks? What's that?"

"Their tails. For showing, especially in halter classes. They like the tails to hang limp, so we inject alcohol around the spinal cord above it. It deadens the nerves and lasts longer than a local anesthetic. Months, sometimes forever."

Umberto was carrying a syringe full of alcohol. "You mean it kills the nerve? Would it work in other body parts, too?"

"I guess so. But it's permanent. The horse would never feel anything in that part of his body again unless the nerve regenerated. There's a high probability for complications. Also, it swells like crazy. It's not even sanctioned, but if I don't do it, the trainer will, and he's more likely to make a mistake. Anyway, I'll call you later if I find out anything about that streptokinase."

He was humming as he climbed into his truck and drove away.

The horses all had fresh water, and wisps of hay remained in their bins from that morning's feeding.

"Maybe Roger's still paying the grooms."

"Where is the mare with the laminitis?" she asked.

"At Tish's dad's place in Coachella."

She looked over the other horses, running her hand down a leg here, scratching a forehead there. "Not a bad bunch," she said. "The gray mare is beautiful. Fandango? What a shame about the eye."

We walked back to watch the rest of the game. Halftime was nearly over. Tish sat in her usual place, arms crossed over her chest, wearing a blue polo shirt and jeans. She had a can of beer in the grass beside her and stared bleakly across the field through impenetrable dark glasses. I introduced her to Kelsey.

"Your husband was all right," she said. "I only got to play in the one game, but he gave me that opportunity. Thanks to Andi, I guess." She flashed a weak smile at me. "And now Roger wants me for the next tournament. He's forming a new team."

"Are you okay?" I asked. "You seem depressed."

"Nothing a twelve-pack won't cure," she said bitterly, taking a sip from the can.

I wondered whether her mood had something to do with Jaime. Surely she wasn't close enough to Ross to be so down over his death. "Are Ross's grooms being taken care of?" I asked.

"Juan went to work for Hats Off about the time Jaime jumped teams. Nacho took off, maybe back to Mexico. Who knows?"

"Then who's been taking care of his horses?"

"Me." She delivered the statement matter-of-factly, not expecting praise or thanks. "Can't stand to see them neglected. None of this was their fault."

"Thank you," Kelsey said. "It's a relief to know they haven't suffered because Ross can't care for them himself. He'd be glad to know they're okay. Are they getting enough exercise?"

"I give them each a turn around the track once a day. That's all I've had time for. I've been taking some of Jaime's out in the mornings while he was in Argentina."

"I didn't know he had his own horses."

"They belong to Crawford, but they're Jaime's responsibility. He doesn't trust the grooms to work them right."

"I understand you're also caring for the foundered mare?" Kelsey asked.

"She's at Daddy's place, not doing too good."

"I'd like to see her, if possible."

Tish shrugged and rattled off directions.

"Want to go with us?" I asked.

"No room in your car, and Daddy's got the Beamer today. Besides, I promised Jaime I'd help him with Gracie's stuff."

"I certainly do appreciate your help," Kelsey said. "If you'll let me know how much to pay you . . ." She stopped, uncomfortable discussing money but wanting to do the right thing.

"Don't worry about it," Tish said. "It's the least I can

do. I'll have the feed man send the bills to Andi. You can figure out what to do about them."

Great. Another of Ross's debts for me to settle.

Chapter Twenty-seven

Kelsey and I sat far enough from the field to ensure privacy. Neither of us was really interested in the game. While she went to get us sodas, I asked the bartender in the clubhouse for his phone book. By the time Kelsey returned I had a plan.

"I couldn't believe it at first," I said, "but I'm convinced Umberto was systematically destroying Ross's horses. I don't know if he hit Fandango's eye on purpose—I can't believe even a nine-goal player could be that accurate. He may have meant to hit Ross, who knows? But the others—"

"Why would he do such a thing? It wasn't for competition, that's for sure—Ross's team never even won a game. Besides, those two that were poisoned? That was before the season."

"I don't know why, but everything points in that direction. We've got means and opportunity. That's two out of three."

"What?"

"Nothing. But listen. Umberto was carrying streptokinase and alcohol, and the alcohol was in a syringe. Hal told me that alcohol can be used as a permanent block—a local anesthetic. Streptokinase destroys tissue. Tendons, for instance. He had no reason to be in Ross's barn at that hour. Wait, there's more." I held up a hand as she started to interrupt.

"The night Umberto was killed, Ross accused him of switching mares. He swore he'd examined one bay mare and a different one was delivered the day of the game. He said he found the original at 'his place in Coachella.' I checked the phone book. Umberto isn't listed in Coachella, but his sponsor is."

"Jackson Crawford?"

"Yes. He's from Kentucky, too. Do you know him?"

"Somewhat. Actually, he's the one who planned to buy Cash before she died."

"What a coincidence," I said dryly. By now I didn't believe in those, and I doubted she did. "A pickup that might have been his was seen at the polo club the night I broke into the AFF van. I'm pretty sure the member who caught me got out of that truck."

"There must be lots of trucks like that around."

"Driven by men fitting his description? Babs described him pretty well. She didn't see a cane, but she said he barely got out of the truck. And it could have been his truck that nearly ran into me the night Ross was attacked."

Even as I spoke, the green Ford in question pulled up next to the twelve-horse vans bearing the Hats Off Farm logo. Kelsey and I exchanged glances.

"We know he'll be here for the next few hours," she said. "He won't leave until his game's over."

We stared at the truck. Crawford climbed out, leaning heavily on his cane.

"Let's go," I said.

We drove the fifteen minutes to Coachella in tense silence. We went first to Hannover Farm, Tish's father's place. It was an unpretentious five-acre ranch with covered pipe corrals and an irrigated pasture. No one was around but we easily identified the laminitic mare. She was lying down in one of the shaded pens and climbed laboriously to her feet at our approach. As on the day I first saw her, she leaned backward to keep the weight off her front feet but pricked her ears expectantly and nickered at us. I suspected someone had been feeding her carrots and was sorry I didn't have one for her.

"Easy," I said. The mare was still officially mine, since Ross had never canceled the promissory note. If her condition did not improve, I might be faced with putting her down. Unless there had been a switch and we could prove it.

We entered the pen. Kelsey pulled a peppermint from her pocket, and the mare took it eagerly. Kelsey clucked and rubbed the dark nose while I bent down to check her digital pulses. Still bounding. We looked her over carefully, noting all her markings on paper. Small, triangular white star, no white on any of her legs. Mane shaved off like most polo horses'. An altogether nondescript mare.

"She's got two whorls on the right side of her neck, one on the left," Kelsey said.

I looked at the spot she indicated, where the hair grew in a circle. We measured the distances from her ears with our hands and documented them. Then I lifted her upper lip and looked for a tattoo. She had none.

"You know," Kelsey said, "if I wanted two horses that looked exactly alike, I'd start with one like this. There's nothing special about her. She's a common color, and plain. But why do it?"

"That's the question. Ready to find the answer?"

"Let's go before I lose my nerve."

I'd written down the address and phone number and kept it in my purse. We asked directions twice and were finally pointed down a long, well-maintained dirt road lined with citrus farms and a few private stables. A wood-burned sign announced HATS OFF FARM WEST.

I eased the Miata along the narrow lane between horse paddocks toward a long, enclosed barn—no ordinary pipe corrals for Crawford's animals. Still, I imagined it was a step down from the white-rail luxury of Lexington. The stable was cement block, the two half-acre pastures surrounded by sturdy wooden fences. To one side stood a beige stucco house, and a smaller, matching structure was visible behind the barn.

We pulled up at one end of the barn as a Mexican man approached from the smaller house. I recognized him as the older groom who used to work for Ross.

"*¿Qué quieren, señoritas?*" he said. "*El patrón no está aquí.*"

"Hello," I said. "Juan, right? Do you speak English?"

He shrugged, though I was sure he understood the question.

I stepped toward the barn, but he blocked my way. There was nothing precisely menacing in his stance, but something in his eyes said not to cross him. I glanced at Kelsey in frustration. Had we really come down here only to be turned away by a groom?

"*Buenos días,*" Kelsey said, startling me. "*Yo soy* Kelsey, *la esposa de* Ross McRoberts?"

Juan turned his sudden broad grin on her. "*¿Habla español, m'ija?*"

"*Sí, un poquito. Queremos mirar sus caballos. Venimos muchas millas. . . .*" She opened her eyes wide and blinked a few times, gazing at Juan and appearing altogether harmless.

He ate it up. Within seconds he was giving us a guided tour. Juan chattered happily with Kelsey, whom he clearly adored, while I glanced in the stalls.

"This one, I think."

Kelsey, social smile in place, drifted over. "*¡Qué bonita! ¿Podemos mirarla?*"

Whatever she'd said, it worked. Juan, beaming proudly, led the mare from the stall: a bay, perhaps slightly finer-boned than the other, with a small triangular star and no white anywhere else. She had only one whorl on each side of her neck, and her color might have been a shade darker than the mare at Hannover's. Kelsey murmured admiringly in Spanish and casually, almost affectionately, inverted the mare's upper lip.

Juan rattled off a staccato comment. Kelsey said something in return, a deep frown creasing her features.

"What?" I said.

"He says Ross was here the other day, looking at the same mare. That was last Sunday." The day he was attacked.

Though the mare's teeth indicated she was about the same age as the laminitic horse, this one had a tattoo. Trying to be unobtrusive, I memorized it. M29361, or the final number may have been a seven.

Kelsey and I exchanged glances. Now what? I was convinced Umberto had switched the mares, but what could we do about it?

"Did he get the papers on her?" asked Kelsey.

"He told me he did, and that she wasn't tattooed."

So we were stuck.

Kelsey turned to smile at Juan. "*Gracias, Juan. Vamos ahora.* We're ready to go."

But Juan wasn't ready to let us go. Judging from his expression and arm gestures, he wanted to show off the horses in the pasture as well. Unwilling to cast suspicion on our motives, we followed him to the fence.

The pastured horses—several mares and a gelding with a big ankle—nibbled sparse grass ten or fifteen feet away. Juan entered the half-acre enclosure and waved his arms at them. The horses started and suddenly took off at a gallop.

The sight was breathtaking. Far from the frenzied, chaotic flight of the loose animals on the polo field—was that really less than a week ago?—these ran for sheer enjoyment. After their initial surprise at Juan's action, they obviously felt no fear. They cavorted in a big circle, one occasionally kicking up his heels or sprinting ahead of the others.

I turned to share my appreciation with Kelsey and saw that her face was totally devoid of color. She stared at the running horses as if they terrified her.

"Kelsey, what's wrong?" I asked.

"That mare, the chestnut, I'd swear—*Juan, traiga la roja por favor*?"

Puzzled but anxious to please her, Juan stepped into the path of the approaching herd and held up his arms. Most of the horses slowed to a walk, but those that went around him did so at a gentle trot, pulling up nearby. He easily captured the mare in question and held her in place with his hands buried in her shaggy mane.

"*¿Cómo se llama ella?*" Even I knew she was asking the mare's name.

Juan looked from the mare to her. "*Su nombre es* Whisper," he said. "*Pero se llama* Cash."

I caught my breath. "Cash? Isn't that the name of . . ."

Kelsey nodded and asked Juan a question. He answered with an apologetic shrug.

"Her name is Whisper, but they call her Cash," she explained to me. "He doesn't know why." She walked a slow circle around the barely winded mare. I saw that her flanks bulged slightly and wondered whether it was all grass or if she was pregnant.

"My God," Kelsey said, "she looks just like her. Almost . . ." She bent to wipe the sand from the right hind foot. The mare picked it up uncertainly, and Kelsey cupped it in her hand, gazing at it with a sadness I could not comprehend. Abruptly she dropped the foot and straightened. "*Lo siento, Juan.* I'm sorry. For a minute I thought this was a mare I once owned."

"Alyourmoney?" I asked.

"Yes. But I was wrong."

"Are you sure? After so long?"

"Yes. This mare's right hind foot is half white. My Cash's feet were all black. Otherwise she's a dead ringer."

I stepped into the paddock and raised the mare's lip. It was badly scarred, the ink smudges unreadable.

"That's what nearly convinced me it was her. Cash cut her lip once on a piece of metal, and most of her tattoo wound up being trimmed out. I still remember how Ross's hands shook while he sewed her up. . . ." She smiled wanly at the memory. "It twists her lip a little, and this one has the same thing. It's incredible." She patted the mare's neck and turned to go.

I let go and the lip fell back. It pulled to one side so the prehensile part—the protuberance she used to pick up her food—pointed to her left instead of straight ahead.

"Kelsey, are you sure? That's quite a coincidence."

"I'm sure," she said. "My mare's dead. I know she is, but maybe I still haven't quite accepted it." She shrugged again, her enthusiasm for our adventure now gone. We climbed dispiritedly into the Miata and drove back in brooding silence. I was thinking that such a scar could be surgically faked.

Finally I asked, "Was Alyourmoney insured?"

"Yes, of course."

"Do you know for how much?"

"Probably the two hundred seventy thousand my father originally paid for her at the Keeneland sale. Ross wasn't likely to have had it changed."

Ross had claimed his father-in-law paid a half million dollars for the filly. I decided not to mention this exaggeration to Kelsey.

My brain kept tripping over the fact that Kelsey was certain the mare in Crawford's pasture was *not* the filly Ross planned to sell Crawford before she died. Everything else fit. Somehow Ross had managed to sell his mare and still collect the insurance. But how?

"How do you prove to an insurance agency that a horse died? I mean, what's to stop someone from claiming a live horse died, or substituting another horse's body for the one that's insured?"

"I'm not sure how they're identified. They'd probably want a good description, maybe a picture? And the tattoo number, of course, if it has one. As far as proving death occurred, you need a veterinarian's statement, and a necropsy to determine the cause. They're a lot more concerned about people killing their horses to collect the insurance, so they're worried about cause of death." She said this matter-of-factly, but I felt my stomach tighten at the thought of murdering horses for money.

"Tell me more about Jackson Crawford."

"I don't know him well. He has a little farm in Versailles, that's west of Lexington? Nice place, and he keeps it up. He's not hurting for money, that's for sure, but he didn't make it in the horse business. He keeps a couple of stallions, one that never proved himself much, so if he gets any mares at all, they're bottom-of-the-barrel. That kind of reputation just gets worse because by breeding only poor mares, a mediocre stallion produces foals no one wants. He'll never attract good mares."

"Didn't you say he had two? What about the other one?"

"He's called Splickety Lit. He's a three-year-old that never ran 'cause of an injury, when he was two? He's got some royalty, but you have to go back a few generations to find it. I think he's by a grandson of Nijinsky, out of a mare that goes back to Citation and Northern Dancer."

"Even I've heard of them. Guess he had to put out some bucks for a colt like that."

"Not really. You'd be surprised how cheap an unproven horse can be, especially one that can never race, no matter how good his breeding is. If you go back far enough in any thoroughbred's pedigree, you're bound to find good blood somewhere. He was the kind of 'bargain' Crawford's always looking for, but I think he planned on buying some well-bred mares for this one. That's why he wanted Cash. Can't say he didn't learn from his mistakes."

As I drove through the gate to the polo club, I thought how lucky I was to have Kelsey as an ally. She could recite the biographies of people she "barely knew" and the bloodlines of their horses—even converse with their Mexican grooms.

"Where'd you learn to speak Spanish, anyway?" I asked.

"In high school," she said. "Where else?"

Chapter Twenty-eight

The one o'clock game pitted Hats Off Farm against Rancho Domino and was well under way when we returned to Las Palmas. Jaime scored to the crowd's polite approval as we approached the clubhouse. His movements had a vicious quality I hadn't noticed when he worked for Ross.

Debbie and Roger Dietrich sat at a table. She sipped champagne; he drank bourbon. They invited us to join them and offered us champagne. Roger proffered condolences to Kelsey. That accomplished, we sat in uncomfortable silence, sipping the too-warm champagne, no one willing to make small talk.

Finally I said, "Roger, do you know Jackson Crawford?"

"You bet. I deal with him quite a bit. He banks with us. Made good money in pharmaceutical research."

Oh, man, how'd I miss that? Who could find out more easily what streptokinase can do to a horse's tendon than someone involved in the commercial drug industry? "Do you know anything about a mare he owns named Whisper? He calls her Cash."

"Red mare? No white?"

"That's her."

"Yep. Picked her up three, four months ago. Not much on bloodlines but a good-looking mare. He seemed to expect a lot out of her."

"Where did he get her; do you know?"

"Bought her from Angus McPherson, the fella that owned the spread Ross was runnin' before we came down here. McPherson died about then, and the farm went on the market."

Too many deaths, too many coincidences. Who was Angus McPherson and how did he fit in?

"Funny thing," Dietrich continued. "Seemed to me ole Jack was awful excited about that mare. Paid a good bit for her, too—more'n I'd of give for her. That's jes between you, me, and this bottle, but I figured he knew what he was about, or thought he did. Guess if she had a good foal or two on the ground, she might suit Jack's purposes all right."

"What purposes?"

"Nothin' special, jes' breedin'."

"Would Ross have been involved in the sale?"

"I reckon he would've got his ten percent. Angus let him run things, give him a commission on sales and fees. Used to keep his hand in more, till his health failed. Young man, too, not more'n forty. Jes' goes to show, eh?"

"What went wrong with his health?"

"That was kinda strange. He kept real quiet about it, wouldn't let anyone visit him right up till the end, 'cept Ross."

Maybe he had some disfiguring ailment and didn't want to be remembered that way. I glanced at Kelsey, but she was staring at her glass. *Oh, sure. He had AIDS. He didn't want them to know.* "When did you and Ross decide to come to the desert?"

He thought a minute. "About the same time, three months or so. His idea. I mean, I come down every year, but I used to team up with Crawford. When he got hurt, he decided he wanted an all-pro team, so last year I didn't come at all. Thought about sellin' the condo. Then Ross popped up and suggested gettin' together. He picked up that fancy car and hired Jaime to buy a dozen or so horses jes' like that." He snapped his fingers.

"I gotta say, surprised hell outa me. Oops, sorry." He shot a look at his wife, then at Kelsey, who glanced impassively back, unimpressed by his mild profanity. He shrugged and continued. "Never thought he had that kinda money. Guess the insurance on that mare helped. Still, he must of laid out two, three hundred K in less than a month, all in a hurry to get ready in time."

The insurance only partially accounted for the money Ross had spent. Where had he gotten the rest? "You say Jaime bought the horses for him?"

"That's the way it's usually done. The pros know where the good polo horses are."

"What about the gray mare, Fandango? He said she was given to him in lieu of payment for vet services."

"She was McPherson's special mare. Angus used to play a bit, too. He give her to him, all right. Maybe it was instead of paying him."

I could forgive Ross for embellishing that story.

So what had we learned? About three months ago Ross faced the death of his employer, who was possibly more than that.

Careful, Andi, you're making a big leap here with not much evidence to back you up.

Call it a clinical impression. A hunch. His good mare died unexpectedly around the same time. He'd already arranged to sell her for more than the insurance paid. The man who wanted to buy her instead bought another mare through Ross, a chestnut that was virtually identical to the Alydar mare he really wanted. Coincidence? Unlikely. I was missing something, though. Ross could have sold Crawford a ringer, but nothing pointed that way. Crawford had told Dietrich he was buying Whisper, and Whisper was in his pasture. So why did he call her Cash? And why was he so angry with Ross?

"Help me understand Crawford a little better," I said. "He was furious at Ross the day of the practice game, and later when Rowdy was injured. He's fairly small-time with horses, right?"

"Yeah, but he's got big aspirations. Wants to be

thought of as someone with an eye. A man who can spot a diamond in a sand dune, he likes to say."

"So he buys cheap horses with good bloodlines and tries to breed another Secretariat?"

"Pretty much. Except he wouldn't recognize a Secretariat if he kicked him in the head." Dietrich chuckled and took a swig of his bourbon. " 'Tween me an' you, an' this-here glass."

"How about an Alydar?"

"What're you driving at?"

"Crawford really wanted to buy the mare Alyourmoney, right?"

"Sure, but she died."

"So we can assume. We know the mare he wound up with isn't her. But would he know that?"

"Course he knew it. He told me he was buying Whisper."

"But wouldn't he get better foals out of his new stallion if he bred him to a royal mare rather than to this plodder?"

"Well, sure, but if she's dead, she won't be producing too many foals." Dietrich sniggered and looked at the others for approval. Debbie smiled supportively but Kelsey's rapt attention was focused on me. She saw where I was headed, and appeared both fascinated and horrified.

"Would he be able to tell the difference by looking?"

"No, but I *told* you—"

"What if Ross convinced him it was really Whisper who died?"

Everyone at the table stared at me, and the moment stretched uncomfortably. On the field someone scored and most of the crowd cheered and shouted. My personal audience remained silent.

Kelsey finally spoke. "He switched the papers so he could collect the insurance on Cash. As a vet, he could have fudged it. Could he have scarred the lip? Of course he could. The mares look enough alike, except for that one foot." Her expression reflected pride, with faint embarrassment thrown in. I could understand how she felt—the plan was brilliant, using a man's greed against him. Still, he had cheated Crawford.

"We know it really was Cash who died," I pointed out. "Or at least, that's not her in Crawford's paddock."

"And I guess Jackson Crawford knows that now, too," Kelsey said. "I wonder how he found out? He would have been delighted at the prospect of breeding his unproven stallion with what looked on paper like a mediocre mare. A good colt would prove his horse; a bad one could be blamed on her."

Debbie spoke up. "Please, could someone explain this to me? I understand why you might switch a poor horse for a better one, but I can't see why anyone would fake inferior papers for a spectacular mare."

I glanced at Kelsey, who put it simply. "Crawford wanted to breed his stallion with a mare who was better than she appeared. The foals would turn out better than expected, and his stallion would then take the credit."

"That sounds like a tremendous gamble," Debbie said.

"Everything in the horse industry is a gamble," I said. "He was looking for prestige, wanted to be thought of as a man with an eye. Money was immaterial."

Kelsey smiled. "But Ross went one switch further, sold him Whisper instead. The *real* Whisper, exactly the mare he'd paid for, even if he paid a little more than he might have otherwise."

Dietrich cleared his throat. "You're forgetting, there's blood tests to catch that sort of thing."

I caught my breath. Was I really making all this up?

Kelsey waved a hand. "Every thoroughbred has its blood typed," she explained to me. "Before it can be registered. The numbers are stuck in a computer, and it takes practically an act of Congress to get them released. That stuff is guarded like the crown jewels."

"In other words," I said, "even if there was a discrepancy—which there wouldn't be, because the mare was exactly what her papers claimed—but if there was, nobody would catch it unless an identity were challenged. The identity of an offspring."

"You got it. Unless Crawford decided to check himself. Which seems unlikely, since he would have been calling attention to his own little game."

"Still, he would've found out sooner or later," Dietrich persisted. "When the first foal hit the track and someone suspected it was too good. He'd have come after Crawford, who would have pointed them right back at Ross."

Kelsey and I exchanged glances. *That would take years. Ross knew he wouldn't be around to worry about it.* We shrugged simultaneously. "Would anyone check because a foal was too *good*? Blood tests are for when the offspring are a disappointment."

"But that wouldn't matter," I said. "Remember, Ross didn't switch mares, he only *claimed* he did." He'd lied about lying. *That's my Ross.*

"I wonder how Crawford found out," Kelsey said again.

"We may never know," I answered. "But he was angry enough to come after Ross in his own barn."

"Angry enough to kill?" Kelsey asked in a low voice.

We all looked at her.

"Umberto worked for him," she pointed out. "He might have ordered him to sabotage Ross's horses. After he poisoned the first two he probably figured it was less risky to get someone else to do the actual damage."

"Why kill him if Umberto was acting at his direction?"

She looked at her hands, clasped around her champagne glass, which was still full. "It was just a thought."

I placed a hand on her forearm. "And a good one. I didn't mean it couldn't happen, but why?"

"We know Umberto did it, right?" she asked.

Roger and Debbie looked inquiringly at us but we ignored them.

"Right," I said.

"And he played polo for Jack. Somebody killed him.

Maybe Jack was paying him off and he got too greedy." She shrugged. "I don't know."

"Neither do I," I said. "But one thing's for sure. Crawford's got some explaining to do."

"How you gonna go about questioning him?" demanded Dietrich. "You can't prove a thing, far as I can tell."

He had a definite point, and since I wasn't sure what had been done, I couldn't even figure out what I wanted to prove.

Slow down, Andi. History, exam, assessment, plan. What was my plan?

"Where do you think these animal rights people fit in?" Debbie asked. "Or do they?"

"Good question," I said. "Maybe we should talk to them. Bob Talbot might have their addresses." I'd seen him go into the clubhouse earlier, so I excused myself and headed that way.

I spotted him in earnest conversation with the bartender. The tail end of their conversation reached me as I approached. "She's underage, goddammit," Talbot was saying. "If I find out you've been serving her, I'll have to press charges."

I hung back but he spotted me, so I fixed my mouth into a smile and offered my hand, which he shook somewhat reluctantly.

"Do you have the names and addresses of the Animal Freedom Fighters?" I asked. "I'd like to ask them some questions."

"I expect I got 'em somewhere," he said. "Only I can tell you, they didn't kill your friend."

"Why do you say that?" I asked, privately wondering what had prompted this statement. I hadn't said anything about murder.

"I got ears, I hear what you girls are up to, and you're barking up the wrong tree."

I studied him for a moment. "Mr. Talbot, if you know something about either attack, and you're withholding it—" I stopped because I really had no idea what would happen, but the implied threat hung in the air.

His eyes grew increasingly belligerent. "Let me tell you something, young lady. I love that little girl of mine, misguided though she might be. You may not agree with my methods, but 'less you been in my shoes, you got no cause to criticize."

I was stunned. Babs wasn't a suspect. Was she? "Um, I'm sure you've done your best for your daughter," I muttered inanely. "Do you think you could give me those names and addresses sometime today?"

He seemed anxious to get rid of me now, and nodded wordlessly, then headed out the front door.

"Come on," he said.

I followed him to his car and rode to the trailer. He scribbled some addresses and shoved them at me. I couldn't get him to expand on his earlier statement, and he seemed to regret saying anything at all.

Chapter Twenty-nine

"A man's got to believe in something," Wade Sanders said, and took another toke.

We sat in the living room of a brown stucco house, anonymous among a litter of similarly run-down dwellings. Its single salvation was a shaggy olive tree that overhung the front yard, lending the house a shady, domestic quality often missing in desert dwellings, especially in poorer neighborhoods like this one in Indio. The sidewalk out front was cracked and buckled; weeds grew through and around it. The inside badly needed paint, the ceilings were nearly black, and crisscross lines of masking tape adorned the room's one curtainless window.

This address was listed as AFF headquarters and was almost certainly home to the Gerings. I'd called the courthouse from Las Palmas and learned they had been released on bail the previous day. Bob Talbot had had no phone number for them.

We had been nervous approaching the house, thinking there was a good possibility one of these people had killed Umberto, broken into my clinic, stabbed my dog, and tried to murder Ross. Twice. The gray van was nowhere in sight, but having coaxed our courage up, we knocked anyway.

A cloud of marijuana smoke preceded the man who'd discovered me rummaging around in the van Monday night. He was less menacing in daylight. In fact, with his plain brown hair and slender frame he was downright nondescript.

"Help youse?" he asked. Then his brown eyes narrowed as he recognized me. As he moved to slam the door I stuck a foot in.

"I'm Andi Pauling," I said. "And this is Kelsey Vallice. We've come for some answers."

"I'm not the spokesman," he said. "Come back when Tom and the girls are home."

"We'd like to know where you were on certain nights this week. Surely you don't need Tom to tell you that?"

"I don't have to talk to you." But he backed out of the doorway and didn't close it. I followed him in. After some hesitation, Kelsey did, too.

"It's us or the cops," I bluffed. "If you aren't hiding anything, you might as well use this opportunity to convince us." I glanced around for signs of other people, even though he'd said he was alone. Of course, if someone was in another room we'd never have known. "We might be able to help each other. What's your name?"

"Wade Sanders." He sat on a filthy sofa of uncertain color. "Christ, I never expected this. I just joined the Freedom Fighters a coupla weeks ago. Seemed like the thing. Jesus."

"Why did you join?" I asked.

That's when he said, "A man's got to believe in something."

"It's what separates us from animals," Kelsey put in. Sanders and I both glanced at her. It wasn't the smartest remark under the circumstances, and Sanders couldn't let it pass.

"There will come a day when the human race will look back on the fight for animal liberation and shake our heads in dismay at our own ignorance. Our fight is like the civil rights movement. One day it will be a felony to murder a steer for its meat, or a mink for its fur, or to experiment on dogs and rabbits. They can't speak for themselves, so right-thinking humans must speak for them. The righteous must sacrifice so justice may prevail. The struggle to enlighten people is never-ending."

I sat on the other end of the sofa, on the edge. His convoluted argument made me weary. "Wade, what about the mare who died after you 'liberated' her?"

His hooded eyes flashed dangerously. "You killed her."

"You'd prefer she suffer? She'd have died of shock within hours. Even if she somehow survived, both front legs would have had to be amputated. Horses can't go around in wheelchairs. She should never have been out in that street."

He shrugged. "We expected some losses. She's a martyr. She died free. She'll be written up in our next newsletter."

What could I say? He truly believed that made it all okay.

Kelsey spoke up from where she stood near the window. "Is that why you killed Umberto? Because he was abusing horses?"

"That polo player? I wasn't even with the group then. Tom wouldn't kill anyone. Our weapons are words and activism, not guns and bullets. Killing a human would distract from our purpose, which is education. That's where Hill screwed up."

"Who?" Kelsey asked.

"Paul Hill," I said, remembering the article I'd removed from the van. "He's the one they convicted for murdering the doctor in Florida."

"That was justifiable," Sanders said. "One life for many. But it was poor strategy. It distracted people's attention away from the point they were trying to make." He drew deeply on the joint and offered it first to me, then to Kelsey. We both declined. He pinched off the live end, studied the roach for a second, then ate it.

I couldn't wait to get out of this house. But I needed

a few more answers. "What about the night I was looking around in your van? Did you break into my clinic later?"

"You never should have done that," he said, suddenly agitated. "Tom and the others were still in jail. You stole things. They blamed me. It was all your fault."

"I'll give you back your articles," I said, "if you'll tell me what you did after I left."

"Didn't do anything. Think I'd go to the cops?"

Kelsey and I exchanged glances. This wasn't going like we'd hoped. "Did you break into my clinic? Just to get even, or to look for your articles?"

"No way, man. Only reason we'd do that would be to set the prisoners free. And I wouldn't do it alone."

The few animals boarding at the time had been undisturbed. Only the euthanasia solution went missing. If murder was against their principles, and they certainly wouldn't use it on an animal, what reason would they have for taking it?

I was amazed to note that I had accepted everything he told me. I believed him, because once I understood the group's basic premise, the rest followed easily. The trick was to think like one of them. "Where were you later that night?" I asked.

"Here, prob'ly."

"What about the next night?" The night Ross was attacked.

He shrugged. "That's Tuesday, right? The day Tom and his sisters got out of jail. Well, that night, anyhow." The anticipated lawyer must have shown up after all, once Lara and I had left. "We had a late meeting. Tom didn't much like jail. We'd gotten kicked off the polo club grounds, so we were making plans for our next target."

"What's that?"

He grinned, the first sign of humor I'd seen. "Wait and see."

"Tell me something. What would you people do if you

got your way? If all the animals were free to roam and no one ate meat anymore?"

His eyes flickered, a brief moment of panic, then narrowed. "We'd celebrate," he said hesitantly. "That's our goal."

"I doubt it," I said in disgust. "What would you do for attention then?"

He shrugged listlessly, the pot having removed his ability to stay agitated for long.

I didn't ask about the second time Ross was attacked. Something about the way he moved—quick, jerky motions—convinced me it wasn't him I'd seen in the hospital room swathed in blue. What would this guy know about potassium, anyway?

Who knew how to kill with potassium? And who would kill with Euthanol? The same questions, over and over. *Am I asking the wrong questions? Or asking them of the wrong people?*

We stood up. Sanders seemed more relaxed than when we arrived. It might have been the pot, but I thought he was also relieved to see us going. Had I missed a key question? Maybe there was more to be learned, after all.

"By the way," I said at the door, "why the sudden upsurge in activity? I mean, the group has been protesting for years. Why the pamphlets and the spectacle now?"

"We got a big contribution earmarked for specific activities."

"From whom?"

He wouldn't tell me. Maybe he didn't know.

"What's Jackson Crawford's relationship to the AFF?"

"Who?" He seemed genuinely puzzled.

"The man in the green Ford pickup, who walks with a cane."

"J.C. He bailed Tom and his sisters out, and he gave me a ride to pick up the van that night. I guess he's a sympathizer."

Before he closed the door behind us I took from my purse the two articles and handful of flyers I'd "borrowed," and handed them to him.

As we drove away I felt disgusted with myself. I'd been so ready to blame the AFF for all that had recently gone wrong that I'd neglected to pay close attention to other possibilities.

Kelsey said, "I bet the big contribution came from Jack."

"I bet you're right. Why would he do that?"

"Why don't we ask him?"

"You mean, just *ask* him?"

"Sure," she said. "We made it through this interview okay. We'll do it at the polo club, where there are lots of witnesses. In case he gets any ideas."

I smiled at her seriousness, then frowned, realizing her concern was well founded. "Okay, let's go."

The Hats Off Farm game was over, and the final contest of the day beginning. We found Crawford overseeing the cooling down of his horses from a vantage point in the Corvette Jaime had driven earlier: his baseball cap perched on his head, the cane resting against the seat by his right leg, a soda can wedged in his crotch to be used as a spittoon. He was barely aware of me before I climbed in beside him. Kelsey watched from the Miata.

"Hello, Mr. Crawford." I reintroduced myself, but he seemed to remember me. "Nice car. What happened to your truck?"

"Jaime's using it to clear out Berto's place. Him and his sister and girlfriend. What do you want?"

"I'm curious," I said. "Why have you been donating money to the Animal Freedom Fighters?"

"What're you talkin' about?"

"This animal rights group that's been disrupting the games. They were never a problem until you began giving them money. I'd have thought your sympathies lay at the other end of the field."

"I'm busy. You'll have to excuse me." He started the engine, clearly expecting me to get out.

"We saw the mare," I said quietly, not moving.

He glared at me, conflicted. He wanted me to go away, but he needed to know what I'd seen, what Kelsey and I had put together. Curiosity won out. "What mare?"

"Both of them, actually. The one Ross examined and paid for but did not receive. And Whisper."

He gave an elaborate casual shrug. "Whisper's a pregnant broodmare. Brought her down from Kentucky. Should have left her there; the bluegrass is better for growing colts. I don't know anything about the mare Berto sold your boyfriend."

"Let's skip that for now, though I didn't say anything about Umberto having sold it. Kelsey spotted Whisper because she looks so much like a mare she used to own. A mare named Alyourmoney. When Ross first arrived in the desert you were asking him about her. Like your mare, she was called Cash."

It wasn't much of a leap, and his reaction told me I was right on target. He needed to know what I'd overheard, but did not want to ask.

"We figured out what happened," I went on. "You wanted the Alydar mare, and he was willing to sell. He had a look-alike on the property, a mare that belonged to Angus McPherson. The Alydar mare died. Then Angus died."

"They were queers together," he said. "Betcha didn't know your boyfriend was a faggot."

Looking at him, I understood why Ross had encouraged people to think he and I were more than friends. Why he never moved out. He desperately wanted them to think he was "normal." Heterosexual. He'd done the same thing in vet school. A great weight moved off my shoulders, and I realized I was no longer angry at Ross. I hoped with all my heart I'd have a chance to tell him it didn't matter, that I loved him anyway.

"How would you know something like that?" I asked.

He looked away. "Everybody knew," he said.

So there had been rumors. Of course there had.

"When Angus died, he left Ross in charge, didn't he."

"Hell, he did more'n that. Ross inherited everything. 'Cept there wasn't much left. McPherson'd been sick awhile. The place was heavy in debt, but he'd put the horses in McRoberts's name."

"And he convinced you Whisper had died instead of Cash."

"The dirty little—yeah, he said he switched 'em 'cause the Alydar mare was insured and the other one wasn't. Said I could have her for a good price but with the wrong papers, since he was gettin' his money from the insurance company. He knew I'd jump at it. Shoulda known I'd catch on, though."

"How did you figure it out?"

"Shoer came to trim her feet, saw the right hind was blacked. I'd never a noticed if he'd just left it white."

"So you killed Ross out of revenge?"

"Huh? *Kilt* him? You kiddin' me?"

"Isn't that what happened?"

"Hell, no. I wanted him to squirm. Get him in the barn, where he'd feel it. What good's revenge if he ain't around to know about it?"

Also, he'd never get his money back. "What about Umberto?"

"You think I kilt him, too?"

I didn't answer right away. I sure liked that cane as a murder weapon, but where was the motive?

"He was destroying Ross's horses," I said.

He chuckled. "Yeah. Cost me more'n the mare to get him to do that. Two-thirds in advance. But *that's* good revenge for ya. He'd a lived, we'd a got the whole string. Left him with a barn full of cripples and a pocketful of dust, and no lady friend to keep him warm at night."

"What?"

"Heh, heh. You thought it was your irresistible charms Berto was after that night, eh?"

I hadn't given it any thought—Umberto's sudden interest in me the night of his death. So he was only trying to get at Ross from another angle? Just following orders. The irony hurt.

"What was the streptokinase for?"

"You're a vet. Do your homework."

"It destroys tissue. Tendons, for example. Like Rowdy's. By using an alcohol block he kept the horse from feeling pain and ensured the breakdown looked sudden and spontaneous, once the tendon was too weak to hold his weight. I think Jaime noticed the leg was swollen that morning—he tried to say something about it after Rowdy broke down, but Ross didn't want to hear it."

"That's Ross for you. He probably figured he'd missed something and didn't want his hired help making him look bad in front of you."

He was probably right, I thought sadly. "I'm disappointed in Umberto's and your lack of creativity. He was repeating the same trick the night he died."

He shrugged. "We had some left. That stuff's expensive."

The air inside the car was becoming claustrophobic, even with the windows rolled down. But I wasn't finished.

"You poisoned those two horses back in Lexington, too, didn't you?"

His stony expression told me not to expect an answer.

"I think you paid the Animal Freedom Fighters to stir up trouble for him. Those flyers were no accident. Neither was the paint they splashed on my house."

"You live with a cheat, you take your chances."

Ross had only cheated a cheater. Did that make it okay? A dying man making a last desperate fling at the lifestyle he'd always coveted, taking advantage of another man's sly greed—were the circumstances mitigating enough? I was disgusted, and out of questions. I started to get out.

He didn't look at me as he got in the last word. "Anybody asks, I'll swear this talk never happened."

Chapter Thirty

Hungry and discouraged, we agreed to adjourn for the day. I offered Kelsey dinner at a restaurant before taking her to visit Ross, but she vetoed that idea quickly.

"Let me cook!" she said eagerly.

"At my house?" I thought of the untended kitchen. Though Ross had managed to deal with its shortcomings.

"Please, I never get to! Mother's cook always fixes these real heavy southern dishes, ham and fried stuff? Stop by the grocery and I'll get everything I need!" Her childlike excitement made it impossible to say no.

I almost asked why she lived with "Mother" if it was so bad, but it was none of my business. We stopped by the hospital—no change in Ross's condition—picked up Ross's car, detoured to the grocery, and she followed me to Palm Springs.

Kelsey hadn't seen my house before, so as we approached the front door I tried to prepare her for its perpetual state of disarray. I neglected to prepare myself, however.

"Oh," Kelsey said as we entered.

"Oh no," I said. "Velcro, I thought we were over all this!" How could I have forgotten and left him inside?

He sidled over and prostrated himself at my feet. But his tail stub kept wiggling, and his facial expression merely reflected anxiety, not guilt.

"Oh, how cute!" Kelsey bent down to scratch his ears, then his belly. He sniffed the bag of groceries in her hand, finding nothing of interest among the rice and vegetables.

"Ross's things!" I said, realizing what lay at the center of Velcro's rampage. One of Ross's suitcases, which he'd left closed, lay open-faced, its contents scattered.

"What's that?" Kelsey asked.

She picked up a sheaf of torn and slightly damp papers from among the socks and underwear, and I went to investigate a canvas bag whose holdings lay strewn across much of the room.

A large pill vial held capsules of the drug azidothymodine, or AZT, the drug Ken O'Grady had asked me if Ross was taking. The rest of the bag's contents was even more interesting.

"I know why he had an IV in his arm!" I said, examining the labels. Most were in German or some Scandinavian language, but medical terminology is similar everywhere. "Trichozanthine. Compound Q. Intravenous administration only. Babs said he used to park at the polo club at night. I wondered why. It didn't sound like him to just sit. He was medicating himself."

"There are receipts here from Sweden." She handed me one.

"Getting the drugs from overseas meant he could treat himself without being monitored. No going in and out of AIDS clinics, or taking chances on being seen." It didn't stop him from swiping materials from my clinic, though. I found the missing bottles of Di-Trim—nearly empty—and Nizoral, one nearly empty but the other unopened.

"Here's where more of that money went, too." She held up a handful of receipts. "He had laser surgery twice. He has an appointment on Monday for more." An appointment he wouldn't be able to keep.

"The Kaposi's sarcoma."

"And more drugs, going back almost two years."

"The killer didn't have to put an IV in; he just switched drugs. He only had to pull the tubing out of the bag and pop it into the bottle of Euthanol." This widened the possibilities considerably, since switching bottles required almost no skill. One merely had to know how easy it was. A memory picked at my brain.

"Did you know Ross had a safe deposit box?" She was examining yet another receipt.

"Come to think of it, I did see a little key in his glove compartment. It had a number on it. Maybe it's still there."

I went out to check while she continued gathering her ex-husband's belongings. Her face reflected sadness and the same sense of loss I'd witnessed on Ross's face in unguarded moments.

I found the key beneath the other miscellany in the Porsche's glove box. On top was a canceled airline ticket to Mexico City in Ross's name. He'd gone down Monday and returned Tuesday, not long before calling me at the clinic. I was glad Lara didn't know—leaving the country while out on bail was definitely a bad idea. Unless you don't plan to come back.

Why go from the Palm Springs airport to Indio, then call me for a ride back to Palm Springs? Was he really so incapacitated he couldn't drive? How did he get to Indio, then?

I opened the trunk, hoping for more clues. There lay a half dozen bags of saline solution, a handful of butterfly catheters, and several sets of IV tubing. All were brands I used at Dr. Doolittle's. He must have been self-administering fluids—my fluids, naturally—to counteract the diarrhea.

He went to work for me to gain access to my pharmacy. No wonder he didn't care whether I paid him. I was *paying him.* Still, none of this stuff cost much, with the exception of the Nizoral, and he would have paid me back if he'd been around when the bill came. It was more a matter of accessibility. And I felt sure his reasons were more complicated than that.

A factory-labeled bottle contained Cipro, a broad-spectrum antibiotic too expensive for routine use in veterinary medicine. Another contained Isoniazid, which I remembered as an antituberculosis drug. The labels were in Spanish—at least part of the reason for his hasty trip to Mexico.

I went back inside and handed Kelsey the key. "Maybe you can open it on Monday. We'll ask Lara."

"Why did he come here, Andi?"

"What do you mean? There's no polo in Lexington in the winter, is there?"

"He never cared about polo before. Not that much. Now suddenly he's spent all his money and even resorted to fraud to get more. All to form a polo team. Why?"

I set down the stuff I'd been examining. "Were he and Angus McPherson lovers?" I asked.

"He never told me so, but I'm almost certain they were. I was happy Ross had someone."

"Then maybe when Angus died . . ."

"I know he signed a lot of his property over to Ross before he passed away. To protect it from creditors. But by then there wasn't much left. Ross was scrambling to keep the farm going, sold some of the horses to pay the bills. When Angus died Ross quit making the payments."

"AIDS is an expensive disease," I said.

She held up a handful of pharmacy receipts from the clutter she'd picked off the floor. "Tell me about it."

"What must it be like," I mused, "being gay in Lexington, Kentucky? Wanting to be part of the horse industry—are they all like Crawford and Dietrich? Add the fact that he was a vet who couldn't practice. Trying day after day to fit in."

Her eyes clouded. "He never really tried after I left. He only pretended to fit. He blamed his problems on me. I didn't mind, really, but we knew the same people, and I'd lived in Lexington all my life. He didn't convince many people. He only alienated most of them."

"So when McPherson died—"

"—Ross was all alone."

"What about Dietrich?"

She shook her head. "You've talked to him. He's all bluff and glad-handing, no substance. He's probably the only person Ross knew who never caught on to his double life, but he's not much of a friend. I've wondered how Debbie puts up with him."

"So Ross went on a spending binge."

She grinned. "Sure looks like it."

"He was pretty high when he got here, like he had a big secret to keep. No, that's a poor analogy. He was just bursting to tell me how much everything cost, like a kid who got a fancy new toy before any of his friends."

"You know what I think?"

I looked at her, questioning.

"It was suicide."

"What do you mean? You yourself said Ross could never—"

"I don't mean he hooked himself up to the Euthanol. You're right; he couldn't. And he kept taking the drugs, he wanted to stay as healthy as possible. But he knew what was coming. He took care of Angus while he got worse and worse. Who was going to care for Ross?"

"Maybe that's why he chose the desert. We have a huge gay population here, and I understand the AIDS Project is one of the best in the world."

She shrugged. "Maybe. Or maybe he just liked the sound of it. Living in Palm Springs? Or dying here. And there was you."

"Me?" I'd assumed that was just a coincidence.

"He thought a lot of you, Andi. You always looked out for him in school. He knew you well enough to persuade people the relationship was, well, more." Kelsey had moved into the kitchen and begun chopping vegetables. "I think he wished it was more."

I wasn't ready to talk about that. My feelings needed sorting out. "So he was putting up a front," I said. "He'd done that for years. It doesn't mean he wanted to die."

"He had to know Crawford would find out about that

mare. Jack Crawford has a reputation as a man who gets even."

"You think Ross wanted Crawford to chase him down and kill him?" My skepticism must have shown in my voice.

"Yes. Maybe not consciously, but it was a death wish."

"But Crawford *didn't* kill him. Try to, I mean. Damn, we're talking like he's already dead. Anyway, I don't think it was Crawford."

"Jack may not have given Ross the drug that put him in his coma, but he set off the cascade."

"Maybe," I said, "but I don't see how he could foresee the chain of events. We still don't know who attacked him."

"He went around angering people. Almost randomly. Umberto, the Animal Freedom Fighters. Eventually someone was bound to come after him."

"He *was* acting reckless," I agreed. "I thought it was, I don't know, just him."

She touched my wrist and looked at me. "Andi," she said, "why are you doing all this for him?"

I looked at my hands. "I care for Ross, too."

She shook her head. "But that's not enough. You've put everything you have on the line for him. Why?"

I thought about the reckless classmate who'd made me feel at ease in a strange town and threatening surroundings, maybe kept me from giving up before I started. I remembered my polyester waitress uniform and a truck stop in southern Illinois, where the boys grew up to work in the steel mills or—for the truly ambitious—owned bars with pictures of football players on the walls. The women had babies and worked at the checkouts in Kmart and dreamed of running away with country-western singers. Smoke from the coke pits could choke a town on a windless summer day. "I know a thing or two about running, myself."

The phone rang. Glad for the distraction, I followed

the shrill of the cordless handset, which I found in the bathroom.

"Hello?" I said just as the answering machine picked up. As I turned it off I noticed there was already one message.

"Andi? Hal. I got that information you wanted. Streptokinase is used in research to induce bowed tendons. If you want to meet me somewhere, I'll give you the articles."

"I think I've got it figured out. Can you just tell me about it?"

"I was hoping we could go out for a bite to eat, at least a cup of coffee. I spent almost an hour looking for them, and I've still got work to do. It's my busy season, you know."

I struggled against my annoyance. After all, he had gone to some trouble to do me a favor. It wasn't his fault I didn't need the information anymore. I could meet him someplace. But where? He didn't drink, so The Tenth Goal was out. "Tell you what. Kelsey's fixing dinner. I'll meet you at the polo club after we eat, and we can take it from there. Okay?"

"Great! I've got to go look at a couple of horses out at Hannover's place in Coachella, then swing by the hospital here in Indio." At first I thought he meant where Ross was, then realized he meant the equine hospital. "See you around eight?"

I heard the enthusiasm in his voice and hated myself for encouraging him. It would be fully dark long before eight, and even though it was a game day I thought the grounds would be deserted. I wondered if he was dangerous but couldn't make myself believe it. "I'll be there. I might have time for a cup of coffee, but then I need to meet Kelsey. She'll be expecting me," I finished, and made sure he understood she'd know where I was going and why.

As I hung up I hit the playback button on the answering machine. It was Trinka Romanescu asking me to call her at home sometime Saturday. I dialed the number she'd given. She picked up on the fourth ring, sounding slightly out of breath. Loud rock music jangled across the wire, and we both had to raise our voices to be heard.

"Andi, glad you called."

"Did I interrupt something?"

"I'm working out. Hang on a sec." The music was abruptly silenced and she came back.

"Reason I wanted to talk to you was, a woman came into your clinic today asking about a dog. Velcro?"

Oh, damn, I thought, *Mrs. Barton has come back to haunt me.*

"Ruth Artimas."

Double damn. "What did she want, exactly?"

"Apparently she wants Velcro. She said she's ready to deal, and you'd know what she meant. Isn't she the one who had me put that cocker down a few weeks ago?"

I told her a quick version of the story of Velcro, Ross, and Mrs. Artimas.

There was silence on the line for several seconds, then, "You still owe me lunch. I want to talk to you about your clinic." She was breathing rhythmically, probably pumping dumbbells with her free hand.

My right hand involuntarily reached over to feel the soft flab over the opposite triceps. Then my fingers traced the scratch on my palm. I'd almost been able to put it out of my mind that day. "What about my clinic?"

"You need help, right? Now that McRoberts is out of commission. I'm thinking of getting into a daytime place. I've got money saved for a down payment. You want a partner?"

It was my turn to fall silent. "Let's talk," I said finally. "Maybe I do."

We agreed to get together on one of her nights off. I hung up feeling almost giddy.

Kelsey had completed dinner, a vegetable stir-fry over Minute rice with soy sauce. I ate two helpings.

I told her I had to go back to the polo grounds to meet

Hal. She planned to visit Ross, and I told her I'd meet her there when I was through. She took his keys and grabbed his medications to show the nurses. Then she headed for the door, paused, and turned to me. "He's never going to recover, is he?" she whispered. I could only look at her as this knowledge passed between us. Slowly, Kelsey walked out to the car and I was left alone.

It was a bit early, but I decided to head out anyway.

Chapter Thirty-one

As I drove I thought about what we'd learned that day. We'd ruled out our most likely possibilities. I needed a new list.

Mentally—and not for the first time—I tried superimposing suspects on the figure I'd seen in Ross's hospital room. It could have been almost anyone who wasn't fat or lame. Besides Crawford that left out Babs, who was too short, and her father, who was too heavy. What about Jaime? He knew potassium could kill—I'd told him so myself. He had the bottle of tablets Hal had given him—a simple matter to dissolve a few in water. And he'd seen me switching fluid bottles for the mare, Bella.

I might have taught him how to kill. I pushed the thought away. People killed every day. It was easy.

He could have slipped into the car beside Ross, so weakened by diarrhea he could barely drive. So weak he couldn't keep his assailant from exchanging his medication for the lethal injection? Wouldn't he remove the needle? Or did he even know?

But surely Melanie or the nurse would have noticed Hispanic features. And how could anyone mistake Jaime for a woman? Besides, he claimed to be out of the country when my clinic was burglarized and during the first attempt on Ross's life. How hard would that be to check? Jaime could have killed Umberto, but if he was at Umberto's funeral, he couldn't have attacked Ross. And I was sure the same person had done both.

I felt a grudging respect for whoever had slipped into

the hospital room and injected Ross with potassium. That definitely took guts.

The kind of guts Hal would need to kill me while Kelsey waited? I shoved the thought away. I simply couldn't imagine my colleague murdering someone that coldly. Besides, where was his motive?

What do you really know about him, Andi? He could have motives you'd never think of and wouldn't understand if he explained them to you.

As expected, the polo grounds were deserted. I parked near the road under a tamarisk tree and killed the engine. Sitting in the dark, I tried to reconstruct Ross's last night, but no new ideas came to me. I began to feel claustrophobic, so I got out of the car and strolled over to the Bluegrass stable.

The spotlight on the corner nearest Ross's barn was dark—burned out or maybe broken. The added shadow gave me a sense of security somehow, but I wished Hal would hurry.

I knew I'd missed something, some clue that would point me toward the killer. I kept getting turned around. Again I considered Hal, that missing twitch. He could have used it to bludgeon Umberto and then ditched it. I tried to picture him in a panic, first placing the polo mallet by the body to divert suspicion away from himself, taking care to get blood on the head without leaving fingerprints. Later realizing the evidence would never come out of the twitch's wooden handle. So he disposed of it and claimed it was lost.

He drives a Ford pickup. Can you swear the truck that passed you the night you found Ross didn't have a vet pack?

But why kill Umberto? Jealousy? Because he was flirting with you? Come on, Andi.

Who had access to Ross's keys?

The Mexico trip. Someone may have driven him to the airport and picked him up. That person would have had his car Monday night. His car and his keys. Who would he ask?

Fandango nickered and thrust her head over the rail of her pen. "Sorry, girl, no peppermints," I said, but entered the enclosure, stroking her nose, allowing her presence to calm me. From her good side, in the dim light, the damage was invisible.

"What a waste," I murmured. "What sort of bastard takes out his vendetta on a horse? If anyone deserved to be killed, it was Crawford." I felt a little ashamed of this sentiment but couldn't shake it.

"Anyway," I told her, "I don't think it's too smart for me to wait here. If you see Hal, tell him I'll meet him at The Tenth Goal, all right?" Surely they served coffee. I'd phone Hal's service from there, drink a cup, and call it an honest try.

Just as I unlatched the gate, headlights swept the drive.

"Too late, I guess." But the truck passed beneath a spotlight, and I saw it wasn't Hal's. New Ford, no vet pack. How could I imagine that wasn't obvious? Could be green. Crawford's truck? I was virtually certain it was. It stopped in the road, then turned toward my half-hidden Miata.

"Damn," I whispered to the anxious mare. "Whoever it is knows I'm here."

An explosion cut the stillness, and the driver's-side window of my car disintegrated in a crash of glass. Horses danced and snorted on all sides.

What the hell . . . ? I stopped myself from shouting. *That son of a bitch shot my car! Thought I was sitting—? Tried to kill me?*

It had been the dull blast of a shotgun. Like the one hanging in the rear window of Crawford's truck.

The driver saw the car was empty. Wheels churned the weedy ground and the truck spun around to the road.

I ducked behind Fandango as the headlights swept over her.

Who's driving? Not Crawford.

Crawford told me Jaime had his truck today.

Impossible. Jaime was in Argentina when Ross was attacked.

Not Jaime. Jaime's replacement.

Damn, that's what I missed. Who would Ross loan his car to but the player who worked for him. Tish. She'd been there, watching, while I treated Bella, so she knew how the IV worked. She had access to Jaime's electrolyte tablets since she cared for his horses while he was in Argentina—a simple matter to dissolve a handful in water to be injected into an existing IV line. She had no car of her own, depended on her father's BMW. Jaime wouldn't question her use of the pickup, nor Ross her use of his car while he was in Mexico.

And when I asked him about his keys he knew. He'd confronted Tish and she'd tried to kill him.

But *why*?

I touched the scratch on my palm, almost as if for luck. If I didn't find a way out of here quickly, it wouldn't matter if I had HIV.

The truck had begun a circle of the stables. For a couple of minutes the lights would be headed away from me. Time to escape? To where? If I tried to run for the car, I'd be in the open for a good fifty feet. I'd have to pass under a light or waste time going wide. Either way, she was bound to see me. She could run me down or shoot me—it wouldn't matter.

Where was Hal when I needed him? Probably still at Tish's father's farm. I imagined him boasting about meeting me here when he finished treating her father's horses, Tish finding enough work to keep him busy awhile longer, then racing to get here first. Well, damned if she'd do to me what she'd done to Umberto. Or worse, what she'd done to Ross.

Without much of a plan, I climbed the fence and swung onto Fandango's bare back. It startled her and she leaped through the open gate, trotting nervously down the aisle.

Along the way I leaned over and unlatched other gates. Two horses followed us. The animals fed on each other's panic. Once free of the barn they broke into an all-out run toward the playing fields. I clutched Fandango's neck hoping my one-eyed mount didn't stumble in her headlong flight through the darkness.

We hit field five before Tish spotted us. The truck bore down at reckless speed, its headlights bobbing wildly on the dirt road. I nudged Fandango's sides, hoping for even greater effort.

Tish had a shotgun, but we had an advantage, too. Fandango leaped over the short divider between fields as if paced. Pickup trucks can't jump. Tish was stuck on the road.

I leaned to the right, hoping to steer the mare away from the road. Her stride faltered and I scrambled to stay on. One of the other horses pulled up beside us about the same time as the truck. I flattened myself against Fandango's neck as the shotgun exploded.

The other horse went down. Over the pounding of hooves and my own heart, I heard Tish's furious scream.

She shot a horse. Tish can't handle that. Would she hold her fire now?

The horses swerved right, away from the noise. As I struggled to stay aboard, we leapt another divider and sped at a sharp diagonal down field three.

The truck pursued us down the field. I could do nothing to alter Fandango's course. The journey down the hundred-yard green took a long time, the pickup's headlights throwing ever starker shadows before us. I dared not look back for fear of falling.

We bypassed the far-end goal at a full gallop. The riderless horse reached the tree line first and planted her feet. Her sudden stop gave me a split-second warning that saved me from going over Fandango's head as she propped and skidded into the brush.

Lights from the truck engulfed us as Fandango tossed her head back and reared. I struggled to hold on as tamarisk branches scratched my face and the mare searched frantically for an escape route. The other horse had vanished through a clear spot to our right, but Fandango couldn't see that way and I couldn't pull her head around. Her forefeet hit the ground, and she tried to go left. A huge, horizontal limb blocked her path. I felt her brace to rear again as the truck pulled in close, completing a three-sided barricade.

"You made me kill a horse!"

Tish's shriek cut the night as she dropped down from the cab. She held the shotgun against her right shoulder, leveled at my chest.

"Stop, Tish! You can't keep killing forever!" I nudged Fandango's flanks, encouraging her to force her way through the foliage. But her feet were rooted in equine panic. She trembled violently and I sensed she might self-destruct at any moment.

"You should have stayed out of it!" she screeched. "This had nothing to do with you!"

"Stayed out of what?"

"You and that southern girl, asking questions you shouldn't. Things are finally going right, and I won't let you screw it up!"

"You killed Umberto! Why?"

"He crippled Jaime's horses. Deliberately. He had no respect for horses. He was in Jaime's barn, about to inject another tendon. That stuff they found, he gave it to Rowdy the night before. It was only supposed to bow a little, not blow apart. He got the dose wrong. The bastard just shrugged his shoulders, ready to experiment on another one. He didn't care if a good horse died 'cause he got it wrong. He did it for the money."

The shotgun had dropped slightly. Could I . . . "Crawford paid him."

"If you know that, how come you're asking around?" She raised the shotgun's muzzle, and even in the darkness I imagined I could see her finger tighten on the trigger.

"What's going right that you're afraid I'll screw up?" Using present tense, deliberately.

"I'm finally on a team. Roger wants me to go back to Kentucky and play for him permanently."

I wasn't about to tell Tish what I thought Dietrich really wanted from her. Trying to make my voice reasonable, to calm myself and therefore Fandango, I said, "What happened that night? How did you know what Umberto was doing?"

"I went to the barn to talk to Jaime. He was so angry at me."

"About what?"

"Nothing. It was nothing." She was panting. I braced myself for the blast of buckshot I knew would kill me at this range. "It started with the mare, Bella. He shouldn't have ridden her so hard. He knew it but it pissed him off when I told him. He doesn't like me to tell him anything."

The mare's trembling had lessened. Could I steer her out of here without alerting Tish? "You went to the barn?"

"I saw someone there, thought it was Jaime. Then when I saw . . . I knew what Berto was doing; he was hurting the horses. Jaime hurt Bella, but not on purpose. This was deliberate. I grabbed Hal's twitch and hit him. I didn't mean to kill him. I should have killed Crawford instead. Maybe I will."

"Then you planted the polo mallet to frame Ross." I was desperate enough to try to kick the shotgun out of her hand, but she was out of range. Fandango ignored nudges from my left heel.

"I was framing *Jaime*. He *hit* me; I wanted to get even. I kept the twitch so I could get him off later. It didn't go like I thought. But it would have been okay if only you'd stayed out of it. Ross would be in jail, and no one would care." She was fighting tears and jerked the shotgun in frustration.

Fandango's muscles bunched beneath me and I stroked her neck. Tish saw the movement and tensed.

"Wait," I said. "It was Crawford's fault. He was paying Umberto to do what he did. And you're the most important witness there is. With your help we can get him punished. Think about what he did."

In the distance, headlights entered the barn area gate. Hal had finally arrived.

"I've killed two people, Andi. They're not going to make any deals to get me to testify against a man whose only crime was against animals."

"Tell me how you gave Ross the euthanasia solution."

She winced like I'd slapped her. "I only stole it for insurance, in case he got too close. He suspected me but had no proof until you told him about the keys. I had his car when I broke in. He called me and I made him let me explain. I'd seen him at Babs's. That's how I knew what to do. He'd park under the tamarisks and put in the IV. He was so sick, really I did him a favor. Saving him from suffering. Like you did for Jojo. I'm sorry I have to kill you, Andi. We have a lot in common, and I wanted us to be friends."

Hal's truck was sitting next to my Miata, a half mile away. Surely even he could tell something wasn't right.

"I stayed in Babs's trailer till he quit waiting and hooked himself up. Pretty soon he fell asleep. He did that a lot. I just slipped in next to him and changed bottles, like you showed me. He never even knew. It will be much worse for you." She sighted down the shotgun like a rifle, the barrel pointed at my face now.

"He isn't dead, Tish. Ross didn't die!" I ducked left as I shouted.

She gasped and the muzzle jerked as she fired. My right side ignited in agony from the scattered buckshot, but the worst of it flew over me.

The close-range explosion galvanized Fandango. She tried to bolt forward in the instant my hand flailed near her good left eye. I slipped sideways, fighting to stay on her back. She spun to the right and reared.

I felt myself fall even as I heard the final explosion

from the shotgun. Fandango stumbled toward the truck, went down on all fours, tried to rear again, and collapsed.

Her thousand-pound mass pinned Tish against the truck. The shotgun landed near the Ford's rear tire. I dragged myself to my knees and moved it out of her reach. Then I checked pulses.

Tish's was strong.

Fandango was dead. She'd fallen on her chest, but I could see an edge of a gaping hole in her rib cage and blood was everywhere.

Where was Hal? I needed his help. My left hip was badly bruised in the fall, and my side hurt like hell where the buckshot had grazed me. Tish needed an ambulance, and somehow we had to get the mare's body off her.

Then I spotted his headlights creeping along the road. Finally. He must have seen Tish's taillights. Maybe he'd called for help after seeing my car—I heard a distant siren, growing louder.

For once I was glad to see him. He drove around the fields and came in from behind the clubhouse. His headlights illuminated the grisly scene, and I had to look away from Fandango. Hal got out and stared open-mouthed first at Tish, then the shotgun, the dead mare, and finally at me.

"Jeez, Andi," he said slowly. "What happened?"

"She tried to kill me. She murdered Jaime and almost killed Ross. But she's alive. I'll need your help."

"You attacked her with a horse? She had a shotgun and you got away?"

"Yes, Hal. Now, *please* . . ."

"Well, darn. I guess this means you're not gonna have coffee with me, huh?"

Chapter Thirty-two

The monitor continued to indicate a normal ECG and reasonable oxygen stats, though lower than before the pneumonia had set in. The ventilator marked cadence for a dirge. The blanket covering Ross had slipped down, exposing the incision along his sternum, swollen and greenish red from infection. I tugged the blanket up to cover the scar.

Now? Dr. Hostettler asked the question with his eyes.

Kelsey nodded, swallowed several times, and said, "Please."

Ken O'Grady switched off the respirator. The resulting silence engulfed us. The four of us stared at Ross or at the floor, anywhere but at each other.

The silence grew until the monitor alarm sounded. It had taken far longer than anyone expected, but Ross was finally at peace.

I put my arm around Kelsey. She buried her face in her handkerchief.

"This is the right thing, isn't it, Andi?" she asked for the hundredth time.

"I would have done the same," I said.

"He was never going to get better?"

"No, never."

"Thanks, Andi. I wish his father had come."

The man had grudgingly signed the papers, and that was the extent of his participation.

My palm itched where the scratch had healed. The menace of AIDS rode my shoulder like a parrot, whispering in my ear so that it affected everything I did. I'd been tested once—negative, thank God—and would be tested monthly for six months or until the results changed. Even then I couldn't be certain I didn't carry the virus—a few people don't seroconvert for years. I felt like I couldn't make long-term plans of any kind, particularly regarding partnership with Trinka, who worked the clinic this morning. I wasn't ready to tell her why and had resorted to increasingly weak excuses. I was afraid she would drop the whole thing out of frustration.

Ken O'Grady removed the leads connecting Ross to the monitor and pulled the blanket up to cover his face. They wouldn't move him until we left. I led Kelsey from the CCU into the wide, impersonal hallway, made more bleak by the few plastic Christmas decorations some well-meaning administrator had put up.

Bud Thorpe was waiting. "Just wanted to get your feelings on this," he said.

"We have nothing to say," I snapped at him.

"Got to get the story."

"Anything bigger than a paragraph with the bare facts and the editors at the *Desert Sparkler* will know who stabbed my dog."

He faltered. "I don't know what you're talking about."

"The picture of Velcro could only have been taken by the one who stabbed him. At first I thought someone tried to break into my house and he got in the way, but I figured it out later."

"I told you; I've got my sources."

"You took that picture."

"Bullshit."

"You wanted to steer attention away from your buddies in the AFF. Velcro wouldn't attack anyone. You just walked in and stabbed him. The light was still on in the picture. When I arrived it was broken. You did that when I pulled up, so I couldn't see you."

"It must have been the Hannover broad. She'd have the key the same way she had the one to your clinic."

"The thing that really convinced me, once I thought about it, was that Velcro growled at you the next day when you came into the office. He's never growled at anyone."

"That doesn't mean anything." There was no force behind his words. He left, muttering under his breath.

Kelsey smiled wanly. "I'll keep you posted on what happens with Jack Crawford."

I suppressed a grin. The Animal Freedom Fighters had received an anonymous note detailing "J.C." 's part in sabotaging Ross's horses. The ensuing campaign of harassment was the AFF at its best. Four of Crawford's horses were kidnapped and subsequently released in a Nevada wilderness that was home to a protected herd of mustangs. His house and truck were paint-bombed, and several thousand dollars' worth of polo equipment was destroyed. All anonymously, of course.

"You know," Kelsey said, "I enjoyed playing detective. I might do something like that when I get back to Kentucky."

"Like what?"

"I could specialize in tracing horses, or tracking their identity in cases like this one. I can use the money from selling Ross's horses to start my own business."

"Kelsey Vallice, private horse detective."

We laughed. It felt good.